A TIME OF PREDATORS

OTTO PENZLER PRESENTS . . .

God Save the Mark
by Donald Westlake

The Quiller Memorandum
by Adam Hall

Hopscotch
by Brian Garfield

A Time of Predators
by Joe Gores

Peregrine
by William Bayer
(forthcoming)

Grandmaster
by Warren Murphy and Molly Cochrane
(forthcoming)

JOE GORES

A TIME OF PREDATORS

A TOM DOHERTY ASSOCIATES BOOK
NEW YORK

TO MY PARENTS WITH ALL MY LOVE

A TIME OF PREDATORS

Originally published by Random House, Inc., New York, in 1969.

This book is printed on acid-free paper.

Edited by Otto Penzler

A Forge Book
Published by Tom Doherty Associates, LLC
175 Fifth Avenue
New York, NY 10010

www.tor.com

Library of Congress Cataloging-in-Publication Data

Gores, Joe, 1931–
A time of predators / Joe Gores.— 1st ed.
p. cm. — (Otto Penzler presents—)
"A Tom Doherty Associates book."
ISBN 0-765-31050-3 EAN 978-0765-31050-7 (hc: alk. paper) — ISBN 0-765-31051-1 EAN 978-0765-31051-4 (trade pbk.: alk. paper)
1. Married women—Crimes against—Fiction. 2. Witnesses—Crimes against—Fiction. 3. Revenge—Fiction. 4. Gangs—Fiction. I. Title. II. Series.

PS3557.O75T56 2005
813'.54—dc22

2004056320

First Forge Edition: March 2005

Printed in the United States of America

0 9 8 7 6 5 4 3 2 1

INTRODUCTION

It was 1970, and something was about to change in the world of mystery fiction. A writer living in the San Francisco area had been struggling with a variety of jobs, most notably private detective and repo man, as he wrote short stories and sold a few for which he received critical acclaim but not too much money.

Having received encouragement from such noted critics as Anthony Boucher and Frederic Dannay (half of the Ellery Queen writing team), Joe Gores quit his job and devoted himself to writing full time. That first novel was *A Time of Predators*, and won the Edgar Allan Poe Award from the Mystery Writers of America. In the same year, he won the Edgar for the best short story of the year, "Goodbye, Pops."

The short-term historical significance of winning two Edgars in the same year is that no one had ever before (and, indeed, not since) achieved that extraordinary success. The long-term significance is that a writing career had been launched with fireworks, and Gores soon went on to produce a new form of detective fiction.

Private eye stories had been around a long time before Gores created DKA (Dan Kearney Associates). But just as there had been police novels before Ed McBain came along to create the 87th Precinct, this was a colorful variation. There was no single hero in a McBain cop novel. The entire precinct was the hero, with various members of the squad stepping up for starring roles in various books. The hero was a team, not an individual, and that formula has been part of McBain's success for nearly half a century.

The hard-boiled private eye was the invention of an American pulp writer, Carroll John Daly, and it was soon made popular, as well as literary, by the more famous Dashiell Hammett. Hammett knew how private eyes functioned, since he worked for the Pinkerton Detective Agency for some years. In the same vein, Gores understood the workings of a private detective agency, since that had been his job for twelve years. And it was a job for which he was clearly cut out. "I loved detective work," Gores once said. "I truly loved it."

The firm for which he worked took on many assignments, but among the most common were repo jobs. This involved recovering property, almost always cars, for which the putative owner had failed to make payments. When all other avenues of collecting payments had been exhausted, the car company turned to its last resort—hiring an agency to repossess the unpaid-for automobile.

This could be dangerous work, as many people didn't want to have their cars taken away. One of those reluctant to give up his Cadillac was Jimmy "The Weasel" Fratianno, a Mafia hit man. As it happened, Gores' best opportunity to repossess that particular car happened to occur on his first date with a young woman who eventually became his wife of more than a quarter of a century. Dori Gores was nervous but thought it was fun. Joe Gores was just nervous.

The years as a private dick provided lots of experiences, most of them hilarious. They provided the raw material for dozens of short stories and elements of novels. But raw material is not the same thing as a finished piece of fiction. The difference, as Gores states it, is "A detective digs around in the garbage of people's lives. A novelist invents people and then digs around in their garbage.

But it was those days that enabled Gores to produce his innovative series about a detective agency in which the firm itself is the protagonist, and each of its members step front and center for their own star turn.

The novel at hand, *A Time of Predators*, is not a DKA novel. Nor is *Interface*, one of the great crime novels of all time, with a surprise ending that has rarely been equaled. Nor is *Come Morning*, for which Gores received an Edgar nomination in 1985. Nor is *Hammett*, in which the great novelist's early experiences as a Pinkerton are the basis for a complex novel that was filmed in 1983, five years after the book's publication.

Francis Ford Coppola produced the adaptation for Orion Pictures/Warner Brothers after a painful series of screenplays. Brian

Garfield had a hand in the screenplay, and so did the great Ross Thomas, as did Gores as Dennis O'Flaherty, Thomas Pope, and doubtless others gratefully lost in the mists of time. Although it was a beautiful movie made from a beautiful book, it became an utterly incomprehensible mishmash, as German-born director Wim Wenders evidently had no concept of a story line. It is worth watching for the superb sets, good dialogue, and characters so colorful they seem to have been created by Crayola, but I defy you to provide a rational account of what actually happened and why.

Other non-DKA novels are *Wolf Time* (1989), *Dead Man* (1993), *Menaced Assassin* (1994), and *Cases* (1999).

Oddly, the DKA novels seem to have dated a little less than *A Time of Predators*, which, in its sensibilities and use of language, is very much of its time. The criminals, entirely dark souls with hardly any redeeming qualities, use a colloquial English that smacks of a time before vulgarity was so casually accepted at virtually every level of society, especially among teenage hoodlums.

Four young punks, vicious as can be, in dialogues among themselves, never use language stronger than "cool it," "let's split," and "fruiter" (for a gay man).

The girlfriend of the main punk has interior dialogues in which she decides how far to let him go. Although she is in college, and they have been seeing each other for some time, she continues to coyly kiss him good night, and a bit of tongue sends him wild with desire. It is clear that the book was written about people at the very brink of the sexual revolution, but in a community in which the first shots bad not yet been fired.

A Time of Predators is a straightforward revenge novel. A man's wife witnesses a brutal attack on someone the hoods mistakenly think is gay. They fear she can identify them, so call on her home and repeatedly beat and rape her, after which she commits suicide. When the police fail to apprehend the thugs and even bluntly tell her husband that they won't continue to pursue them, he decides to seek justice on his own.

There is suspense to spare, and some scenes are quite violent, especially for their time. Gores's protagonist is reminiscent of some of Mickey Spillane's heroes. It is possible that a television producer saw this same quality in Gores' work and in his ideology, as he hired him to write twenty-two episodes of the 1984–1985 CBS series *Mickey Spillane's Mike Hammer*.

Gores worked on numerous television cop shows, including *Kojak*, for which he won another Edgar for a teleplay, a one-hour episode entitled "No Immunity for Murder." Other shows that Gores wrote teleplays for include *Magnum P.I., Columbo, Kate Loves a Mystery, Remington Steele, Eischied, The Gangster Chronicles, Scene of the Crime*, and *T.J. Hooker*.

Joseph Nicholas Gores was born in Minnesota in 1931 and led a peripatetic early life, heading off for Alaska between his sophomore and junior years at Notre Dame, where he received his B.A. He then spent a year in Tahiti and a couple of years in Africa, teaching in a program that predated the Peace Corps. While getting his master's degree at Stanford, he took the job as a private detective that was to help form his professional life.

Once he began his writing career, all the other jobs, all the travel, essentially ended. He was a professional writer now, and a hardworking and successful one, with TV scripts, short stories, screenplays, and novels filling his life, though nothing in that life was as important to him as his wife, Dori, with whom he has had a love affair since the day they met.

His writing style is clean and pure—a modern-day Hammett who doesn't waste time and space with frills and overwritten prose. He is that rarity in the mystery writing world: a first-rate writer who can also plot. It's a deceptive style. It is so lean and so real that it seems that there are no other words that will do the job as well as he has done it. It takes numerous rewrites to make all those sentences seem inevitable.

Donald E. Westlake, one of the all-time great professional writers in a wide range of styles, has complimented Gores by calling him "dogged and brilliant"; "dogged" he works his prose over and over again to get it right, to make it seem so simple and effortless, and brilliant because the end product is so glorious.

A Time of Predators may be read for several reasons, all of them good. Here is an excellent reflection of a time just before the world changed forever, and here is an absorbing suspense novel, and here is the book that launched the career of one of the finest crime writers alive.

—Otto Penzler
New York

BEFORE...

FRIDAY, APRIL 18TH

BEFORE...

Professor Curtis Halstead yawned, looked at his watch, and settled back into his ancient leather easy chair. Paula hadn't been on the 12:30 A.M. bus, or she would have called from the depot; the next, and final, wasn't due from San Francisco until 2:10. He stretched a heavy arm toward his glass of red wine, planning to read the dozen mimeo'd papers he'd collected that evening from his graduate seminar in anthropology at Los Feliz University.

But sitting there in the pool of light from the floor lamp, with the living room of their big old house creaking homely about him, Curt felt his eyelids getting heavy. He surrendered, draining his glass and setting aside his papers to slide lower in the chair. In a few minutes his breathing was even and steady.

"You ever had a guy try to queer you?" asked Rick Dean idly.

Rick was nineteen, lean and dark and intense, with a Barrymore profile. Sitting in the front seat of Heavy Gander's 1956 Chevy station wagon, he turned so the remark would include the two in back as well as Heavy. One of them, Champ Mather, worked his big callused hands and frowned with the effort of expressing himself.

"Christ, Rick, a guy do that to me, I . . . I'd break his neck."

"Well, it happened to me," said Rick, suddenly moody. His dark eyes stared at the cars straggling from the broad V-shaped lot of the drive-in movie. "It was two years ago, I was just a junior in high school and really dumb. I was walking home from this movie, see, and this guy came along and asked if I minded company."

He stopped, as if realizing that the lights of a car swinging toward the exit might show the tautness of his features, and tipped up his beer can. They had drunk three six-packs during the movie. Since Champ Mather was twenty-one, he could buy it for them legally.

"Then, as soon as we got on a side street, he reached right over and *groped* me! Right there on the sidewalk!"

The boy beside him stirred. Heavy Gander fit his nickname, for he was obese and sweating under his light windbreaker. Merely because he was behind the wheel, his belly was jammed up tight against it.

"So what'd you do, Rick?"

Before Rick could answer, the other boy in the back seat, Julio Escobar, made an elaborate and well-practiced movement, and a switch blade was lying along his palm. It was unopened but deadly looking merely by its six-inch folded length. Julio had straight black hair and an olive face whose coarse features included a long down-turned nose and a thick-lipped mouth. The lower lip was loose and petulant.

"I would have stuck him!" Julio exclaimed intensely.

In the concealing darkness, Rick's fingers tightened around his beer can. "Well, I didn't stick him, but I beat hell out of him. I damned near killed him."

The others made approving noises, and Rick tossed his dead soldier out the window into the nearly empty drive-in lot. Actually, he had floundered away from the sidewalk across the sandy loam of a vacant lot, chased into darkness by the queer's laughter. Funny, he hadn't ever before let himself think about that night. His mouth tightened. "Say, you guys wanta have a little fun?"

"Sure, Rick," Champ said immediately. Despite his hulking size, Champ had the alert, devoted, empty eyes of a fine retriever. Rick was the one with ideas. Rick always thought up things to do that were fun to remember afterwards, until he forgot. Champ forgot stuff easy.

"How about you, Julio?"

Julio shrugged his narrow shoulders with great nonchalance. "We should get some more beer, Rick. Or if we knew who had some pot . . ."

"No hash," said Rick sharply. He had blown pot only twice, but it had made him feel vague, made him want to drift. Tonight he didn't want to drift. Tonight he wanted to be sharp and hard and tight. He laid a hand on Heavy's meaty shoulder. "Let's go, man. We'll drive down by the university somewhere, see if we can find us a queer. Then we'll give him a hard time, just for the hell of it."

Heavy emitted a sudden terrific belch, and Julio started giggling. Heavy was forever breaking a guy up with all the wild noises he made.

"Geez, Rick, I don't know . . ." Heavy began cautiously.

"It's Friday—no school tomorrow. But if you're chicken—"

Heavy grunted and twisted the ignition key sharply. He had a roundly cherubic face, but when he brushed back his long blond hair, a skull-and-crossbones ring glinted dully on his right hand. Rick grinned to himself. You could always shame chicken Heavy into doing stuff.

"I'll pay for the beer," Rick offered happily.

What the hell, his folks gave him a good allowance while he was going to junior college, even though he lived at home. As Heavy started the car, Rick thought with a sort of warmth that these three guys were still better friends of his than anyone he'd met at Jaycee. Julio and Heavy would be out of high school in June, and would be draft bait unless they signed up at Jaycee as he had last year. Champ was too dumb for the Army anyway; he'd even flunked all their tests and everything.

"You can tell fruiters by the way they walk, every time," said Rick with spurious authority. "Drive down El Camino, Heavy . . ."

Paula Halstead hung up the phone and stepped from the booth behind the darkened Greyhound depot. Her spike heels rapped staccato messages from the blacktop, deserted except for a young man wearing a cheap suit and an undistinguished tie. He was blond and willowy, with a weak angular face.

"Did you get your husband, ma'am?"

"Yes. The big bear had fallen asleep in his chair."

Paula might have added, over his wine. If she knew her Curt, he probably had drunk too much dago red and would have been sitting with his head back and his mouth open, snoring gently. At forty-three he couldn't shake it off as he once had; and every night he seemed to take that glass or two too many.

"Would you like me to wait until he gets here, ma'am?" persisted the blond youth.

Paula laughed. She was thirty-six, one of those slender yet well-rounded women who remain sexually attractive into their fifties. Her mouth was generous but thin-lipped, her nose short and straight, and her eyes a startling blue in a face made tawny by the Peninsula's inevitable sunshine.

"Lord, no! It's only about ten minutes from our house at this time of night. But it is so *very* nice of you to offer . . ."

He shook her hand, formally with a slight bow, and she watched him start walking east toward the railroad tracks. A rather effeminate young fellow by his looks, clerk in some county office, but married and with a new child. They had begun talking on the bus because they both had been carrying that evening's program to the San Francisco Spring Opera; his baby son had prevented his wife from accompanying him to the city. Not often young people were opera enthusiasts now.

An old green station wagon squealed into Brewer from El Camino, with shouts and laughter from the boys inside. Paula shook her head and smiled to herself. In her high school days the jalopies had carried such signs as *Don't laugh, lady, your daughter may be in this car;* the world had worn primary colors then. Even sex, with its hurried fumblings in back seats, had seemed exciting then, not the messy, boring business that marriage had proved it to be.

In the next block the brake lights brightened and there was the harsh grunt of tires sliding over gravel. There was a single shout, very clear in the chilly mid-April air. Then Paula was running, toward the station wagon and the four figures which had converged on the young man who had ridden the bus with her.

"Stop!" she cried, flying toward them, too outraged to taste fear. "*Stop it!* You can't . . ."

Rick had twisted the victim's arms up behind his back, so high that he was bent almost double. Champ's knee worked three times, like a piston, driving up into the strained, contorted features level with his belt buckle. Champ grunted with effort each time his knee connected.

Heavy tore at his shoulder, yelping in a voice made reedy by fear, "Quick, you guys! Champ! *Run!* Somebody's coming . . ."

As the others scrambled for the car, Rick, transported, drove the heel of his shoe into the back of the fallen youth's head. He twisted his leg, so he could feel the face grinding into the gravel of the railroad right-of-way. Then he too ran, bursting from the shadows just as Paula arrived.

For a moment they were face-to-face, the streetlamp shining directly on Rick's features. Then, with a little mew of belated terror, he swept her aside and almost dove for the open rear door of the wagon. It squealed around the next corner and was gone as Paula tottered toward the fallen youth.

His breathing was shallow and labored. With sudden resolution she tugged at his shoulder to roll him over onto his side. Only then did she see what Champ's knee and the gravel had done to his face and his eyes.

She gagged, staggered away a few steps, and threw up violently. Her body contracted jerkily with each spasm. Then heavy running footsteps raised her head. Curt's chunky shape was pounding toward her from the bus depot where his VW was pulled up with the motor running and the driver's side door hanging open.

"Oh, thank God," Paula sobbed in a half-whisper.

PAULA

MONDAY, APRIL 21ST–
WEDNESDAY, APRIL 30TH

CHAPTER 1

Rick Dean had inherited his mother's dark good looks and his father's nervous energy. Waiting for Debbie Marsden in the Jaycee cafeteria, he realized that he was tapping rhythmically on the tile floor with his right foot. Relax. Last Friday was over, couldn't be changed. By the newspaper reports, there was no way they ever could be tied in with what had happened to that Harold Rockwell.

No way, that is, except one.

He wiped a hand across his forehead. Where in hell was Debbie? Of course, she had to get a ride up from the university after her nine o'clock, but he had told her ten-thirty sharp in the caf, had cut his Survey of Western Civ to meet her. He shouldn't be cutting even gut courses, not today. Not the Monday after . . .

Could that Paula Halstead have gotten their license? Hell, it had been dark, she'd been running . . . He wouldn't have panicked and tromped that Rockwell if she hadn't come running up that way. Who could have known he was married, for Christ sake, with a kid and everything? And then that crap in the papers about him being blinded. You couldn't blind a guy just by pushing him around a little, could you?

Rick's leg was jiggling again, his foot tapping the tiles. In sudden vivid recall, his heel was against the yielding neck muscles, he could feel the face being ground into the gravel. He shredded the glowing tip of his cigarette in the ashtray; what sleep he had lost over the weekend had been from fear, not remorse.

Rick stood up suddenly and waved, sloshing coffee across his tray. The girl was just his age, with long toffee-colored hair worn absolutely straight and framing a heart-shaped face. She moved like a filly.

"I'm sorry I'm late. I had to wait for a ride, and—"

"That's okay, Deb." Rick made his voice nonchalant so she would not know it was important. After all, Paula Halstead could identify *him:* maybe not the car, maybe not the others, but *him.* They sat down.

Debbie Marsden had expressive blue eyes, wide-set. Her nose turned up too much and she had a long upper lip, and though her mouth was accented with too much lipstick, she still looked younger than her nineteen years. All except her figure. Her body really had filled out in the nine months since he last had seen her.

"You made it sound important on the phone, Rick." There was vague petulance in her voice. "After not hearing from you for *months—*"

"The folks have really kept me hitting the books this year. Ma's afraid I'll get drafted."

What did she expect, for Christ sake, a hot-line to her dorm? He'd taken her to the high school senior prom, then dated her a couple of more times before last July, when they'd gone swimming out at Sears Lake. She'd let him get all steamed up afterwards, on a blanket up from the beach, and then had left him hanging. Still, she was the only person he knew going to the university. He made his voice casual.

"Say, Deb, do you know a prof at the U named Halstead?"

"Curtis Halstead?" She was not a beautiful girl, but when she smiled, her face came vibrantly alive. "Know *of* him. He's a full prof in the anthropology department. One of my girl friends, Cynthia, has him for a course. I met his wife at a faculty tea last September."

Rick made himself stir the cold coffee left in his cup. Talk about blind luck! "Could you . . . ah . . . get his home address?"

"Why, I suppose so, Rick. Wouldn't it just be in the phone book?"

Wow. That woman, that Paula, must have shaken him up worse than he'd thought. *He* should have come up with the phone-book idea. The woman was frozen in his memory like a fly in amber, that was the trouble: her gleaming blond hair, her startling blue eyes, her high cheekbones, the thin parted lips with the teeth gleaming between them like . . .

"Is anything wrong, Rick? You look so funny . . ."

Good old Deb. He stared at her, as if seeing her for the first time. Man, she'd really grown up during those months. He hadn't meant Paula to be mentioned, just Halstead himself, since Debbie might have read about that Rockwell creep in the newspapers and seen Paula's name, as Rick had. But he remembered from high school that she had only been interested in international affairs, all that crap, like his Dad was in the stock-market reports. She thought he looked bothered, huh? He raised his head to give her the look that worked on his Ma even when she was sore about something.

"Well, you see, Deb, there's this sort of mix-up . . ."

"Rick, are you in *trouble?*" Her eyes shone; she took his hand in both of hers as if it were a fragile treasure. Her lips were parted. Hell, he should have thought of this right away; she'd lived just two streets away when they'd been kids, had always acted a little gone on him.

"Not really in trouble, Deb, just . . ." His facile imagination took over then, as it always did when he was conning some chick, even his Ma. "You remember the Triumph that Dad gave me for graduation? And remember what he said about having an accident with it if I'd been drinking?"

"Rick, you *didn't* smash up your car!"

"No, nothing like that. It's just that, ah, yesterday I'd had a couple of beers and was coming from the parking lot at the bar I'd been in up by Five Points, and I just touched fenders with this other car."

"And Professor Halstead was driving the other car?"

"His wife was." Rick's imagination was in full flight now, he could almost see the tall slender woman getting out of her car—a Mercedes, say—with a flash of shapely woman leg and a dazzling smile. "This morning I got thinking that if she went to her insurance company and it got back to Dad, somehow . . ."

He stopped there, watching her. Women were really dumb about cars and insurance, anyway, and Deb knew his old man was a broker.

"But . . . what can *I* do, Rick?"

"Do you think maybe you could find out when she'd be home alone? I mean, I wouldn't want to ask her in front of her *husband* to not report an accident to her insurance company, and just let me pay her for the repairs. Not with her old man a college prof and all."

Men were such babies with their precious male pride. Just in her one year at the U, Debbie had learned that a wide-eyed look of rapture during class lectures meant a better grade from any male prof, even the old ones past thirty who should know better. But she was really glad that Rick had come to her for help; she'd been crushed last summer when he'd dropped her, after she'd gone further with him than she had with any other man before.

"All right," she said, smiling abruptly. Her teeth were white and even; Rick could remember when she had worn braces. "I'll pretend I'm interviewing him for the student newspaper or something." She stood up. "I'll be late for glee club rehearsal, Rick, but you can call me tomorrow at Forrest Hall."

Leaving, she wondered if he had called her *just* for help in straightening out about the accident. Maybe, when he called tomorrow . . . She wondered if he still ran around with those icky kids, that Julio who gave her the creeps, and that fat one, Heavy, and the big dumb one with the funny eyes who'd quit school before he graduated. Champ, that was it. They'd always been the ones who were sent down to the principal's office to be disciplined.

Watching her slip away through the crowd with a wave of her hand, Rick suddenly realized that she was really a wild-looking chick. In the months since he'd last seen her, she'd started wearing her hair different, and her figure sure had filled out. But then, unexpectedly, he thought of Paula Halstead. Blue eyes burning in a brown, slender face. Maybe if he just went over to her place, alone, told her how it had happened, maybe she'd just agree not to tell the cops about him. And then maybe she and he could . . .

Wiggy, for Christ sake. That's what he was, wiggy. She was a hell of a big danger to him. Period. What did they do to you for blinding some guy? And it all had started out so simple, too; just a little fun, like they used to have with kids in high school from the lower grades, getting them down behind the boiler in the basement and taking their lunch money away from them. Instead of wiggy ideas about Paula Halstead, he ought to be figuring out how he could make sure she couldn't identify him. If she couldn't, he was safe. If she could . . .

Well, if she could, he somehow had to make sure that she *wouldn't*. That meant he had to find some leverage, something to scare her with.

But how? Maybe he could get old Debbie to help him, he thought, with the vague outline of a plan forming in his mind. Without her knowing what he *really* was doing, of course.

And when all this was over, maybe he'd start picking up on old Debbie again. She'd developed into some real prime stuff.

CHAPTER 2

"All right, all right," growled Curt Halstead. He jerked his tie savagely, bulging the flesh over his shirt collar. His muscular, thickening body was encased in gray slacks and an old flannel sports jacket with leather patches over the elbows. "So you'll go down to the police department and look at more pictures on Monday. Why?"

"Because they blinded that boy," Paula said in a cold voice.

She was leaning in the bathroom doorway, arms folded. They were on the second floor of the old isolated frame house that had been their home since Curt had joined the Los Feliz University staff in 1954. Their bedroom windows overlooked the university golf course.

"I'm sure they didn't *mean* to blind him; it probably was some horseplay that got out of hand. And since it happened a week ago, why would you be able to recognize any of them if you *did* see them again?"

"I'd recognize that one," she said grimly.

Curt finished with his tie, and ran a comb perfunctorily through his black, close-cropped hair. It hadn't yet begun to gray, but it was thinning, especially around the crown of his head. He looked impatiently at his watch. "Why do you always start these conversations when I'm late for my Friday night seminar?"

She met his brown eyes steadily. "Because I want you to understand my position. I'm going to keep looking until I find that boy. Stopping to grind Harold Rockwell's face into the gravel was the most vicious thing I've ever seen anyone do to another human being."

"Why do you insist on words like 'vicious'? Sick, maybe, but—"

"I saw his face when he did it," she flared. "You didn't. Evil: naked, willful evil. I want that boy caught, and I want him punished."

"The lady doth protest too much, methinks," grunted Curt. He got his briefcase from the spare bedroom he had converted years before into a study, and was followed by Paula to the head of the stairs.

"What time can I expect you home, Curt?"

He grimaced; he had more than the beginnings of a double chin. "I might be a little late," he said judiciously. "Young Chuck Belmont is reading his paper on 'The Relation of Culture to Human Evolution'—a damned brilliant piece of work, actually—and I imagine there'll be some discussion afterwards."

Paula said dryly, "I'll set out a bottle of wine before I retire."

"Always have to get your little dig in, don't you? Because I enjoy a glass or two of wine . . ." He cut off the rest of it, shook his head, and went down the stairs. Paula watched him cross the living room to the front door, almost hungrily, but he didn't look back. She sighed, went down the stairs herself, and turned right through the double doors leading to the dining room and the lighted kitchen beyond.

Could Curt be right? About her protesting too much? Ever since the attack on Rockwell, she had lived with a strange . . . what? Excitement was too strong a word: anticipation, perhaps. Expectancy. Involving herself completely in the search for the attackers, pushing the police in their investigation. Could Curt be right?

Over the years they had modernized the kitchen with bright new stainless-steel fixtures, metal storage cabinets, and maroon vinyl tops on the flat surfaces to give her plenty of work area. She began the supper dishes automatically, getting out the dishpan and draining rack, shaking out soap powder, sousing glassware in steaming suds.

Perhaps she was being unnecessarily alarmed over teen-age horseplay, as Curt put it, which had gotten out of hand and had ended in tragedy. Perhaps she was merely a frustrated woman seeking some outlet for a mild discontent with her life, her marriage, even herself.

Paula paused, holding a plate under the hot-water tap and barely feeling the smart of the steaming water running over her hand.

No. She had seen it in that boy's face, along with the fear. Pleasure. Excitement. The sort of excitement that the big lie propounded by mothers to their daughters and women's magazines to their readers claimed was to be gained from sex.

Paula dried the dishes, put them away, and carefully set out the accusing bottle of wine on the coffee table by Curt's reading chair. Then she went out onto the narrow front porch, nearly buried in the thick overhang of live oaks, and listened to the frogs chorusing in the ditch between the drive and the golf course.

It seemed important, suddenly, to know whether she actually *was* using the attack on poor Harold Rockwell for some obscure inner satisfaction. Know thyself, as . . . who had said? She smiled in genuine pleasure. Plato, or Socrates, or Pythagoras, or Chilo, or Thales. It had always amused her that no one knew whose sage advice on knowing it was.

What was the answer, then? Another affair? The first had been five years before, with a visiting English professor whose courting had been the direct antithesis of Curt's bearish lovemaking. Candlelit suppers at remote rendezvous; flowers; passionate poems cribbed so shamelessly from the classics that she had found it unflattering. And the denouement in unfamiliar motel room beds? Distressingly familiar: counterfeiting orgasm as she did with Curt, to heighten her lover's pleasure while experiencing none herself. No, an affair was no answer at all.

Through the screening bushes she could see the flicker of approaching auto lights on the blacktop below. They caught the bright yellow sweater of a girl coming up the road from the university. Strange to see a girl walking along this isolated road at night, alone. A girl who looked pretty, with toffee-colored hair, worn long, visible only in flashes through the foliage. The car passed, dropping her back into darkness. Then Paula heard the aluminum folding door of the phone booth across the road creak shut. That explained it. An insistent date, a slapped face, a phone call to the folks. But the light in the booth went on only momentarily, showing the girl, then the door reopened.

It was like watching a home movie, where the flickering figures were familiar yet remote, without real relation to one's own life.

Restless, Paula spent some minutes prowling the bookshelves that flanked the old brick fireplace. Her mind kept returning unbidden to Curt's remark. Yes, he *was* right: her avid pursuit of the investigation somehow was unhealthy. She would look at the last batch of "mug" shots on Monday, but then would let Rockwell's poor ruined face and that other young, strained, defiant one slip back into the limbo where they belonged. The attack on Rockwell really was no concern of hers.

She ought to be thankful for Curt, not dissatisfied with him. He was older now, less demanding sexually; and despite their bickering they were fond of one another. No matter what they said, Paula doubted that other women got any more than that from *their* marriages. If she sometimes felt that life was wrapped in too many layers of padding, it probably was the psychological onslaught of premature menopause. Her marriage might, after all, be like Sally Redmond's. Poor Sally, convinced that her husband's occasional evening at the chemistry lab was actually being spent in some heavy-busted grad student's bed.

Now that she thought of it, Sally had said something about perhaps dropping by this evening while Curt was gone. Good Lord, she hoped not. Sally was more than she could cope with reasonably tonight.

Paula sighed, contemplating with resignation the possible martyrdom of her evening.

CHAPTER 3

They were to meet at a drive-in on El Camino Real, that old regal highway that once connected the California missions and now is the artery for a dozen Peninsula cities between San Francisco and San Jose. It was Friday-night crowded, which was the reason Rick had chosen it. His fire-red Triumph was parked a block away; Heavy's station wagon would serve for the evening's foray.

Champ Mather was second to arrive. Rick watched him slouch across the blacktop lot between the carloads of exuberant kids—among them yet forever set apart by something that brooded in his tanned, Indian-beaked face. Despite his awesomely powerful body, his dark deep-set eyes were weak and tentative, with a tiny mouse of chronic panic peering from them.

"Hi, Rick." He slid into the booth and put permanently grimy hands on the table. "Guess I ain't late, huh?"

"No, you're okay. How did work go today, Champ?"

He considered it seriously. He had spent two years in ninth grade, two in tenth—Rick had shared the second with him—and then had quit school because he no longer was eligible for football. Old Mr. Bailey, the principal, had gotten him a job as gardener on four large contiguous Hillsborough estates, with a room in a boardinghouse a short mile distant.

"I had a good time today," he finally admitted. "I, uh . . . it's spring, y'know? They . . . the flowers are comin' up good now, an' the trees need prunin', an', uh . . . yeah, the spring's a good time, Rick."

Even in high school, Champ had been scouted by the pros—switched to guard, his solid 220 pounds would have been enough—but he just had not been bright enough to learn the complex defense patterns of pro ball.

Rick, glancing outside, felt his gut muscles tense. Heavy's two-tone green station wagon was pulling up across Entrada Way.

"Okay, Champ, they're here. Let's split."

Dusk had fallen, and Heavy had the headlights on. Despite its faded paint and dented body, the wagon was in perfect mechanical shape; Heavy did all his own work. Rick and Champ got in the back seat. Julio was in front with Heavy.

"Where to?" Heavy had to raise his voice nervously above the blaring pops station he always was turned to.

"Out by the university golf course—Linda Vista Road. And turn down that damned radio." Rick's voice was ragged with the effort of hiding the tension in it. "Drive slow. We want it plenty dark."

Julio Escobar looked back at Rick. Before being drawn, along with Heavy and Champ, into Rick's orbit three years before, Julio had been a savagely self-sufficient loner with only his switchblade for companionship. Sometimes, such as tonight, he wished he still was.

"You sure about the professor being gone tonight, Rick?"

"Very sure. He teaches a seminar from seven to ten, and he stops for coffee afterwards with some of the students."

"What if someone sees my car?" Heavy demanded.

By the lights of an overtaking auto, Rick could see sweat on the fat boy's neck. "We'll park a quarter of a mile away."

Entrada Way dead-ended at Linda Vista Road in a T-junction. Heavy turned south toward the university.

Champ's brows were furrowed. "Why do we gotta come out here to her house?" he demanded.

"To see if she recognizes us."

"What if she does?" Heavy cut in uneasily.

"I've got that all worked out," Rick assured them.

The trouble was that he *didn't* have it worked out. Sure, he had the approach to the house all plotted out; he knew how to find out if Paula Halstead could recognize him or not; but then it all got hazy. If she did, then what? An idea of how they could make sure she wouldn't identify him to the police had been dancing uneasily in the back of his mind ever since Monday, when he'd talked with Debbie. But he had continued to reject it in conscious thought. Paula Halstead was damned near as old as his *mother*, for Christ sake, no matter what she looked like.

He leaned forward to put his forearms along the back of the front seat. To hell with it. Things always worked out. "Right up here," he said, "is another T-junction, Heavy. Take a right into Longacres Avenue Extension, and I'll tell you where to stop."

Longacres skirted the northern edge of the golf course. Rick kept watch on the edge of the road, suddenly exclaimed, "Turn here." Heavy slowed, turned into a small dirt area beside the road. "Pull up under those trees and douse the lights."

The wagon stopped on a carpet of narrow brown leaves fallen from the eucalyptus trees, facing back toward the blacktop. With the lights and motor cut, the night washed over them with the scrape of crickets, the rustle of a breeze in the trees overhead.

Rick checked his watch. "Okay. Eight o'clock. Let's move out, you guys."

By the weak illumination of the interior lights, Rick proudly watched the others get out. They were *his* outfit, like the commando-type group way back in World War II that they'd seen in the drive-in movie last week. He really dug war movies, always saw himself as the commander of whatever group was featured.

As he reached for the door to shut it, there was a whirring along the blacktop, and a small hunched dark shape hummed by. They saw a pale flash of face turned toward them, and all ducked involuntarily.

"What the . . . was that a *kid?* On a *bike?*" hissed Julio.

"Christ, Rick, we was standing right in the light," quavered Heavy. He emitted a sudden explosive belch which for once did not crack up Julio. "We gotta leave. We can't—"

"We aren't quitting now," snarled Rick. "Hell, it's dark; he was by before he could see anything."

For a moment they wavered, group discipline shattered. Champ was the one who saved it for Rick. "We coulda been up to the house by now, you guys wasn't always arguin' with Rick."

That did it. In a compact group they crossed Longacres and went out across the golf course. Rick, in the lead, glanced back at the others. Here they were, because he had wanted them to be, not for any other reason. He was in command. He stopped and they gathered around, their eyes gradually adjusting to the semi-darkness of a first-quarter moon.

Rick gestured down the long alley of the fairway. "See the lights just showing through those trees? Not another place within half a mile of it. We'll go right down the fairway, across the fourteenth green, and up the driveway to the house."

"What if someone else is with her, Rick?" Julio's question was not a challenge this time, but a request for tactical information.

"Then we get a signal to hold off."

Before they could frame their questions, Rick went on. The soft, already dew-wet grass was springy under their shoes, muffling any sound of their passage. In Rick's mind, he led a commando into enemy territory: for a moment, fleetingly, he wished they had blacked their faces. Five minutes later they crossed the green, skirted the sand trap, and then stopped at a strip of weeds, some fifteen feet wide, that separated the course from the edge of the Halsteads' gravel driveway.

"*Down!*" hissed Rick suddenly.

They hit the dirt. There was the growing hum of an auto, the spreading aureole of its lights above their backs. Then it was by, with the oddly abrupt drop in decibel level that always accompanies a passing auto.

Heavy spoke in an urgent, frightened whisper. "Rick, there's a *girl*, just sitting in that phone booth across the blacktop with the door open and the light out. I saw her when that car passed!"

"That's Debbie. She's our lookout. As long as she keeps the door open, so the light in the booth is out, we know no one is coming. If she shuts the door like she's making a phone call, we split."

Julio had stiffened like a retriever finding the scent when he had heard Debbie's name. She had been in Rick's class, a senior when he'd been a junior, and had always been too good for Julio Escobar. She'd never worried about showing her legs to the crowd as a cheerleader, but she'd never even looked at Julio. Cheap goddamn tease.

"You should have told us that our safety would depend upon a woman." In his excitement, Julio's voice had taken on a Spanish singsong.

"Deb doesn't know any of you are here," Rick said. "Once I call her in that booth, she won't even know *I've* been here."

He led them across the wet shallow ditch and up the winding drive through the trees. The house, as they came up under its dark bulk, proved to be an old, rambling, two-story frame building from a more leisured era of California's history. They stopped at the foot of the wooden steps leading to the porch where Paula had stood shortly before.

"When I ring the bell, stay out of sight. She'll open up, I'll ask directions. If she doesn't recognize me, we just leave. If she does, we go in, all except Heavy. He stays on the porch and watches in case Debbie gives the signal that someone's coming."

At the head of the wooden stairs, Rick peered through the foot-square glass panels in the heavy oak door. His heart pounded wildly. Paula's back was to him as she moved slowly down the row of bookshelves in the far wall of the living room. To her left were broad oak stairs; between the stairs and the bookshelves was a passageway leading to the rear of the house.

The graceful line of her neck, partially hidden by her shimmering blond hair, flowed into the line of her back and flank and finally the taut curve of her thigh as she moved indolently along. For a giddy moment Rick thought she was being openly sensual, aware of his scrutiny; then he realized that it was just her natural grace. Her brown legs were bare under a flaring peasant skirt of some brocaded material, and he could see the taut straps of her brassiere through her cotton blouse.

Rick jabbed the bell. It was so simple, suddenly: just do what he had fought against all along. He ducked back as she turned, so she wouldn't see his face through the glass.

Paula opened the door with a false briskness and the words, "Sally, I was *hoping* you'd drop by and . . ." She stopped at sight of the pale, handsome, boyish face just level with her own. "Oh, I'm sorry, I thought you were someone . . . else . . ."

Their eyes met and locked, as they had in Brewer Street the week before. Rick saw sudden recognition dawn in the piercing blue eyes. He took a short step forward and drove his right fist into her stomach. Her lungs emptied with a pneumatic *whoosh* that flecked spittle against his cheek, her eyes rolled up, and she crumpled. He caught her as she went down, grappling awkwardly at her dead weight.

"Champ!" he yelped. "Quick! Help me hold her, for Christ sake!"

Champ went by him, got an arm around her from behind, and they quickly shuffled her out of the doorway. Now Julio also was inside, pulling the door shut, while Heavy remained on the porch. Rick was very aware of Paula's warm, heavy weight; his excitement was heightened rather than lessened by the beginnings of fine lines at the corners of her eyes and mouth.

"Have you got her okay?" he panted.

"Yeah."

Champ's heavy forearm, encircling Paula and pressing up under her breasts, had burst the top buttons of her blouse. Rick couldn't keep his eyes from the deep cleavage above her bra. Champ held her full weight easily, with only one arm, without apparent strain.

"Just hold her for a second," said Rick.

He crossed to the hallway, found an open door just to the right, and stuck his head inside. There was a rheostat control rather than a switch for the overhead light, set so the room was almost dark but not quite. Rick could see more bookshelves, a flimsy-looking straight-backed chair like the one his ma had next to the piano, a couch, a small three-legged stool covered with a bright woven slip-cover, and a side table bearing an ornate lamp and an electric clock. An oblong rag rug covered the center of the floor.

"Bring her in here, Champ," he called unevenly. He was going to do it. *Do it, do it, do it* kept echoing in his mind. He probably would have done it even if she *hadn't* recognized him.

Paula was gasping, still not conscious enough to be struggling, but Champ dragged her across the living room one-armed so he could hold a hand over her mouth to muffle possible outcries.

"Dump her on the couch," said Rick. "It doesn't matter if she yells—I don't think anyone can hear her in here anyway."

"But . . . what are you gonna do, Rick?"

All pretense of sophistication left him as he stared at the limp, sprawled woman on the couch. He was engulfed by adolescent fancies about this voluptuous woman laid out like a feast before him.

"I'm going to screw her." His voice creaked on the verb as if it wanted to break into a higher register, and he felt blood shoot to his cheeks. Then he herded Champ to the door and shoved him from the room, ignoring the big man's hungry stare as realization dawned.

In the gloom, Rick turned back toward the woman. Should he wait until she was fully awake? Or just take her now? Would she fight him? If he waited, maybe she would help him. Undress herself slowly, tantalizing. Hell, in bull sessions the older guys always said that older women always were hot for it, no matter what they said.

As he bent over her, Paula picked up and swung the decorative three-legged milking stool at his head. Rick blocked the clumsy blow with a forearm, so the stool went around him and was wrenched from her grasp by its own weight.

Aroused by the attack, Rick slashed a fist at the side of her jaw with a fierce exultation. She fell back away from him in a sort of slow motion. He went in after her. Mouthing obscenities, he tore at the frail material of her panties. Now she would find out what it meant to oppose Rick Dean.

CHAPTER 4

They were gone. Paula, huddled on her side on the couch, kept her eyes tight shut and listened. Her legs were drawn up in the fetal position; her ripped panties were lying on the floor by the couch and the straps of the one sandal she still wore were hanging loose. Her ears were like separate little animals, independent of her, which listened and probed and evaluated sounds while the voice of the one called Rick bragged in her memory.

"She *still* doesn't know who we are. And even if she finds out, she won't tell. She won't dare, because she knows we'll be back then."

Which should have been silly, because if she told, the police would make sure they never would be back. But they were lucky. For reasons that the one called Rick was, she was sure, incapable of understanding, Paula would not tell.

She listened to her memory again. The casual retreat of swaggering footsteps—jackbooted Nazis leaving a looted Jewish shop on *Kristallnacht*—then, oddly, the phone being dialed, Rick's voice using words that made no sense, to someone named Debbie, the front door closing.

Her listening ears probed the old house for reassurance. Creak of ancient timbers. Sigh of old and faithful joists. Outside, the rustle of oak leaves. Nothing else.

Paula explored split lips with a careful tongue. Blood-clotted. Teeth loose. Was this how a hibernating animal felt when the snow had melted and it began checking how it had come through the winter?

Poorly, thank you. I came through it poorly.

She groaned and pushed herself into a sitting position. The pit of her stomach ached, her face and neck were gritty enough for an involuntary grimace of distaste. It was the body that betrayed you.

Paula ran automatic fingers through her hair, found that the plastic clasp that had held it back against her skull had broken, so it was a blond flood around her shoulders. She looked at the clock.

9:40. That would be P.M.

Curt would be finishing his seminar soon, folding his papers and ramming them sloppily into the briefcase, talking all the while and not getting the papers in until he finally thought to look at his hands.

Curt, big frowning bearlike man.

"Please come home," she said to him solemnly in the empty house.

But she knew deep inside that Curt wouldn't, not in time. She sighed and got carefully to her feet. Not *really* too bad, physically. Just the sort of stiffness she would expect if she had played some hard sets of tennis after a winter layoff. How had it happened to her, when after Rick, the first time, she still had felt only revulsion? She still had been Paula Halstead then, had gasped "No!" when he had swaggered to the door, zipping up his Levi slim-fits, and opened it to call out "Next?" in a parody of a barber with an unoccupied chair.

Maybe it had started then? Realizing, then, that they were all going to do it, and that Rick was going to stay and watch them?

"I'm sorry, Curt," she said aloud.

The clock's bland electric face murmured 9:47 to her eyes. Curt still would be in the seminar room, with its long wooden table and tube steel chairs with plywood backs. And talking. Curt was good at talking.

This is in *your* half of the court, kiddo, not Curt's. A sizzler. Up on the toes, swing the racquet, send a hot flat drive over the net . . .

9:51. Eleven minutes to get up off a couch. Rome was not built in one day. Good old John Heywood. You could always count on John for a platitude or two. The fat is in the fire. She picked up the ripped panties, found her other sandal in a corner as if hurled there by an explosion. She went out carrying both items.

At the foot of the stairs she paused. Seeing, really seeing, the living room. To her left, the windows that in daylight looked out across the drive and the fringe of woods to the golf course. Below the windows, the couch. Nearer, its back to Paula, Curt's reading chair. Please, Curt, come home. The coffee table, Paula's snide bottle of wine, her disordered stack of paperbacks. Dark wine-colored rug. To her right, through double doors, the dull sheen of dining-room oak.

Nowhere any sign of their predatory passage. Oh, fingerprints, probably. On the doorknob. Perhaps on the phone. And, of course, on her soul. Grimy ones, there, that wouldn't wash off.

The skinny Spanish-looking one had been second. Hot eyes, hot hands to force her knees apart. She whimpering, then willing herself to relax, to watch the ceiling as she had hundreds of times beneath Curt, to forget that this indignity was happening to a complex and subtle being named Paula. Three minutes, perhaps, worrying her like a terrier. And then, when his moment arrived, crying out like a rabbit struck with a stick.

She'd still been safe, even then. Still unfeeling.

She mounted the stairs slowly, shoulders sagging, to run a tub full of steaming water. Her blouse was ruined but the skirt was still intact. She hadn't been wearing a slip. Her bra was holding with one hook. She removed everything, chucked it all into the woven wicker clothes hamper they had bought one year during a Mexican vacation, dumped in more bath oil than she usually used.

The steaming water, touching abrasions and sore places, forced little cries from her; but she resolutely lowered herself into it. Her body flushed a bright pink. She began lathering with an intense and useless concentration.

It was no good. You couldn't wash it off.

The fat one hadn't even gotten his pants down before he was finished, was still standing in the middle of the floor. Rick had hooted with laughter and had gone to the door to tell the others about it.

Paula stood up, lathered her body until it was creamy with suds. It was the body that betrayed you. She looked involuntarily down at her breasts, sore to the touch and marked with angry red finger marks that soon would be purple. The broken skin around the toothmarks in her right shoulder already had turned red and puffy. Wasn't a human's bite supposed to be more septic than a dog's?

If that one really had been human at all.

Curt, damn you, why weren't you here? She sloshed away the soap, sighing. Who was she kidding? Curt had fought a good war once, a quarter of a century ago; but now, tonight, that big animal one would have taken care of Curt with one hand.

Yes, it had started with him, the big animal one who had hurt her. Started with his hateful empty grin, his hard breathing as he bent above her, the agony of iron fingers gripping her breasts almost impersonally. When she had screamed, then he had lunged forward to enter her. Twenty minutes, so they both had been slippery with sweat. No watching the ceiling that time. Then his oily face had been jammed down against her neck, forcing her head to one side; and then, when he had come, his teeth had sunk into her shoulder.

She still might have been all right, if she just had been given time. But Rick, aroused by watching the big animal one on her, had taken her again, immediately.

Paula carefully dried her brown, beautifully female body with a huge woolly towel, merely patting at her bruises. She pouffed an extravagant amount of powder over herself and then, still nude, went to listen at the head of the stairs like an insecure child suddenly convinced that its parents have abandoned it. Was there any more terrible feeling than that universal childhood terror? Yes. The knowledge of having abandoned oneself. Abandon all hope, ye that enter here.

10:39.

In the bedroom she brushed out her hair, then chose her frothiest negligee, one with a pale blue peignoir that fit over it and tied at the top with a blue nylon ribbon. She sat at her dressing table to carefully make up her face, applying eye shadow, mascara, and lipstick with calm, sure little strokes.

Just this once, Curt, leave them early. Come home and explain it to me, convince me that I couldn't help it.

She turned her face from side to side, examining the effect. The lips had been a problem, but the splits were inside and the lipstick tended to minimize the puffiness. She put her tiny jeweled watch, an anniversary present from Curt, on her left wrist, pausing to admire its twinkling against her tanned flesh. Eleven o'clock.

Still at the dressing table, she smoked a cigarette partway down, knowing that her deadly calmness was not natural and stemmed at least partially from shock, but also knowing that the abyss that had opened inside her was too fetid to be tolerated.

11:06. Sorry, Curt darling. Too late now. Much too late.

Paula completed her penultimate chore quickly, with a classical allusion she was sure Curt would appreciate, and taped it to the mirror. To the bathroom medicine chest, return, sit down, examine the effect again. Not with a bang but a whimper. My, so literary tonight. First Master Heywood, then Signore Alighieri, then Citizen Tacitus in her own literary effort, finally Mr. Eliot. Hurry up, please, it's time.

And past time. She might have supported even her partial sexual arousal by the animal one's savaging, if it had stopped there. If she had stopped. But Rick had taken her that second time, immediately.

And she had reached her climax.

In fourteen years of marriage she had never had an orgasm. Where Curt's blunt but deeply personal love-making had failed, where candlelight and verse had failed, a vicious gang of teen-age boys had succeeded. In the brutality of this mindless coupling she somehow had found fulfillment. So what sort of disgusting little beast crouched inside Paula Halstead to peer out with wild, beady eyes? What sort of perverted woman was she?

Paula shuddered with a bone-deep revulsion.

She laid her right hand, palm up, in her lap, with her left hand drew the razor blade across the wrist coolly and without qualm. It just stung a little. She dropped the blade, let her hand hang down to aid the flow. Then she sat motionless in front of the mirror and watched the subtle change flow into her face. Too bad, kiddo, she told her suddenly sleepy image. You were pretty good in there a time or two. But not tonight, when it counted. Not tonight. Sorry, Curt darling. At least you won't ever know that I had to fake it with you, but that . . .

She fell face forward and a little to her left. Her face struck the glass tabletop and knocked off a bottle of hand cream. The bottle bounced on the rug and came to rest by the limp fingers of her left hand.

It was 11:33 P.M., four minutes after she had cut her wrist.

CHAPTER 5

Curt glanced at his watch and quickly drained the last of his coffee. Already 10:59, and Paula had been querulous.

"Warm up that coffee, sir?"

Curt hesitated. "I *really* should be going . . ."

Just then Belmont, who had delivered that evening's paper, said from across the booth, "I understood you to imply tonight, Doctor, that the social sciences ought really to deny hereditary influences on the development of human personality, and stress environment instead."

The waitress poured coffee. Curt leaned back with a sigh.

"Well, Chuck, I'd go even further than that. I would agree with Ashley Montagu that human nature is the result of gradually supplanting instinctual primate drives with intelligence. In man the instincts, through lack of use, have withered away."

"Isn't that implying an unbridged behavorial gap between us and our closest relatives?" Shirley Meier was short and overweight, but Curt knew there was nothing sloppy or undisciplined about her mind.

"Culture fills the gap." He leaned forward across the narrow booth; some three hours before, Rick and Champ had shared a similar booth in the same drive-in. "Modern man's uniqueness *is* that he has been freed from instinctual behavorial determinants."

Belmont nodded raptly, but the Meier girl's face was stubborn.

"Instinctual *influences*, Dr. Halstead, are not *determinants*. I think man has an inborn hostility, for instance, which urges him to—"

"That's where you're wrong, Shirl," said Belmont complacently. "No kid is *born* aggressive; his hostilities arise from frustration, every time." His thin, intelligent face was self-satisfied as his dark eyes turned to Curt for approbation. "Wouldn't you agree, Doctor?"

Curt nodded. "John Dollard's classic, titled *Frustration and Aggression* and first published in 1939, points out that aggression is an *inescapable* consequence of frustration—i.e., the ghetto, where Negro frustration explodes like an unvented gas heater bursting from a buildup of fumes. More important, however, is Dollard's point that the opposite also is true: aggression *always* presupposes frustration. Without frustration in the environment, there would be no hostility."

"You said that was published in 1939," Shirley Meier remarked flatly. "Wasn't that the year that Hitler invaded Poland?"

"Come *on*, Shirl," hooted Belmont. "That's ancient history."

Curt surreptitiously checked his watch. 11:17. He really *had* to leave. With an apologetic little cough, he slid from the booth. "I'd best get along, or my wife will display some aggressive behavior of her own." He shook hands with Belmont. "A terrific job on the paper, Chuck." And then he smiled at Shirley. "Young lady, I'm afraid some of your ideas need rethinking before you carry them out into the world."

It was a pleasantly tough smile on a face itself pleasantly tough, despite the blurring of line that overweight and the passing years had brought, and Shirley's answering smile lit up the corners of her personality. "I'm sorry, Professor, but I think it's a jungle out there and I think that man, by nature, is the chief predator."

Curt drew in a deep breath on the way to his car. The air, even at night, had the faintest tinge of industrial haze. Thank God for the universities, last enclaves of sanity in a hurried, pushy, grinding America. With tenure at Los Feliz, Curt was secure from it all. He would spend the summer thinking through his book on man's nature.

He turned the VW left into Entrada Way, which cut through a presubdivision residential area to Linda Vista Road. The streets were deserted and dark except for the glow of televisioned living rooms and an occasional porch light left burning by a watchful parent.

That Shirley Meier, bringing up Hitler's naked aggression against Poland as a subtle refutation of the argument that hostility presupposed frustration! Belmont hadn't even caught her point. Curt's grin faded. He had caught it. 1939. He'd been fourteen then, attending secondary school in England because his father was a visiting professor at the London School of Economics, and the shadow of war, despite Chamberlain's "peace in our times" return from Munich, had hung heavy.

Ancient history, Chuck Belmont had called it.

To a generation that found nothing distressing in swastikas, iron crosses, or Nazi helmets, it probably was. Certainly Curt's three years in the British military were something he seldom recalled himself, these days. The desert war in 1942, the clandestine landings in Sicily, these seemed to belong to a different Curtis Halstead.

He turned left onto Linda Vista Road, putting the bug through its sprightly gears. Just five weeks until finals; then, the book. No summer classes this year, nothing whatsoever to interfere.

He passed Longacres Avenue Extension, glancing off to his right across the dark expanse of golf course. Pity he didn't play, living where he did. Perhaps this Sunday he and Paula, who used tennis to stay in condition, could start taking a bit of a hike again. He hadn't taken a ramble through the heavily wooden strip beyond Linda Vista, which marked the meanderings of San Luisa Creek, for over two years.

Curt braked, swung into his drive, made the switchback and sent the VW chuffing up the grade in second to the darkness below the porch. He sat in the car for a few moments after killing the engine, listening to the creak of cooling metal and the chorus of frogs from the ditch by the golf course. Shirley Meier had brought the past drifting back to him in shreds and tatters. Not a bad thing, actually. Dealing habitually with students, it was easy to forget the past's validity: for youth always saw its current problems as unique in man's history, and thus as susceptible only to newly formulated solutions.

Curt checked his watch—nearly midnight—sighed, fumbled out his keys, and climbed to the porch. In the deserted living room, an unopened bottle of dago red waited on the coffee table for his disapproving head-shake. Paula was becoming a nuisance about his evening glass of wine. He crossed to the hall, stuck his head into the reading room, where the overhead light still glowed. The couch was rumpled, the throw pillows bashed out of shape. He had reached for the rheostat control before he saw the rag rug bunched up in accordion pleats as if a runner had used it as a starting block, and the Swiss milking stool on its side in the center of the room.

Well, now, that was damned odd. What . . .

Curt whirled and went to the foot of the stairs, moving silently on the balls of his feet, before he stopped. Reflexes honed a quarter-century before apparently were not totally forgotten. But really, now, the rug and stool would have a perfectly simple explanation; and meanwhile, he was glad Paula hadn't witnessed his ludicrous thirty seconds as an overweight James Bond creeping about his own home on tiptoe.

He clumped stolidly up the stairs and into their bedroom. Paula was at her dressing table, just in the act of bending over to pick up a fallen bottle of hand cream.

"What the devil happened downstairs? What . . ."

Blood. Ten pints of blood in a woman Paula's size, and half of it on the floor. More blood, it seemed, than a human being possibly could hold.

Curt was across the room in three strides to lift her by the shoulders away from the dressing table. Her body was still warm, but her head flopped back inertly against his supporting arm. Her lower jaw gaped idiotically. One front tooth was chipped, and there was a puddle of saliva on the starred glass where her face had rested.

Very slowly and gently Curt laid her down again. The eyes had not been Paula's eyes; they had been those of a corpse. His onetime long familiarity with death had taught him that "mortal remains" is a very precise concept: with the act of dying, every shred of glory flees from every human corpse.

He put his hands over his face and rubbed them slowly up and down, feeling it now like a gunshot wound when the air gets at it.

How? Why?

Curt turned back, raised Paula's flaccid forearm and twisted it so the wrist was up. He regarded the rubber-lipped gash for a long moment. That was how. A ragged sob torn from his chest surprised him. But why? Would he ever come to any understanding of why?

He turned away without even seeing the note taped to the mirror, and went stiffly down the stairs again without any awareness of making bloody footprints in the hall and on the risers. In the living room, his hand closed over the phone receiver, blotting out the prints left by Rick while phoning Debbie in the booth across Linda Vista Road.

Curt dialed the operator to ask for the sheriff's office.

CHAPTER 6

The room where the actual killing took place was slippery with blood. Flies buzzed everywhere, and the hot North African air seemed almost septic. The goats were sent crowding and bleating down a wooden ramp to the gate, which was raised to let one animal through at a time. The goats had no other direction in which to go.

"Show one more time," promised the head slaughterer. He was an Arab with a seamed, gentle, knowing face.

He seized the goat's topknot with his left hand and twisted the hard bony head up and to the left. This presented the jugular to the view of the half-dozen uniformed men who were his audience. The goat returned their gaze with totally expressionless eyes.

"The throat . . . *so*," he said. "Then the knife . . . *so!*"

The broad, double-edged knife flashed once, the animal gave a convulsive start; its hoofs drummed briefly on the floor. The Arab stepped back with the slightest suggestion of a flourish, extending the knife handle-first to his audience. The goat's eyes had not changed, yet somehow now they were dead eyes, unspeakably so.

No one moved to take the knife. The lieutenant, like the rest of them heavily sweat-splotched under the arms of his uniform jersey, cleared his throat. His voice was too high-pitched for effective command. "Cutting a man's throat is the quickest way of finishing him. We've all been extremely, ah, efficient in practice; this is a good opportunity to . . . um . . . for the real thing, actually."

The enlisted men remained silent; only the flies responded. Something gurgled dismally inside the dead goat. Curt, at seventeen the youngest of the lot, made a sudden impatient gesture. It couldn't be all *that* bad; the effing wog did it for an effing living, didn't he?

"Give me the knife."

Another goat was led into the enclosure. Curt looked into its calmly omniscient eyes, and looked quickly away. He seized the rough top-knot, twisting up and to the left as the Arab had done.

"Good . . . good . . ." murmured the slaughterer in approval.

Curt slashed. The goat, its throat half severed, tore from Curt's grasp to whirl about like the Rifiya dervishes they had seen in the *meidan* at Alexandria. Blood from the gushing jugular splashed over all of them, and a hot salty spray of it hit Curt in the mouth.

The goat stopped and stiffened, head lowered, legs braced against the unseen foe that sought to upset it. Then it began a burring noise, which seemed to issue from the gaping throat rather than its mouth . . .

Curt moaned and rolled over and scrubbed at his mouth with the back of his hand. He was soaked with sweat. His eyes opened and were staring at the old-fashioned beamed ceiling of his study.

The goat's burring began again, only now it was the doorbell. Thank God. He hadn't dreamed about the war in years. Why didn't Paula answer the damned door? Why didn't . . .

It all rushed back.

He swung his legs off the rumpled couch and sat up, gripping the edge fiercely with his hands until the urge to throw up had passed. His shoe skidded an empty wine bottle across the floor, bringing the rest of it back. Drinking steadily all day; must have passed out finally.

The doorbell burred again, patiently. Curt lurched to his feet, forked shaky fingers through his hair while the dizziness passed.

Hadn't undressed, hadn't even removed his shoes. Passed out. Paula was dead.

Paula was dead. Goddamned doorbell again. Ought to . . .

He went unsteadily down the stairs and crossed to the front door. It opened to let spring into the house like the voice of a friend long absent. He stared at the man on the porch, a tall stranger.

"Maybe you remember me, Professor. Monty Worden. I was in charge of the men from the sheriff's office on Friday night."

"Of course." Curt stood aside, searching impressions blurred by shock, by the interim drinking, by his incredibly pounding head. "That is, a . . . Detective-Sergeant Worden, isn't it?"

Worden, he decided, must have stopped on his way home from Sunday services. The policeman's suit was a dark blue with a wicked gray stripe in it, and his tie was tasteful enough to have been picked by his wife. He was a good four inches taller than Curt's five-ten, with thick-fingered hands and the bull neck of a wrestler. By his presence in the middle of the living room, he made it a position he was defending. The busy gray eyes were a cop's eyes, full of sadly won wisdom and totally observant. All of the exceptional combat officers Curt had known in the military had regarded life through similar hard and wary eyes.

"Sit down, Sergeant. I drank too much yesterday and last night . . ."

"That dago red really puts the blast on you, all right."

So those observant eyes had noted and catalogued the bottle Paula had put out on Friday night. Curt said, "There's coffee or tea . . ."

"Tea's fine." Relaxed on the couch, Worden brought out and extended a manila envelope. "Her note. The lab boys are through with it."

Curt carried the note down to the kitchen, ran the teapot full of tap water, hot, filled the kettle with cold and put it on a burner, and then smoothed the note on the countertop. He had not been allowed to handle it on Friday night. It was a measure of Paula, he thought, that her writing had not been at all shaky.

> Curt darling,
>
> Here it is, the traditional note with the touch of sadness assumed appropriate for such occasions. Please understand that I am doing this because of something intolerable in myself, not in our marriage. I would like to do it in style, like the worthy consul of Bithynia, with light poetry and playful verse; but time is short, and to be brought back when halfway there would be degrading. It has been good over the years, darling, so please try to forget this.
>
> Paula

Something intolerable in myself. What? What could she have discovered in those few hours that would explain such a terminal act? He shook his head, set cups, sugar, spoons, milk, napkins, and lemon slices on a TV tray to carry into the living room.

"The water will be hot in just a few minutes." His mind was clearer now, but his head ached abominably; perhaps he would lace his tea with brandy. He measured his next words to the detective. "You mentioned that your criminology lab was 'through' with the note. Might I ask what they were doing with it?"

"Paper often takes good fingerprint impressions, so we checked. We found only your wife's on the note and on the pen which was used."

Curt was stirred by a breath of emotion almost too slight to be identified as anger. "What other prints were you expecting to find?"

"You said you hadn't seen the note." He shrugged. "Routine."

"What about the razor blade?" Curt demanded sarcastically. "Why didn't you check *that* for prints, too, see if I—"

"Too much blood for impressions."

"You mean that you actually—"

"Just routine, Professor. Like I said." Worden's apologetic tone did not reach his eyes. "A suicide is a crime against the person, so it comes under the jurisdiction of the Criminal Division. The investigation is carried out by the Detective Bureau, Homicide Detail. Since I was in the barrel on Friday night, I got the case."

"That still doesn't explain why you fingerprinted Paula's note."

Worden shrugged heavy shoulders. "Since I'm in charge, Professor, subject to review, and one or two little points bothered me—we checked fingerprints."

The teakettle's mournful whistling brought Curt to his feet. Out in the kitchen, he emptied the pot, spooned in strong black Keeman, covered it with boiling water. His hands were shaking: Worden was probing wounds that still were bleeding, and Curt didn't know why. He carried a bottle of Korbel into the living room along with the tea.

"Would you like some brandy in yours, Sergeant?"

Worden shook his head. His gray eyes watched Curt with such a pitiless and avid concentration that it was almost contempt, and Curt paused with the cap halfway screwed off. The spark of anger glowed more brightly. To hell with you, Worden. Plain tea for me, then, too. Then a new thought struck him with the force of a bucket of ice water dashed in the face.

"Paula's suicide *was* a suicide, wasn't it, Sergeant?"

Worden sipped his tea tentatively. "Say, this *is* good; you'll have to tell me what kind you use." Without waiting for Curt's reply, he went on, "Yeah, it was suicide. I've been in the Detective Bureau for ten years, Professor, and I've found that pills are the usual for a woman unless she's spiting—then they'll use the damndest things. But your wife chose the razor blade instead." Then he rapped out, "*Why?*"

"Why . . . why because . . . Her note explained it, she didn't want to be brought back when she was halfway . . . was halfway there . . ."

Curt stopped; the hand holding the teacup was shaking again. His face felt like carved stone. Was this why criminals so often broke down under police questioning? Because of the steady relentless pressure that only a cop knew how to exert? But Curt wasn't a criminal. Paula had killed herself, so why was Worden pressuring him?

"Okay," conceded the detective, "say that explains the razor blade. But what about this, ah . . . the consul of something . . ."

Curt found himself answering almost eagerly, for the ground was less painful here and he felt an absurd urge to justify himself. "Consul of Bithynia. Paula is—was—the daughter of a professor in classics. The reference is to the *Annals of Tacitus*, I can't remember which book—anyway, where he mentioned Caius Petronius, consul of Bithynia and Nero's Master of Orgies. When Petronius fell from favor, he chose to kill himself by bleeding to death a little bit at a time, conversing with his friends meanwhile, eating, drinking—even sleeping—and being entertained by frivolous poetry and light verse until he died. Paula . . . the passage always appealed to her as sort of epitomizing the civilized man, so I suppose . . . when she wanted . . ."

"Yeah." Worden's eyes were flat and gray as stagnant water. "But there's one other little thing, Professor. No hesitation nicks. Usually suicides, they got dozens of little cuts near the veins where they were getting up the nerve to do it. Your wife didn't have any."

"But I told you, Paula was very . . . very strong-willed."

"Yeah. You know, Professor, we performed an autopsy on her."

Curt was out of his chair. "*Autopsy?* You mean that you . . . *Paula?* But goddamnit, man, I didn't give any permission—"

"It ain't necessary in deaths by violence, Professor."

Curt started to speak again, then stopped. Something in Worden's tone had turned his rage to ice. The detective had hit him with the fact of the autopsy in a purposely brutal way, just so he could study Curt's reaction to it. And Curt had been playing Worden's game, giving him the initiative, unconsciously seeking the detective's approbation or at least sympathy.

Well, he wasn't going to do that anymore. Paula was gone, his personal life was now a bewildering shambles, all right; but there had been a time when Curt had of necessity been pretty bloody-minded, to survive. Maybe he still could be. At least, he wasn't going to let this sadistic cop trample around through his emotions. He sat back down, slowly, and poured out more tea for both of them. He was pleased that when he spoke, all emotion had been denatured from his voice.

"I see. And what did the pathologist's report show, Sergeant?"

Worden had begun frowning at the tone of Curt's voice. He almost snapped, "How long had it been since you'd had sexual relations with your wife?"

"*How long* . . ." Curt heard his voice rising, and just quit speaking, completely.

Worden seemed pleased by this. "Oh, come on now, Professor." There was a wink and a nudge in his voice. "That ain't a real hard question to answer, is it, just between us men, like?"

"I don't know how long, Sergeant. Some weeks, probably."

"Yeah. How about a lover? Did your wife have a lover?"

Curt squeezed his eyes shut for a moment. This couldn't really be happening. Paula dead in a pool of her own blood two days before, and now this sadistic bastard was . . . He made himself open his eyes. "Isn't the husband supposed to be the last to know?"

Worden, momentarily baffled, said, "Yeah, that's the truth, ain't it?" Then he leaned into his swing, trying for the fence. "Did you have a fight with your wife on Friday night before you left?"

"Fight? No, there was a bit of acid on each side, but—"

"You didn't hit her? Kick her? Knock her down?"

"Now see here, Sergeant," Curt began in cold fury, "I won't lis—"

Worden's voice cut through his like a torch through foil. "Your wife had three loose teeth—not counting one chipped by hitting her face on the tabletop—and split lips on the same side of her face. Probably done with a fist. A deep bruise on the lower abdomen, again from a fist—some internal bleeding there. Secondary bruises on her forearms, breasts, upper belly, inner thighs. Abrasions on her back. On her right shoulder, a damned nasty bite."

"But . . ." Curt felt a terrible bewilderment. "But . . . she . . ."

"The pathologist also took vaginal smears and found abnormally large deposits of spermatozoa. Suggest anything to you, Professor?"

Curt was reminded of one of his own lectures on the fossil bones of some Australopithecine hominid dug up in a dusty African gorge a thousand millennia after its death; but this man was talking about *Paula*. He saw that his knuckles were white, absently returned his teacup to the coffee table. "I finally understand what they mean by police brutality, Worden. Not rubber hoses in back rooms—oh, no, it's more subtle than that these days. I hurt, down in my guts, because Paula is gone. I'm confused and bewildered as to *why* she's gone. But . . ."

"You'll live through it," said Worden bluntly. "*Somebody* staged a gangbang here Friday night. I want to know who, and I want to know why. As far as why your wife killed herself, I don't really give a damn, since the physical evidence confirms suicide. Maybe when they got done with her, she found out she'd enjoyed it, I don't know. But—"

"God*damn* you, Worden!" Curt came erect in a rush, his sleeve catching the rim of his saucer and flipping his teacup upside down on the rug. Worden, his cup still balanced on his crossed knees, didn't bother to move at all. Curt wanted to lash out, destroy the big detective, but twenty years of conventional living inhibited the impulse. All he could use were words. "I'm not going to take . . ."

His voice ran down as a sudden realization struck him. Paula, name and photo in the newspapers, returning time and again to look at police mug shots. Paula, determined to find Rockwell's attackers. *Why do you insist on words like "vicious"? Sick maybe* . . . Well, Paula had been right. Vicious. Paula, facing them alone while he . . .

In a cold and deadly voice he said, "If you weren't a sadistic incompetent who couldn't investigate an overtime parking meter, you'd know who assaulted Paula."

"Any facts, Professor?" Worden seemed singularly unmoved.

"A week ago Friday a man named Harold Rockwell was attacked on Brewer Street in Los Feliz. He—"

"Brewer Street ain't in our jurisdiction," said Worden quickly. "City cops handle it." But his face had become thoughtful.

"Paula was the witness—the *only* witness—to that attack. It was carried out by four juveniles. Suggest anything to *you*, Sergeant?"

Worden nodded in disgust. "Yeah. Damnit, I *knew* there was something I should of remembered. You wouldn't know which police sergeant is handling the Rockwell investigation, would you?"

"Why don't you go to hell, Sergeant?" Curt asked, suddenly weary.

When he was halfway up the stairs, he heard the front door shut behind the departing detective. By turning quickly, he caught a glimpse of the tall, hard man just disappearing briskly down the front steps. Monty Worden, Curt thought hotly, was not at all like the television cops. Worden, in fact, acted as if he would be reduced in rank and would lose his seniority if he ever apologized to anyone for harboring mistaken ideas about them.

That was the trouble, of course. Curt's reaction to Worden's probing was at least in part a result of the secret feeling that his loss should have made him immune. He was enraged because Worden had refused to observe the proper hushed tones, the cast-down eyes, the murmured condolences. Worden had been a cop, doing a cop's job, and no matter what his shortcomings as a human being, Curt had an idea that he probably was a damned good policeman.

Which said something very sobering about the society that Worden was hired to police.

CHAPTER 7

"Thank you, sir," said Debbie Marsden gaily.

She slid into the Triumph with a quick flash of thigh, and smiled at Rick as he closed the door behind her. When he had called the dorm she had agreed to a drive immediately; Rick wasn't a boy you could stay mad at for very long.

He got in under the wheel. "Whither away, fair lady?"

"Just someplace on El Camino for a soda. Tomorrow's Tuesday, and I have heavy classes."

"El Camino it is."

The flashing red Triumph dug out of the semicircular drive in front of Forrest Hall, which had been named after the frosty-chinned old lady whose portrait hung over the fireplace in the common room.

"I was really sore at you last Friday, Rick."

"I'm sorry, kid." He looked sideways at her from dark, heavy-browed eyes, seeming properly shamefaced in the momentary illumination of a campus streetlight. "But I told you on the phone that night what had happened. I was up to Julio's for some help with my Spanish, and on the way down to the Halsteads' I had a flat on the freeway. I called you as quick as I could get to a phone . . ."

"I don't like that Julio very much," said Debbie irrelevantly.

Rick smiled to himself. Nothing to be scared of, now. Paula Halstead wouldn't dare tell on them, especially not after the way he'd turned her on that second time. Hell, if he could get alone with her he bet she'd let him do it again, because those old chicks really dug the young studs like him. Everybody said so.

He looked over at Debbie's clear, fresh profile. He'd like to get her into the pad, too, but after somebody like Paula Halstead she'd probably be—what was the word?—insipid. Then, on an impulse that surprised him, he reached over and gave her hand a squeeze. Old Debbie. She'd really grown up since the last time he'd dated her.

"Hi, doll," he said softly.

Surprised also, and a little startled, Debbie said, "Hi, yourself, Rick Dean." She laughed with the sheer joy of living; the wind of their quick passage down palm-lined University Way ruffled her hair. She almost timidly returned the pressure of his hand. "I'm going to have the biggest, gooiest sundae you've ever seen."

Rick took the Triumph across El Camino on the overpass, to join the northbound traffic. After a couple of miles he spotted a little café on the right-hand side where he could pull in without crossing lanes.

Inside, in a booth, Debbie returned to the previous Friday. "It was creepy, sitting there in the dark and waiting for you to call or something. And then seeing my folks' old *paper* boy . . ."

Rick caught himself just starting to ask if she meant the boy on the bike, which *really* would have been stupid. "Paper boy?"

"He came right up to the booth like he wanted to use the phone." Looking at Rick, she felt her heart quicken. Even as kids growing up in the same subdivision with him, she'd had a sort of thing about Rick. Her folks had waited until after her graduation last June to move across the Bay to San Leandro, so she wouldn't have to switch high schools her senior year. "It was just as a car passed and I could see him real plain. And then when I heard what happened later . . ."

If Debbie only knew what *really* happened later! Anyway, now they didn't have to worry about the kid on the bike, because Paula wouldn't ever go to the police about them. He felt so good that when the waitress, who was old, about twenty-five, brought their orders, he winked at her. Cheeseburger and chocolate malt for Rick, something called the Awful Delight for Debbie, with three kinds of ice cream and nuts and sauces.

"Will there be anything else, kids?" asked the waitress, pencil poised over her book of stubs. Her blond hair, he saw, was dyed.

"That'll be it, ma'am, I guess," Rick said politely.

She wrote, totaled, tore out the check and laid it face-down on the table. As she turned away, with her back to Debbie, she very deliberately returned Rick's wink.

Feeling great about that, he tore into his cheeseburger and said around it, "So what happened later, Deb?"

"It's all over the campus, with Professor Halstead teaching at the U and everything, but there was just a paragraph in the papers . . ."

Rick felt something freeze inside him. Slowly he lowered the ravaged cheeseburger to the plate, mustard diluted with beef juice running unnoticed over his fingers. "What . . . happened to the professor?"

Debbie was enjoying herself. "Oh, nothing to *him*. It was Mrs. Halstead." Rick had stopped chewing; he was afraid the skin over his temples would burst. "She killed herself. On Friday night, it couldn't have been very long after I left the booth . . ." Her voice trailed off. "Rick, what's the matter? Are you sick or something? What . . ."

Rick clamped his teeth together in a desperate effort to keep back the surge of bile. *Killed* herself? But she . . . the way she'd been with him that second time, she *couldn't* have . . . couldn't . . .

"What *is* it, Ricky?" Debbie's face was stiff and frightened. "Rick, you're just *white!* What . . ."

"I—ah . . . just felt awful sick all of a sudden. I . . ."

"I bet you're getting the flu, honey." She used the term of endearment automatically; he had been so vulnerable there for a moment, the look on his face wrenched at her heart. "You ought to go right home and get into bed."

In a sort of sleepwalking, Rick paid the cashier and took Debbie out to the Triumph. She just *couldn't* have. Maybe the professor had come home and she'd told him and . . . Maybe he'd killed her, made it look like suicide.

But then, after he'd handed Debbie into the squatty sports car and had started around to the driver's side, he had a flashing vision, compellingly clear, of Paula's face: the high cheekbones, the wounded mouth, the eyes so startlingly blue against her tawny skin, and so filled with sick knowledge and with self-loathing. Not loathing for Rick, not even contempt for him. Seeing him as nothing more than the almost impersonal object that had caused her degradation.

No. His mind rejected the image. He personally, he, Rick Dean, had aroused her. She'd dug him, really dug him. She had killed herself for some other reason. She had cancer or something.

He forced himself to move on, get into the car, drive Debbie back to the dorm. No goodnight kiss; barely aware that she had expected one. Later, at home, he was hours getting to sleep; hours of turning and tossing, watching restless leaf shadow-patterns cast on his window shade by the streetlight outside. Suddenly he sat bolt upright in bed.

The paper boy! He had seen them, had seen the wagon, had seen *Rick*. What if the cops found out that Paula had been with a man—his mind already rejected rape—and started looking, and found that kid . . .

In his restlessness, Rick didn't think of Debbie, lying awake in her bed at the dorm a few miles south. Lying awake and wondering about Rick's odd sudden sickness, just when she was giving him the really rather prosaic news that Mrs. Halstead had killed herself. Not that his illness had anything to do with her death.

After all, hadn't Rick only met the woman once, when they'd chanced to scrape fenders in the parking lot of an El Camino bar?

Hadn't he?

CURT

TUESDAY, MAY 13TH–
TUESDAY, JUNE 17TH

CHAPTER 8

When the phone rang in Curt's office at the Sciences Building, he glanced at his watch: 4:30. He debated momentarily whether he shouldn't already be gone. Doris Reeves, the Anthropology Department secretary, had a remarkable facility for catching him with a two-hour chore just when he finished for the day. But duty won, as usual.

"Halstead here."

"Hi, Professor. Monty Worden. I was wondering could you drop around to the sheriff's office. Few little things, easier to talk about in person than on the phone . . ."

Had they finally found Paula's attackers? It had been eighteen days since her death. He was aware that he was trembling—not enough sleep, despite his thrice-weekly workouts. Those damned nightmares . . .

But no use giving Worden the satisfaction of knowing how hard it had been to wait. "Can it keep until tomorrow afternoon, Sergeant?"

"Huh? Oh, sure. No hurry. Say—three o'clock, county sheriff's office, five-oh-nine Jefferson? I'm in the Detective Bureau."

Five minutes later Curt went down the new cement walk to his VW in the faculty parking area. Less than a month to finals, then the empty summer stretching ahead. Before Paula's . . . death, he had looked forward to it; now he dreaded it. How would he fill its endless hours?

The afternoon was cloudy, gray to match his mood, with a sky so indigo over the Coast Range to the west that it was nearly black. A gust of wind whipped at his hair and tipped up one lapel of his jacket like the edge of a lilypad in a pond. He went down University Way to Los Feliz, fed a parking meter, and climbed the long straight flight of stairs to Floyd Preston's gymnasium. It was on the second floor above the Western Union office. Curt had signed up the Tuesday following Paula's suicide; he hadn't slept a moment since Worden's Sunday visit, and had read somewhere that weight-lifting was so strenuous it could numb the mind as well as the body. It hadn't worked, but at least he had been losing weight.

The gymnasium had once been a dance studio, a great boxy room with high ceilings and polished hardwood floor. The right-hand wall was windows, starting chest-high and extending upward; every few feet around the other walls were full-length mirrors. Between the mirrors on the left wall were racks of weight-graduated barbells; the racks of dumbbells were under the windows, at right angles to the wall. At either end of the gym were raised wooden platforms, mirror-backed, on which were the heavy competition-style Olympic barbell sets. Scattered about were a dozen vinyl-covered benches and various chrome pulleys and other apparatus.

Curt ignored the dozen or so men working out, going by them to the locker and shower area in the rear, separated from the gym by a partition and curtained doorways. He didn't see Preston, but he saw that the upper half of the office Dutch door was open, so the gym owner could check who was on the floor without leaving the office.

Curt got sweat pants and sweat shirt from his locker, then stripped and stepped on the scales: 209. Down thirteen pounds altogether, which was oddly satisfying. He sighed as he drew on the sweat clothes; so much in his life he would have done differently, if he had known that Paula . . . that Paula suddenly would be gone.

Curt followed Preston's typed program of exercises with singular intensity, starting with three sets of sit-ups on the incline board—lowest rung—and then going on to the dumbbell clean and press. By the middle of the second set he was puffing; by the end of the third, red-faced and blowing.

"You handle yourself as if you used to know your body pretty well, Halstead."

Curt started; Floyd Preston had approached as silently as a cat. He was like a cat in other ways: lithe, graceful, deceptively muscular and enormously strong. His face was broad, hard-chinned and angular under a thatch of thinning blond hair—a face that would have been Indian if it hadn't been dominated by cold blue eyes. He was about thirty-five but moved like a teen-age athlete.

Curt wiped a forearm across his face. "At least I'm working up a good sweat."

"Usually only body-builders preparing for a meet work out as hard as you've been going at it these past two weeks."

"I . . . lost my wife recently, so I . . . some trouble sleeping . . ."

He ran down. He had come to hate the stock, pat condolences one invariably was offered, and had been pleased to keep his discussions with Preston limited to reps, sets, poundages, lats, pecs, delts, presses, curls, squats.

But the gym owner surprised him: no sympathy. He merely said, "Must be a hell of an adjustment to make." His voice was very deep; he had thin lips and a broad sensitive mouth.

Curt finished his workout, stripped, weighed. Down three pounds—most of it, of course, merely water loss from sweating. Driving up El Camino in search of a bearable drive-in supper, he turned his thoughts to Worden for the first time since leaving the university. Would he be given faces to fit on the attackers tomorrow? Perhaps even names? The depth of his own emotion surprised him: he wanted to see them tried, and imprisoned, and the key thrown away. The society that had spawned such predators owed that much to Paula and to Harold Rockwell.

Curt parked on curving Jefferson Street, and walked back through bright May sunshine to the newly completed civic center complex. The sheriff's office was in a pink stucco building with three floors and a large sign announcing it as the Hall of Justice and Records. A cement mall separated this building from the County Courthouse. Curt entered a glum and drafty hallway and saw a hand-lettered sign directing him to his left. The room had a wooden counter down the center, to Curt's left, and more hand-painted signs indicating the elevators, the Criminal Division, Corrections, and the County Jail.

"Can you direct me to the Detective Bureau?" Curt asked.

Behind the counter was a very large red-headed man in a pale blue shirt with the Sheriff Department's emblem on the shoulder. He had a two-way radio mike in a right hand that made the mike look small. His sunburned, craggy features wore a slight look of exasperation. At Curt's question, he gestured toward the ceiling with the mike. "Third floor. Criminal Division."

Curt thanked him and went on. The elevator was deliberate, moving with the slow majesty of the law; it had an outsized cage that Curt guessed was for the transporting of prisoners between the jail and the courthouse. At the third floor was a reception desk with a small switchboard directly in front of the elevator. The receptionist was a thirtyish blonde with heavy hips and go-to-hell eye makeup.

By contrast, her voice was very subdued. "Can I help you, sir?"

"I have an appointment with Detective-Sergeant Worden."

"Certainly. If you'll wait a moment, please, sir."

The girl, who had a well-filled blue sweater and meaty dimpled knees under a flaring black skirt, took Curt's card and went through a door directly behind her desk. She shut the door carefully behind her. DETECTIVE BUREAU was painted on the opaque glass.

She returned in less than a minute. "This way, Mr. Halstead."

The Detective Bureau was brutally functional. There were three interrogation cubicles against the rear wall, windows along the right. The left wall was totally without ornament, the way a totally bald man is without hair. There was another door directly beside that through which Curt had entered; LIEUTENANT DORSEY was painted in one corner of its glass panel. Inside the cubicle, a thick-bodied man was champing a dead cigar and bending over a littered desk, writing.

Down the center of the main room was a double row of twelve gray metal desks with three-foot aisles between. On each desk was a telephone and beside each a typewriter stand. There were only four typewriters. Each desk bore an *In* and *Out* basket, and a plaque giving the name and rank of the desk's occupant. Five desks were in use.

"Sergeant Worden is—"

"Yes, thank you, ma'am. I see him."

Worden's desk was the fourth one on the left-hand side; he rose as Curt started toward him. On the desk was a small framed photo of a work-faded woman and two towheaded kids. They shook hands and sat.

"Good of you to come, Professor."

"I appreciate being put in the picture."

Somehow the conventionally banal exchange was like the crossing of rapier blades. Worden grunted as if skeptical of Curt's appreciation.

"You've lost some weight. Little trouble sleeping, maybe?"

"I've started working out at a gym in town," said Curt.

"Well, we all oughta get more exercise." He slapped a gut that sounded like an oak tree struck with a club. "Floyd Preston's place, huh? One tough cookie, that Preston. I remember when he opened up ten, twelve years ago, a lot of the barroom boys tried to pick a fight with him. Not many of them do anymore."

It was the longest digression Curt had ever heard him make, and he wondered if Worden was having trouble getting started. "I see. I'd like to know what your investigation has uncovered to date, Sergeant."

"Yeah. Well." Worden's eyes lost their momentary faraway look.

"I checked with the local cops on this Rockwell thing. Blew one there; should of remembered that your wife was the witness. It's messy, okay. The guy's blinded for life. He saw the guys who jumped him, sure, but he'd never seen 'em before—and sure as hell won't see 'em again."

"Does he know *why* they attacked him, or—"

"Naw. Juveniles. The whole thing took one, maybe two minutes." He paused to consult a folder. "Two-tone green Chevy station wagon, an older one—that's from your wife to the Los Feliz cops, Rockwell can't even give us that much. That's all we got there. But on your wife's thing, I got a little break. It seems a Mrs. Anderson called us about her kid. He'd been out to Sears Lake on his bike, and on the way home had the crap scared out of him by four guys near the golf course."

"This was the Friday night that Paula . . ."

"Yeah. About eight o'clock. His ma made it sound like dicky-jerking—you know, child molestation—so we talked to the kid. He made most of it up, we find out, to explain gettin' home late and to keep from gettin' a spanking. But he *did* go by four guys just getting outta their car north of the golf course, little turnaround—"

"I know the place." Curt was gripping the edge of the desk.

"It's gravel, lots of eucalyptus leaves; no identifiable tire casts, no assurance that what marks we did find were made that Friday night. Interesting thing is, the interior light was on, and the kid says it was a fifty-five or fifty-six Chevy station wagon. He's sure of that. No description of the guys, of course, just *big* guys—but to a ten-year-old, anybody over fourteen looks big. One of 'em fat, one of 'em short—like that."

Curt said thoughtfully, "They would have parked just after dark, walked down the fairway, cut through the ditch to our drive . . ."

"Yeah. By the fourteenth green. Again, no usable casts, just a place where several guys went across—could of been four." Worden leaned forward, gesturing with his big, thick hands. "Then we got lucky again. Just for the hell of it, I had the lab boys print that downstairs reading room where we figure the assault took place.

Got three clear prints, plus a partial, plus half a palm print, all of the same hand. Not yours, not your wife's—but we got enough for an ident if we ever have a hand to match 'em up with. Got 'em off the wall behind the sofa, where you might expect a guy to put his hand when he . . ."

Curt drew a deep ragged breath as Worden stopped. "Well, it sounds to me like you've made a good deal of progress, Sergeant. Where do we go from here?"

Worden shifted in his chair. Then he began playing with a ball-point pen from the desk. When the silence had become oppressive, he looked up at Curt again.

"We don't go nowhere, Professor." Seeing the sudden darkening of Curt's eyes, like the darkening of a pond when the first cat's paw of wind touches it, he added hurriedly, "Oh, hell, we'll keep it open. But for all practical purposes, our investigation is finished."

Curt's voice rose sharply, as if a knife had just been jammed through the back of his hand. "But you *can't* just . . . just *quit!*"

Heads turned, but only briefly; raised voices were no novelty in the Detective Bureau.

Worden leaned forward, his eyes suddenly bleak. "Christ, do you think I *like* it? There's just two kinds of people in my book, mister: the worms and the human beings. Law-breakers and law-keepers. These four snotty young bastards are worms. I'd like to get 'em alone in an alley for just five minutes, I'd wipe their noses for 'em so they'd never want to *touch* another woman again. But if I *arrested* 'em, Professor—then I couldn't even hold 'em."

Curt was spluttering. "What the devil do you mean? Why . . . why, they attacked and *blinded* a man. And then, because my wife had seen them, they invaded my home, did . . ." He choked off for a moment; the images flashing across his mental screen were too vivid. ". . . did something to her that was bad enough so she killed herself. And *you* say you couldn't hold them if you did find and arrest them?"

"Okay, let's take the Rockwell assault, Professor. The guy is *blind*. In court, just how the hell does he identify 'em? Braille?"

"But . . ."

"Remember, we're talking about a smart defense attorney being present to cross-examine. Voices? Who the hell was ever convicted on the evidence of *voices*, except maybe that French dame—Joan of Arc?"

"But my wife was *there*. She—" Curt stopped abruptly.

"Yeah. She's dead. The kid on the bike? Great. He saw four guys getting out of a car. Okay, so we got the fingerprints. Hard evidence—of sorts. *If* they were made by one of the gang, and *if* we ever catch up with him, and *if* we can get him to confess and name the others." He snorted. "So the D.A. brings 'em to trial—for assault and rape, remember, neither one of 'em capital crimes in this state—and *then* whadda we have? *Juveniles*, that's what. When the court psychiatrists and court-watchers and newspaper sob-sisters and A.C.L.U. lawyers got through, the D.A.'d be damned lucky to get 'em on probation and remanded to the custody of their parents for a year." He hurled his pen down in sudden culminating frustration. "Juvies, for God sake!"

Curt stood up slowly, unmoved, barely aware of Worden's tirade. His stomach was sour and his head ached. "You're saying that there is damned little chance that they ever will be apprehended, even less chance that they will be prosecuted, and no chance at all that they will be convicted and punished for anything."

Worden spread his huge paws in wry deprecation, once more in control of his reactions. "I'd be a liar if I told you anything else." He stood up, stretched a hand across the desk. "No hard feelings? It's just the facts of life, Professor."

Curt looked at the hand, then into Worden's once more hooded eyes; his own hands were fisted in his pockets. He ignored Worden's hand, very deliberately, to turn and walk from the room. Behind him, Worden shook his head, sighed, then sat down and began thoughtfully worrying his lower lip.

CHAPTER 9

Through the floor of his room, faintly, Rick could feel the throb of the television set. His folks, watching some stupid program. How the hell was a guy supposed to study with all that going on, and finals only three weeks away? He *had* to do well, otherwise he might end up in the Army. Even his old man, who had flown a desk back in World War II, said that the service was a waste of time.

QUESTIONS FOR STUDY:

1) What were the dominant features of the program advanced by the German liberals in 1884?

Had that kid on the bike seen them well enough to identify them?

2) What Christian philosopher wrote De Consolatione Philosophiae?

The newspapers, in telling of Paula's suicide, hadn't said anything about the kid. Did this mean the police didn't know about him?

3) Name the Latin history of England completed by the Venerable . . .

Rick slammed shut the book impatiently. If the kid hadn't gone to the police already, why would he go now? Maybe the police didn't even know she'd made love before she killed herself. Maybe . . .

Why did she have to go and do that?

Dark thoughts pattered busily through the back of his mind, like rats in a cave, but he quickly closed them away. She *had*, that was the only important thing now, and that kid was their only danger now. If he got really scared some way, so he'd be too scared to identify them, they'd be safe. But how to scare him?

Rick drummed his fingers on the desk. A phone call was safest, because then if he *couldn't* identify them, he wouldn't have seen them. A really rank anonymous phone call, threatening . . . say, make the call to his *ma*. That would be better. Rick knew all about how protective mothers could be when they thought their children were in jeopardy.

He slipped from the room and down the front stairs to the carpeted front hall where the phone was. Lucky both his sisters were out and his folks glued to the television; they'd blow a gasket or something if they caught him not studying. His ma was really hysterical about him maybe flunking out and having to go into the Army.

Heavy Gander's old man, who was a sheet-metal worker in Local 272, had moved to California from Ohio right after the war and had gotten an acre, cheap then, of weedy field just off Middlefield Road. He had built the garage well back from the bungalow, with the idea of maybe doing auto repair in his spare time. But after his wife had died, he had found that fishing took up most of his leisure hours. The garage, separated from the house by a weed-choked patch of ground, gradually had become Heavy's domain. There he did auto repair, keeping the station wagon, his beat-up Rambler, and his old man's Dodge in running order. He had bootlegged in a phone extension, using a set he'd bought from a mail order house, and had blacked out the windows so the gang could drink beer there and make all the noise they wanted.

On Saturday morning the four of them met in the garage.

"I *told* you we should of left when he went by on his bike,"

Heavy said nervously. His cherubic face was distressed above his can of beer.

"How the hell could we know she was going to kill herself?" Rick, as leader, couldn't let them see how the suicide had affected him. "So now all we gotta do is make sure that the kid keeps his mouth shut."

"But we gotta *find* him first, Rick," said Champ anxiously. He was sitting on a stool with his elbows on the edge of the workbench.

Julio cut in, "He is a paper boy, he will follow the same route every morning—and we already know one house he will go by. I will use the little green Rambler, and will find out his name and where he lives."

"*My* car? Aw, now look, you guys . . ." Heavy belched suddenly, cueing a giggle from Julio.

Rick, however, growled angrily. "Shut up, Heavy. You're the only guy with two cars."

Rick made a point of leaving the garage with Julio. "How come you volunteered like that? You've still got classes for two weeks . . ."

"Champ is too dumb to do it, and Heavy is too damn chicken." He paused for a moment, his liquid eyes gleaming. "But there is something I must say to you, Rick. We worry about this boy, who probably knows nothing of us, yet Debbie knows you were supposed to be there that night."

Rick felt a surprising surge of anger. Who did this little bastard think he was? Now that Rick remembered, Julio hadn't really helped much in beating up that goddamn queer that night. He hadn't been slow to get his turn at Paula, though.

"Leave Debbie out of this, Julio! I told you: she doesn't know *any* of us were there that night. She thinks I had a flat tire on the freeway on the way down from your house, and—"

"And if she hears the woman was raped?"

"Cool it, for Christ sake!" Rick shot nervous glances up and down the street. Two women were washing a car in a driveway across the street; half a block up, a black man was getting into an old pickup truck. "How's she ever *going* to find out? You think that creep professor's going to spread it around? Besides, old Debbie'll believe anything I tell her."

Julio shrugged. "Okay, Rick. Debbie is your concern—*now*. But if she becomes a danger, she becomes a danger to all of us."

Julio Escobar was parked on curving Edgewood Drive, just as far from the boy's house as he could be and still see the front door. It was a pleasant subdivision on a slanting hillside, with winding streets with such names as Hillcrest, Glenwood, Cedar, and Sycamore. Ranch-style homes, saplings planted in front yards, lawns green from daily waterings. Since finding out, on Wednesday, where the boy lived, Julio had tried unsuccessfully to find out the name of the woman who lived there. Divorced from her husband, or something, and raising her kid alone. That was good. A woman without a man to protect her or her son.

Julio checked the rear-view mirror, slid lower in his seat. Finding and following the kid had been easy, had taken three days to get the right house. But he still didn't have the name. That was why he was here on Sunday morning, waiting for the woman to take her son to church. If she didn't, he'd have to think of something else.

It had made much trouble for them when Paula Halstead had killed herself; but in a way, he was pleased that she had. They had used her like a whore, but in death she had regained her honor. His father talked a great deal of honor, and it was important, even if it did not put any beans or tortillas in the belly.

Thirty-six years old she had been. Only a year younger than Julio's mother. What would he, Julio, do if someone did to his mother what they had done to the Halstead woman? With no conscious action of his own, the switchblade suddenly was open in his hand. He tapped the blade against the Rambler's steering post. Julio would take vengeance then. He was not like this college professor who had been Paula's husband. Such a man was soft, would flutter away like a little bird, or perhaps hide under his desk when trouble came, like a little rabbit.

Julio was not like him. A knife, if you knew how to use it, made you nearly invincible against ordinary men. And Julio knew how to use his knife.

The front door opened and the boy came out, dressed in Sunday clothes. Julio tensed, slid the knife away. The boy tugged at the overhead door of the garage; it slid up easily. In a moment a white Ford Fairlane was backed out, with the woman behind the wheel.

She turned downhill, away from Julio. He sauntered down toward the house, turned in and went up the walk, his heart beating rapidly. Suddenly he was afraid. What if someone else was there, to remember his high narrow shoulders, his beak of a nose?

He faltered, almost stopped, then made himself ring the bell. He could hear it inside, an empty, heartening sound. He rang it again, to show himself he was not afraid, to make the dumb show convincing for the neighbors. He hoped one of them was watching, because . . .

"Hey you—kid."

The man had come out of the garage of the house directly across the narrow subdivision street. He stood on the lawn, with a green plastic garden hose drooping from one hand.

"Ye . . ." Julio cleared his throat. This was what he had wanted, wasn't it? "Yes, sir?"

The face relaxed a little at the "sir"; Julio had learned in school that politeness paid off.

"You looking for Miz Anderson?"

Anderson! As easy as that! "I . . . well, a *Mr.* Anderson, sir."

"Hasn't been a mister there for near two years." He had a round pleasant face, weekend-stubbled, and wore a windbreaker, a white T-shirt, jeans worn under a respectable beer belly, a black baseball cap with SF intertwined on it in orange. "Just Barb and the boy live there . . ."

"I wanted a . . . Frank Anderson, sir."

"Naw. His name was Charlie before they split up. Guess his name still is Charlie, come to think of it."

Julio left him chuckling at his own wit, and returned to the Rambler. He U-turned away from the house of his informant, drove down looping residential streets to El Camino, and went south until he came to a shopping center. It was Sunday-deserted, its white-lined lot so lightly dusted with cars that he could drive diagonally across to the phone booths. He riffled through the county directory. Yes. There was the listing. He carefully copied down the phone number.

"Lemme call her, Rick," begged Champ. He worked his muscular hands, making the cords jump and quiver in his forearms.

"Cutting cards is the only fair way," Julio objected. Like Rick, he was afraid that Champ would foul up the call if he made it. It was Tuesday night, and they were back in Heavy's garage again, with its grease-stained floor and mingled odors of metal and oil and gasoline.

Heavy was sweating profusely; the shirt was plastered over his seal-like body. "I don't see why we gotta cut cards," he whined, watching Rick shuffle. Then, seeing the look in the others' eyes, he went on lamely, "Well, I mean, Champ *wants* to and all, and . . ."

"And you're chicken. We cut cards, like I said. Low man."

"I'll go first," said Champ eagerly.

Rick put the deck on the workbench, under the extension light that hung from a nail in the rafter above. Their hands, arms, and chests were in the glaring light as Champ cut; their faces were just pale blobs in the dimness outside the circle of illumination.

"Aw, hell, a seven. That ain't very low, is it?"

Rick shuffled again without answering. His fingers were smeary when he touched the deck, and he knew he didn't want to make the call. There was something . . . well, uncool, in threatening a little kid. Even when it was necessary. So he blew out a breath of silent relief when he got a jack of clubs; but he turned to Heavy with only sarcasm in his voice. "Let's see what the crybaby gets."

It was a ten. Heavy, who had been eating a candy bar, left smears of chocolate on the cards. He didn't bother to hide his relief. Julio, in his turn, cut an eight.

"Wow!" exclaimed Champ, "that means I win, huh, fellows?"

Rick said carefully, "Ah, Champ, maybe we ought to, ah, like make it three out of five, or . . ."

Champ's face puckered like that of a baby about to cry. The thick muscles swelled in his throat. He looked from Julio to Rick and back again; they were the ones he had to convince. Heavy, he knew, wanted him to have the fun of calling.

"I know you think I ain't smart enough to do it right," he said earnestly, "But I can do it. I know I can. Why, I already . . ."

He already had made those other two calls, the ones to Nancy Ellington. She was seventeen or something, and went to one of those fancy Catholic girls' schools run by the nuns or somebody. This long black hair, see, and a round real serious face, and sometimes she would talk to him when he was working in the garden at her folk's place.

One morning she was off from school for a saint's birthday or something, and he was going by her bedroom window, real early it was, and there she was bare-ass, so he saw her tits and everything.

"You already what, Champ?" prompted Julio.

"I . . . ah . . . nothin'. I just . . . I got a right to do it . . ."

That Saturday he'd called up with his handkerchief over the phone like he'd seen on the TV, just to tell her what he wanted to do to her but she'd busted out crying. He'd called the next day, too, but old Mr. Ellington answered and said the police were tracing the call, so he'd hung up, real quick, and hadn't ever called again.

Rick sighed. "Okay, Champ, you got a right to do it. We'll call right now, while Heavy's old man isn't home."

"Aw, Christ, Rick, from *here?*" Heavy's chins trembled. "What if they trace the call or something, and—"

"They can't trace through all the electronic equipment they use now," Rick scoffed. "Not unless they're all set up ahead of time."

So they clustered around the bootlegged phone extension while Champ dialed. The woman picked up on the third ring. Not even Rick could find any fault with Champ's performance; in fact, at the end of the two minutes he was sweating. Some of the things Champ said would happen, not only to the boy but to the woman herself, if anybody talked to the police about that night by the golf course, made him, in fact, feel sort of sick. When he glanced over, Julio looked the same way.

But Heavy, once the phone was back in its hook, seemed to feel only a slightly lascivious excitement and sense of power. "What'd she say, Champ, huh? What'd she say when—"

"She started to cry there at the last," said Champ happily.

CHAPTER 10

Curt came from the tin-lined shower in the locker room, his skin flushed red from the needle spray of water, and began toweling off vigorously. He felt better than he had for a long time, at least physically. The scales told him he had broken two hundred pounds for the first time in several years, and the mirror told him that the workouts were beginning to make a difference in his appearance, also. It was just a little after noon of a Thursday—June 12th—and the warm summer air brought the minor rumble and squeal of Los Feliz traffic in through the locker room windows. Summer. There was the real trouble. Commencement was on Sunday; what in God's name would he do with his time from now on? There was not even the hope of arrests of the members of the gang to carry him along anymore.

Dressed, he started across the gym floor. Preston was just locking up the Dutch doors of the office. His face lighted up when he saw Curt. Sometime in the seven weeks Curt had been coming to the gym, they had graduated to first names.

"Hey, old buddy, you got time for a sandwich and a beer?"

Curt hesitated. He had been worried about filling up his days; this was one way. "Sure, why not, Floyd? We can even use my car."

Preston directed him to the Pigskin Club, a small bar and restaurant that faced an access road off Bayshore Freeway. Only one car was parked in front.

"Al doesn't serve lunches," Preston explained. "But he'll make us a couple of salami sandwiches."

The heavy front door was leather-padded and brass-studded on the inside; Curt paused, waiting for his eyes to adjust to the interior dimness. Directly in front was a small dining room with a dozen white-clothed square tables set for the supper trade; to the right was an archway leading into the taproom. The bar had red vinyl fronting and red-topped stools with chromium legs.

"Curt, I'd like you to meet Al Ferrano. Al, Curt Halstead."

Ferrano was a short dapper man with bright eyes in a swarthy face. At first glance he was forty; a closer look suggested a very well-kept fifty. He wore a white apron over his shirt and slacks.

"You must work out at the gym," he said as they shook hands.

"I just started a few weeks ago."

Ferrano shook his head; he had a quick ready smile. "This bar keeps me too damned busy. I only get up there twice a week, so all I do is arm and shoulder work."

He had flipped the caps from three bottles of icy beer while he talked; he set them, beaded and glistening, on the bar, and busied himself with French rolls and mayonnaise. He had singularly heavy forearms.

"I gotta work out for arm-wrestling, would you believe it? My main trade in here is working guys, and after a few beers the construction boys always wanna arm-wrestle." He gestured expansively with the broad-bladed French chef's knife. "Well, what the hell could I do? You don't wrestle 'em, you're a shit-heel and they don't come back. You do, you lose all the time, you're giving the house away. So I started working out at Floyd's gym."

Three men came in, nodded to Ferrano, and settled at the back end of the bar. Ferrano set the sandwiches in front of Curt and Preston.

"Now, thanks to Floyd, guys come in just to try and beat me. Win or lose, they're good for a few drinks, so it's done wonders for business. Excuse me, huh, fellows?"

As he was serving the three men, a blond girl arrived, and then another pair of men. Someone fed the juke box. Curt munched salami sandwich, drank beer. For the first time since Paula's death he felt an inner spring of tension begin gradually to unwind. Preston asked what he taught at the university, and Curt realized that they really knew nothing at all of each other's backgrounds. Which struck him as somehow intriguing, since the gym had become a major focal point in his life during the past weeks.

"Anthropology, Floyd. Mainly upper-level courses these days, which is rather a pity. One becomes gradually isolated from the undergraduates, the ones on whom you can most easily see your fingermarks."

Preston turned his empty bottle with a muscle-thickened hand that looked capable of crushing the glass to brown powder. "I never finished high school—was in the eleventh grade when Korea started, so I quit to join the Army. After Korea, I never went back." His marvelous grin suddenly quirked at the corners of his mouth and made his blue eyes light up almost impishly. "I figured there wasn't enough in my head to live on anyway, so I decided to depend on my back." He slid off his stool. "Why don't you order us a couple more, Curt? I'll be right back—my kidneys are floating."

Curt caught Ferrano's eye, nodded for two more beers, and then caught his own reflection in the back-bar mirror. What did they call it? Fighting the mirror. Odd, Ferrano had spotted him as a body-builder—unless it just had been a guess based on the fact that he was with Preston. That seemed more likely.

His elbow was jostled; the place was filling up. How many years had it been since he'd drunk beer in a workingman's bar? Ferrano brought the beers. He had a good thing going here, and knew it. Curt glanced around, saw Preston returning with his catlike tread. In his form-fitting T-shirt and tight slacks, he was a living advertisement for his own gymnasium. Curt also saw that the man who had jostled his elbow had taken Preston's stool despite the weightlifter's change, cigarettes, glass, and newly opened beer on the bar in front of it.

"That's okay," Preston said, coming up as Curt was reaching out to tap the other man on the shoulder. "I'd just as soon stand for a bit." He edged up to the bar between Curt and the other man, and began pouring out his beer.

The man on the stool turned abruptly. "Hey, watch who you're shoving, mac," he said.

Preston eyed him pleasantly. "Sorry. I didn't know you'd bought the place from Al."

He turned back to Curt, but the other man laid a heavy hand on his shoulder from behind. The shoulder quivered under the touch, Curt saw, exactly like the shoulder of a horse quivering under a fly, but Preston allowed himself to be swung around.

"I said watch who you're shoving, mac." He was stocky and dark, with a tough belligerent face hazed with the day's whiskers. A pair of stained and tattered leather work gloves was on the bar beside him. "If I want any crap from you, mister, I'll beat it out."

"Are you looking for trouble?" asked Preston pleasantly.

"Yeah, as a matter of fact, I—"

Preston hit him.

The blow traveled a bare six inches, but man and stool went over backwards and sideways with a crash that froze conversation along the bar. The fallen warrior, sprawled on the rug, shook his head as if to clear it. The action had been so much like a television fight that Curt almost expected a huckster to appear selling cigarettes. None did.

Instead, Preston poked a finger at the other man. "If you want to fight, get up and fight. Otherwise, I owe you a beer."

Ferrano set them up, bustling noisily, making jokes, slapping shoulders, as the man got up and moved down the bar, muttering, with his companion.

Preston sent two beers down to them, righted his stool, and calmly sat down. "If a guy wants trouble, hit him first," he remarked. "But if he has a thick neck and isn't fat, watch out. And if he doesn't fall down—run."

Curt shook his head in amazement. "Does this sort of thing happen to you very often?"

"It used to when I first opened the gym. Guys then still used to think that weight-lifters and body-builders were so musclebound that they'd tear something if they lifted an arm above their shoulder." He shook his head and grinned. "I suppose I used to think the same thing, before I started lifting. That was while I was in the Army—cadre in the infantry in Fort Leonard Wood, Missouri. Little Korea, we called it."

"You sounded like an anthropologist yourself there for a minute," Curt said. Then he added, seeing Preston's blank expression, "That thing about watching out for men with thick necks who aren't fat. You are a student of the physical man—and in the broadest terms, anthropology is a study of man and his works."

Curt meant to stop there, but he had drunk several beers, had eaten only a light lunch after a heavy workout, and had been having a rotten time sleeping at night. He went on to social anthropology, his own discipline in the field, and found he was talking almost compulsively. It was a strange performance, with part of him sitting back and shaking his head while he rocketed on ineluctably toward Paula's suicide. The ease with which Preston had handled the random violence in the bar had loosened some inner brake; he was like a truck left unattended on top of a hill, taking a long time to get started but impossible to stop once he was rolling.

It was nearly three o'clock when he finally ran down, ending with, ". . . and Sergeant Worden says there's no legal way to touch them, even if the police ever would catch up with the ones who did it."

Preston gave him an odd look. "Yeah, it's the old squeeze. The difference between what you satisfy yourself with, and what you have to have to satisfy a judge and jury." He paused for a moment, said offhandedly, "You almost sound as if you'd like to go after them yourself."

"Me?" Curt was truly startled. "Lord no, not me, Floyd. I wouldn't have the slightest idea of how to go about it, and I wouldn't know what to do with them if I would find them. I . . . I guess I'm not a very good hater."

"Yeah? I would have thought . . ." Preston stopped, stretched, and slid off the stool. "I'd better get on back to the gym, Curt. Even on Thursdays the guys start coming in around four o'clock."

After dropping Preston off, Curt tried to hang on to the rather sleepy, euphoric, beery feeling he'd had in the bar; but by the time he had arrived home, it was completely dissipated. He felt singularly useless, somehow dislocated in time. He had always prided himself on his involvement in modern American life: he approved of change, of new directions, new methods at the university. He approved of student involvement in protest marches and civil rights and antiwar agitation. Because of these attitudes, he had always felt himself deeply involved in the goals and aspirations and everyday life of the country.

Yet that afternoon he had felt a gulf separating him from the others in the bar—not a feeling of superiority, just a feeling of apartness. An uncomfortable feeling that his thoughts, actions, reactions to any given situation would not be theirs. How many of his colleagues at the university would dismiss Floyd Preston with witty, cutting, erudite jokes because he ran a muscle emporium? Yet Preston was decisive in everyday situations in a way that Curt desperately wished he could be. *If a guy wants trouble, hit him first.* Preston saw nothing wrong in the idea of taking vengeance into one's own hands.

Curt went into the room where the rape had happened. The weekly cleaning lady had been in there every Monday with her vacuum sweeper and dustrag, but Curt had not opened the door since that night. Now, standing in the middle of the room made dim by drawn shades, he remembered vividly the rumpled daybed, the accordioned rug, the overturned stool. He shivered.

Paula, facing it alone, no way to turn, no hope at all of aid . . .

Paula, whom he had never seen with her head bowed in fourteen years of marriage, defeated, broken, destroyed . . .

God, *why* hadn't he come home early that night? He drew a long shuddering breath and walked out into the hall.

Paula was dead: dead, dead, bloody dead, and there was nothing he could do about it.

Was there?

CHAPTER 11

Debbie drew a deep shuddering breath and pulled back from Rick's embrace. "Darling—please. We mustn't. I have to go in now."

"Just a little while longer," he pleaded. His hand again sought her breast through its protective cup of brassiere.

"No, please, Rick. I just . . . you know, it's just . . ."

Rick sighed in mock resignation and removed his hand. Debbie, her face flushed, quickly closed the top three buttons his agile fingers had undone. Her hands were shaking slightly. Rick smiled his special smile, and hopped out of the driver's side of the Triumph. Then, as Debbie quickly smoothed down her rumpled skirt, he stuck his head in under the canvas top on his side. "Just so long as you aren't sore," he said.

When he got around the back of the car to open her door, she said, "You know I'm not, darling."

The smile she flashed was so full of future delights that Rick caught his breath sharply. When she slid out, he enjoyed an exciting glimpse of her legs well beyond her stocking tops. That was one thing about the old Triumph, all right. It made them show what they had. He put his arm around her waist as they went up the walk together to Forrest Hall.

He started up the steps with her, but Debbie drew him along the front of the porch into the shadows cast by the supporting columns. "So you won't forget me before next time, Ricky," she said.

She raised her face to his; when their lips met, her tongue darted into his mouth for a moment. Her breathing was short and quick when she finally drew away. Rick said, "Tomorrow night, Deb?"

"I've got to spend the weekend with my folks," she said. "They don't even know I signed up for summer school yet. Classes start next week, so we'd better wait until Friday—a week from tomorrow."

"Week from today, actually," said Rick. "Eight o'clock. Here."

"Okay." She pecked him quickly on the mouth, slid from his automatic attempt to embrace her, and trotted up the steps. On the porch she stopped to blow him a kiss, then went in quickly, catching the screen door so it wouldn't slam. Safely out of sight inside, she leaned against the wall to get her breath. Wow! Even her legs felt weak!

Friday. She'd made it a whole week as a sort of self-discipline. She went quickly to the door again, and looked out. Rick, erect and clean-limbed, was climbing into the Triumph. This was going to be some summer! She couldn't tell her folks, of course, that she'd signed up for summer school because she'd suddenly realized that she didn't want to spend the whole summer on the other side of the Bay, in San Leandro. Where Ricky wasn't.

Debbie floated up the stairs to her room. The dorm was nearly deserted, except for the senior girls who would be graduating on Sunday, because the summer session classes didn't begin until Wednesday.

She started to undress. It really would be a fight not to let Ricky do whatever he wanted to her; just his touch seemed to make fears and inhibitions and hesitations melt. She was glad she was going to be attending classes, because she always studied hard and that would help keep it from getting out of hand. She'd almost given in to him last July, out by Sear's Lake that time when he'd gotten her blouse off and her bra pushed up and everything, and had almost lost him because of it. He'd dropped her completely for nine months, until he'd called in April about getting Professor Halstead's address. She was glad, really, because it showed he wasn't just interested in what he could get from her.

Funny. It had started over again with Professor Halstead, and now his wife was dead and the professor was living all alone out in that big house by the golf course. She remembered Paula from that faculty-student tea: a mature blond woman with a really marvelous figure despite her age. Debbie bet the professor really missed her. Look at the way Ricky, who had hardly known her, had reacted to her suicide.

Debbie stopped with her dress halfway over her head. Paula Halstead and . . . Ricky? That was silly, of course, but . . . But it would explain so many things that had bothered her in the past weeks. Like that sort of flimsy reason he'd had for wanting to see her alone. How broken up Ricky had been at her death.

He could have met her downtown, sometime . . . or in a bar. She knew he sometimes went into bars, because he had shown her the false ID that Heavy Gander had gotten for him somewhere.

She finished undressing very quickly, and got into her flannel pajamas. What if . . . She bounced into bed, sat with her arms clasping her up-drawn knees. What if Paula had killed herself because . . . because Rick hadn't shown up that Friday? That would explain so much.

Debbie's lips thinned and her eyes became calculating. Was she in competition for Rick with the dead woman? A mature, exciting woman who could have wrapped an inexperienced boy like Rick around her . . . well, around her finger?

Debbie might not be a mysterious, slinky, smoldering blonde: but she had a good figure if she did admit it herself, and she was right here, right now. Alive and warm and . . . yes, available, if that was going to be what it took to erase the image of the older woman.

Driving away from the dorm in his flashy red car, Rick pressed the cigarette lighter and turned the radio to a San Francisco pops station. His cigarette canted up at a jaunty angle as he approved his image in the rear-view mirror.

That Debbie, she was something else! Insipid, had he thought? Wow. When she'd Frenched him there, by the porch, he'd thought he was going to cream his jeans. Somehow he was going to get into her pants. A motel? She wouldn't go to one with him. Not now, not yet. Maybe his folks' cabin down by the ocean? Take it slow, talk her around to it? He shouldn't have dropped her last summer, but she hadn't been much then.

The lighter popped, he steered one-handed to light up, sending the car in squealing playful sweeps down the deserted drive. She really turned him on, old Deb; not like Paula Halstead had, of course, but . . .

His mood dissolved. He shrieked the car into the down-ramp to El Camino. Now, at nearly midnight, there were great black gaps in the traffic. The beat pounded out sure and strong from the radio. Paula Halstead. He still could remember that second time, her throwing her head back and forth while he'd been doing it. No other chick in his admittedly limited experience had come on that way with him.

Goddamn it, it *wasn't* his fault, what she'd done afterward. At least now, with the ma of that kid on the bike scared shitless, they were safe. If only he could forget about what had happened afterward, to Paula. It shouldn't have been that way. Shouldn't have been at all. He should have met her someplace nice, alone, in a bar, maybe. Streaking down the highway, he let his imagination roam.

Sure, a fancy cocktail place with thick rugs and soft indirect lighting, where they put a little napkin down under each woman's drink. He would see her, send a drink down to her, she would move over and start talking with him. Her husband couldn't satisfy her, she'd say, and then she'd invite him over to her motel room. In the room they'd . . .

Rick slammed on the brakes, shrieked sideways down a hundred feet of concrete, watching with almost clinical detachment the onrushing rear of the car he'd almost tailgated. He straightened her out, got into the right lane. Goddamn old creep, barely moving! His hands were shaking a little. Cup of coffee? Sure. Relax a minute. Ahead was the little café where Debbie first had told him about Paula's suicide. That had really been a shock. But as far as he was concerned, Paula had never happened. He'd never laid eyes on her. Safer that way.

He slowed, pulled into the white-lined parking area to the right of the café. His fear at the near-crash had begun melting into his lingering arousal from Debbie's good night. The trouble with young stuff like Deb was that you had to play the game with them. The older ones, they wanted it and they admitted it, just like a guy would.

Older women.

He peered through the windshield and lighted square window of the little diner. Older women like that blond waitress here who'd tipped him the wink that night. Funny, he'd forgotten about her until right now, but there she was, just putting down a hamburger in front of some guy. Bleached blonde, twenty-five, maybe pushing thirty almost. The sort who'd let a guy try goddamn near anything he wanted with her. He checked his image in the mirror, ran a comb through his hair. Debbie, get him all turned on and then . . . good night, huh? Well, maybe this chick . . . just maybe . . .

CHAPTER 12

Curt awoke early on Friday morning with a profound feeling of depression, like a delayed hangover from the previous afternoon's beer. But the depression was emotional, not physical, compounded in part from the nagging inadequacy he had felt the previous evening, standing in the downstairs room where the rape of Paula had taken place. Without classes, without his seminar to prepare, he walked through the household chores he had set himself; by two o'clock he was staring glumly out a window and through the trees to the dazzling green of the golf course.

Four men carrying their bags in little wheeled carts were trudging up the fairway, dwarfed by distance into plastic toy figures. Up that way on that Friday night would have come the predators, four of them, sheltered by darkness. One of Paula's favorite Latin aphorisms came to mind: *He who is bent on doing evil can never want occasion*. Certainly, if those who had attacked Paula also had attacked Rockwell, they had come here bent on evil.

One of the toy figures swung a club; after a long moment, Curt heard the hollow slap of wood on golf ball, saw the tiny gleaming shape roll to a stop on the other side of the fourteenth green. A good shot.

Feeling suddenly stifled in the house, Curt went down to the VW, got in, slid back the sun roof. That had been Paula's idea; she had thought the convertible ugly but had wanted the sun on bright days. He started the car, went down the drive and north of Linda Vista. As he had come home that night, past the Longacres intersection. Down there a passing boy had seen the four, getting from their car, while Curt had dispensed wisdom in a drive-in booth. No such thing as evil: just poor, frustrated humanity occasionally snapping under the enormous impersonal pressures of society. While Paula's life drained redly to the floor . . .

Stop it, damnit! There was nothing you could have done.

But what if certain maverick students of humanity like Dart and Leakey and Laurens were right: that in man there still stalked about an atavistic, unschooled self from the older, mindless days of his journey? And what if Curt should let his control of that self slip? Then what?

He took a right from Entrada into El Camino, then left into Brewer toward downtown Los Feliz. Time to stop indulging his Bogart fantasies: he was a middle-aged law-abiding university professor whose wife had killed herself and who was feeling guilty about her death. He tried to turn his mind outward, away from his compulsive scabpicking. The town was full of students whom Sunday's commencement would release—from the university, from this town. Out they would go, sky-diving: it would all be free-fall for them then. You tried to prepare them for it, but you never knew whether you had succeeded; the surprise, really, was how well most of them landed.

He realized he was crossing the railroad tracks where Rockwell had been attacked. Some vague urge made him pull in and park across from the laundromat beyond the tracks, and walk back to the edge of the gravel-scattered planks. Right *here* Rockwell had fallen; here the faceless ones had struck. Kids, probably in a stolen car; kids, hopped-up or stoned or drunk, acting out some private fantasy projection. One read of it, the random violence, but never applied it to one's own life.

But it happened. Into fashionable, quiet Los Feliz had come violence. An old green station wagon, driving south, squealing tires on the turn into Brewer. Slum kids from San Francisco, seeking kicks? Curt raised his head to look west at the Coast Range cupping the Peninsula cities against the Bay. Sparkling subdivisions massed the lower slopes. Slum kids? Or well cared-for kids from these shady streets and sleek ranch-style houses?

If this act of senseless violence had come from these homes, he thought, it became even more senseless, because these houses had been built as fortresses against economic want and personal frustration by a whole generation of parents grimly determined to give their kids everything they could. Under current theories, such homes should have been a quarantine against, not a culture for, the germs of violence.

Curt returned thoughtfully to his car, got in. *I want that boy caught, and I want him punished.* Now Paula was dead, and in turn her attackers also would go unpunished. Enforcers like Monty Worden, whose lives were intimately bound up with the swift and brutal collision of man with man, of man with society, seemed to push everyone around except the predators. In this society, they were the ones who struck and got away with it.

A pity, Curt thought, that just for a while he wasn't a predator himself. As Worden had said, find them and get them alone long enough to make them hurt, hard, for the maimed and dead they had left behind. Render them unable to forget the magnitude of that hurt, that fear, so their sharp vicious edge would be gone and they would be lessened.

Curt realized that he was at the far edge of the brief Los Feliz business district. Ahead, on the right, was the old gray limestone building that housed the city library. Preston's fight the day before must have turned his mind to the past again: to the old hectic days of the S.A.S., when you settled arguments in streets or bars with your hands, your heavy jump boots, and the lieutenant calmly ignored black eyes and puffy noses and swollen knuckles in morning parade. Yes, events in another life, to another person.

Certainly not to Curtis Halstead, Ph.D.

There was a free parking meter in midblock, and Curt parked.

He went up the wide steps and into the library's cool shadowed interior. Behind the desk was a teen-age girl, probably summer help, wearing a filmy white blouse that was blushed a pale flesh tint by her skin.

"Could you tell me where the newspaper files are, miss?"

"In the Periodical Room, sir. Go down that hallway . . ." She leaned across the desk to point out a corridor beyond the open stacks. "Third door on the right; you can't miss it . . ."

As she leaned forward, Curt, without conscious volition, stared down the loose neck of her blouse to the shadowed curves of her swelling youthful unbrassiered breasts. He pulled his eyes away, met a face suddenly scornful of his momentary voyeurism, and backed hastily away even as he felt an almost horrifying stab of acute physical desire.

"I . . . thank you . . . miss . . ." he managed to say.

He fled down the indicated corridor, paused only when he was out of sight of the desk. For God's *sake*, she was *truly* young enough to be his daughter. Was he becoming some sort of dirty old man? He went on to the closed door marked Periodical Room in old-fashioned gilt letters. He could begin now to see the ludicrous elements of it: a fortyish professor fleeing from a young girl's half-glimpsed breasts as from some artful Circe's abandoned sexual beckoning. It was, after all, a natural biological urge, and Paula had been gone for two months.

The periodical attendant was safely gray-haired, with new teeth that obviously did not fit her well. She seemed glad of a customer in the stuffy room. "Yes, sir"—she beamed—"we have the April numbers of the local papers. January through March aren't available. They're out being microfilmed, you see."

"April is all I need," Curt assured her.

He paged through the *Los Feliz Daily Times* for Saturday, April 26th, the day after Paula's death. Sergeant Worden was quoted as saying that Mrs. Halstead had died of self-inflicted wounds. Period. Curt was grateful for the restrained tones. The only Monday followup was the obituary notice, for which he had supplied the material himself. The San Francisco Sunday papers carried only a very brief *Woman Slays Self*.

What masochistic impulse had brought him here to paw through the painful dust of memory? There was nothing he could do, damnit. But still, since he was here . . .

He returned to the *Daily Times*, checking Saturday, April 19th. The attack on Harold Rockwell, unlike Paula's suicide, had been News. There was a front-page photo of Rockwell, obviously from a high school yearbook, a newspaper picture of Rockwell's wife, Katherine, and one of Paula blown up from a sports section photo that had appeared when Paula and another faculty wife had won the faculty tennis doubles. On an inside page was a cut of the Brewer Street railroad crossing with an artist's X marking the spot where Rockwell had fallen. Paula had merely been listed as "cooperating with the police" in their attempts to identify the assailants.

That didn't really seem enough to trigger the four assailants into their second attack, a week later, on Paula. Could he be wrong? Could the assault and rape in his home be unconnected with the attack on Rockwell? Could it just after all have been random violence?

He returned to the newspaper. On Monday the editorial had been about Crime in the Streets. The police investigation, though not headlined, still had been front page. Rockwell was blind, probably permanently. This time Paula was mentioned as being sure she could identify one of the attackers if she saw him again, and was said to have gotten "a very good look" at the automobile driven by the gang.

Yes. That might have been enough. The obsession could have begun, and deepened: the need to see if she could identify the leading attacker. If she could, the necessity to silence her would loom very large in his thoughts. So it could have started as a simple assault, a beating, to assure her silence; but then, physically handling her, wrestling with her . . . Paula's tennis-player's body had been almost calculated to arouse desire . . .

Curt folded up the newspaper wearily. The society that had produced the predators had a good deal to answer for. Or did it? He was suddenly impatient with all the sociological muck he was used to reeling off glibly to his students. Society had not blinded Rockwell. Society had not raped Paula. No matter what pressures they may have been subject to—if any—the predators were the ones who had acted.

And what was needed was another predator, as violent as they.

Curt returned the papers, went back down the corridor and through the main library. His teenage temptress was still at the desk; but now she was just an immature girl whose idea of being chic and daring was to sneak out of the house without wearing a bra under her blouse. As Curt went down the front steps and toward the VW, his mind was elsewhere.

What was needed was a predator, but there was none. So Paula's agony would go unavenged, and the same thing might happen to others.

Curt wished that he hadn't stopped at the railroad crossing, hadn't come here to the library to burn the details of it all into his brain anew. Because of it, he was going to have a lousy time sleeping for the next couple of nights.

CHAPTER 13

"It's a piece of bloody cake," said the sergeant-major.

They were in the back of a Long Range Desert Group jeep, bouncing through the darkness toward a Jerry airdrome near the coast. It was Curt's first mission. The jeep, key to this sort of hit-and-run operation, had no top or windscreen. On the back, on the sides, even on the hood were jerrycans of gasoline and water. Coupled twin Vickers K machine guns jutted up into the star-spattered desert night from both front and rear, their interlocking fields of fire covering the entire 360° radius about the jeep.

They were moving rapidly across open ground, without lights; whenever the jeep lurched, curses lashed the air.

"I'd rather make an effing air drop." In the dark, faces were mere pasty smears. "A piece of bloody cake," repeated the sergeant-major. "I've hit these desert airfields before, laddie. A few guards, a few patrols, a bit of wire, the odd machine-gun nest . . ."

They would slip through the wire in the dark, avoiding the patrols and sentries, to fix their high explosives on the planes. The nitro was mixed with incendiary material to make better fires, and would be detonated by half-hour time pencils that were designed to give them a mile or two of desert before the planes went up.

A piece of cake.

Going through the wire, Curt saw a red glow as a sentry drew on his cigarette a bare dozen yards from their entry point. All the man had to do was turn, see the moving shadows, fire his rifle or cry out . . .

Hand-to-Hand Manual was very firm about silencing a sentry. You went in from the rear, thrusting your knife into his right kidney while smothering any outcry; then you withdrew your knife, slashing as you did, and cut his throat. In the *Manual*, your opponent reacted to this silent, swift, tidy slaughter very much like a hundredweight of grain.

Curt touched the sergeant-major on the shoulder and slid away toward the sentry without further signal. He moved silently and without haste, his mind safely blank, concentrating only on the red glow as the sentry drew on his cigarette again.

Eight yards to go. In the clear desert air he could smell the burning tobacco. Five yards. The knife was in his right hand, point forward, guard against the tip of his thumb and edge of his forefinger.

The glowing dot moved erratically, then showered sparks in being snubbed out against the stock of the sentry's rifle. Curt, motionless, now could see his dim silhouette. The sentry sighed, took his rifle from his shoulder, grounded the butt in the sand by his right boot, and muttered something under his breath in German. Curt went in fast under the cover of the man's own movements.

His left hand closed over mouth and nose and pulled up and to the left, fingers digging into the flesh. He could feel the hard line of jawbone under his third finger; the edge of his thumb was pressed deeply against the sentry's left eyeball, so he could feel the frantic rolling beneath the shielding lid. His legs, intertwined with the sentry's, upset their balance so they started down.

The sentry instinctively put out his hands to break the fall, and Curt put his knife in. It went with a terrible ease, to the guard, with a slight ripping noise as it tore the shirt. All according to the *Manual*.

But then the sentry made a muffled grating noise, all of his scream that got through Curt's fingers. He tried to bite, butt, jerk his face free from Curt's terrible clutching strength. The body under Curt tensed to iron, trembled like a retriever coming from an icy lake. The sentry dug in toes, fingers, reached far above his head, dragged their coupled bodies forward even through the yielding sand.

Finally the rock-hard, straining muscles went flaccid. The toes stopped digging, the clenched hands opened. His strap hadn't been fastened, so his helmet had flipped off, and Curt's jaw was gouged hard against the short-clipped hair. The breathing stopped below him, but Curt didn't move. He listened as the rest of the band fanned out across the airfield, but his moment of fierce exultation had turned to lassitude, to a drained, almost sick feeling.

Five minutes passed.

He had been nearly asleep. He rolled off Paula's nude, sated body in the dark, then groped back again toward heavy melon of breast, silken hollow of hip, warm swell of pubic mound.

"Paula!" he whispered softly.

She didn't move, playing dead. Curt chuckled and reached across to her far shoulder, tipped her toward him.

Her head flopped solidly on the pillow and she stared at him in the semi-dark, slack-jawed, with the sentry's dead sand-gritted eyes.

Curt uttered a hoarse, jaw-creaking shriek of terror, his eyes strained so wide open that the whites showed all the way around. He hurled himself back, twisting in midair, and struck the varnished hardwood floor of the study with his chin, hard enough to jar his teeth.

He sprawled there for a moment in his pajama pants, then rolled over and sat up. His eyes still were wild and his jaw ached. A shudder of revulsion passed through him: he still had an erection.

Not bothering with a light, he staggered down the hall to the bathroom and threw cold water into his face. His luminous watch showed it was just a little after four. Monday morning. He straightened up from the washbasin, cold water dripping down his chest.

He knew it then, for the first time, with an icy certainty.

He was going to find the boys who had raped Paula. Find them, break them, physically and spiritually. Make them crawl and grovel, mew with terror and pain. If the law couldn't touch them, he would be his own predator. Why would he do it, for himself or Paula? Who could unscramble it? Who cared? To hell with motivations.

He padded down the hall, opened the door, was halfway into the bedroom before he realized where he was. It was the first time he had entered the room, except to move his clothes, since the night of Paula's death. The cleaning lady kept it tidy, the king-size bed made up.

Curt didn't even pause. He crossed the room, tossed back the spread, climbed between the sheets. Could his continuing agony of spirit merely have been an agony of indecision? He didn't know; but he slept right through until nine o'clock.

Okay, you want them. You've made your decision. Now where do you start?

Sixteenth Avenue was in the old section of town near the tracks, two miles north of the business district. The street was straight, not curving; the curbs were high, angular, not shallow dips for the convenience of trike-trundling kids. Two-storied houses: prewar, Midwestern in flavor. On these streets it still might have been 1938.

Curt parked in front of 1248 16th Avenue and looked it over. The rambling two-story house had white siding that would soon peel, and a lawn that needed mowing. The old-fashioned black iron gate was rusty. He went around in back, and found 1248B underneath the wooden steps leading up to the kitchen of the owner's flat. It would be an apartment, here on ground level, that wouldn't get much light during the day.

Not that Harold Rockwell would be worried much about light or darkness anymore. The girl who answered his rap was at first glance very pretty; at second glance, almost emaciated. Her baggy cotton dress had been cut to be tight; her hair was mousy, her eyes, large and brown and begging to be lustrous, were as lifeless as her hair.

When Curt said he was looking for Mr. Rockwell, she didn't react in any way; so he added, almost as a question, "Mr. Harold Rockwell, is he home?"

She finally heaved a long-suffering, where-else-would-he-be sigh. Even the thin gold wedding band was loose enough to slip off her finger. Love that might be proof against cataclysm is often vulnerable to the slow erosion of a continuing, day-to-day tragedy. "I'm his wife, Katie. He . . . if you could tell me why you want to see him, he . . . hasn't been very well . . ."

"My name is Curt Halstead. My wife—"

Her face suddenly was animated. She turned, called into the tiny apartment, "Harry, Mrs. Halstead's husband is here!" Without waiting for his reply, she caught Curt's arm and almost dragged him inside. "Come in, come in, he'll be so glad to see you!"

The kitchen had walls daubed bright yellow. As if Katie Rockwell had made a vain attempt to brighten the drab apartment. The fridge was ancient, the gas stove the same, the linoleum curling at the corners. The sort of furnished apartment almost every young couple pass through on their way toward the style of life they will live together; but the Rockwells were frozen here now, rocks in a glacier, without much hope of a thaw.

"Don't mind the place, Mr. Halstead. These old apartments . . ."

"I've got the same problem." To Curt, his own voice was falsely and offensively hearty. "My house is very old . . ."

The living room was more of the same: a portable TV on a corner of the coffee table, a couch, an easy chair like those lugged into dorms by students following a visit to the Salvation Army salesroom. Rockwell, in the easy chair, in slacks and tattered cardigan, might have been remaindered himself. Smoked glasses concealed his ruined eyes but could not disguise the petulance in his pale, sensitive face. He had a great shock of blond hair fringing out thickly above the ears.

"I just dropped around . . ." Curt began, when Rockwell bleated to cut him off.

The blind man jerked like a moth impaled on a pin. He had a sharp reedy voice like an heirloom hand-crank victrola. "Well? What do you want? Why did you come here?"

The self-pity stifled Curt's own pity; he had seen too many maimed by battle to sympathize with the self-destructiveness of one who wasn't coping. He was moved by the man's plight, but not by the man. "I came after information. My wife is dead. Before she died—"

"We heard," broke in Katie Rockwell. "We're both terribly sorry. She . . . came to see Harry in the hospital the week after he . . . he . . ."

"Don't say *I'm* sorry!" cried Rockwell shrilly. He pounded his knee in futile rage. "Why *me?* I'm blind! *Blind!* At least your wife is dead! At least—"

"Harry!" she cried, aghast. "Harry, don't you dare say—"

"It's all right, Mrs. Rockwell," said Curt. "I understand . . ."

"Do you?" yelled Rockwell. He jerked and writhed in his chair, fumbled at his glasses, hurled them across the room, where they struck an arm of the sofa and fell on the rug, unbroken. "*Do* you understand? Look at my face! Get a good look! Get—"

Curt picked up the glasses and handed them to Katie Rockwell. The scarred, sightless, milky eyes did not shock or repulse him; all they did was make him angry. With himself, for coming here. With Rockwell, for destroying himself, his marriage, his wife. But blazingly with the predators, for the destruction they had left behind them. The blind man had slumped down in his chair and, behind the glasses his wife had replaced, had begun to sob.

"I don't know anything about them. I hadn't seen them before, they just . . . came at me . . ." He raised his sightless face. "Go away. Just . . . go away . . ."

As if on cue, the sudden full-bodied cry of an infant just awakened from its sleep came from beyond the closed bedroom door.

Rockwell's bony hands stopped moving in his lap; his face behind the dark glasses became attentive and still. In mid-word he stood up and went across the living room, familiar territory, to the door. He opened it. "Just leave me alone," he repeated flatly, and went inside. After a moment the crying changed in tone and intensity, then died away to comforted abstract whimpering.

Katie Rockwell made empty gestures. "Harry isn't . . . he didn't mean . . . I . . . eventually he'll make an adjustment, you know, to things . . ."

"I'm sure he will, Mrs. Rockwell." Curt didn't believe it for a minute; neither did she. "I can find my own way out."

Only when he was back outside did he realize that the apartment had smelled, with the same indefinable defeated odor that clings to the rooms in pensioners' hotels. The smell of men spending their sedentary hours without hope of redeeming this lost portion of their lives.

CHAPTER 14

"No," said Detective-Sergeant Monty Worden pleasantly.

"What do you mean, 'no'?" demanded Curt.

A dull anger grew in him as he looked into the bland gray eyes across the desk. When he had called the previous day, after his abortive visit to Harold Rockwell, he had been told that Worden was out on an investigation. Then today he had waited over an hour, dividing his attention between the very female knees visible under the blond receptionist's desk and the facts on Paula's suicide he would want to review, while Worden had been in conference with the lieutenant. And now . . .

"What good would it do to open the file for you?" continued Worden reasonably. "It is now official; since our investigation has confirmed death by suicide, we have no further interest in your wife's death. So that's all there is to that, Professor."

"Isn't there just a *little* more?" demanded Curt savagely. "Such as a rape, and a vicious assault on a harmless man, and—"

"Professor, at this time we have no—I repeat, *no*,—legally admissible evidence of a felony having been committed against your wife. As for Rockwell—oh, hell, Professor, we've been all through this already."

Curt tried to keep his voice reasonable; he *had* to find some starting place in his search for the predators. "If the file is closed, Sergeant, then surely there's no harm in letting me see it."

Worden spread powerful hands, then dropped them to the desk. "We do seem not to get on, don't we, Professor? I officially don't give a damn what went on before, during, or after your wife's act of suicide, because *she, killed, her, self*." He slapped an open palm lightly on the desk to emphasize each syllable. "Officially, that is. But—"

"I *do* give a damn what went on before, during, and after."

"Your privilege. But let's just say that our function is to *get* information in this office, not give it, and leave it go at that." He smiled nastily. "Of course, you can complain to the lieutenant . . ."

Curt thought about it for a moment. He couldn't really see himself getting much satisfaction out of Lieutenant Dorsey, who was built like an oil drum and looked just about as unyielding. Curt stood up, sighing. His question was only partially sarcastic. "I suppose there's no law against looking around on my own?"

"You mean hire a private man? It's your money, my friend—but don't expect this department's cooperation." He stood up then, too, with an odd look of distaste in his eyes. "You know, Professor, I ran your prints through Washington and Sacramento when I took 'em for elimination purposes; and you weren't on file anywhere. Not even with the FBI. That means you've never served in the military . . ."

"You're being obstructive because I wasn't in the *service?*"

Worden didn't bother to deny being obstructive. "It ain't that, Professor; it's because I got a feeling about you. I think you've decided you're gonna be a hero and find these punks, and take 'em on. Teach 'em a lesson." He jabbed a blunt forefinger at Curt's chest. "But you ain't even served in the Army—ain't had even *that* much training in taking care of yourself. You won't find this gang, I know that, but you go suckin' around teenage hangouts lookin' for information, and you're gonna find out that a bunch of punks swinging tire chains ain't funny. Believe me, they ain't."

"Thanks for the advice, Sergeant," Curt snarled.

He stomped belligerently up the stairs to the gym fifteen minutes later, his sustained anger at Worden thickening in his throat like phlegm. *Damn* him! Of course, he had made one inadvertent suggestion to Curt: that he get professional help in his search.

At the head of the stairs were four weight-lifters, joking and laughing and shoving each other, and also blocking the hallway. They were some of the "big boys" who specialized in the three Olympic competition lifts, and in such power lifts as heavy knee bends, bench presses, and deadlifts. In their street clothes they were chunky and graceless; only when they were stripped were the square, smooth blocks of muscle apparent.

". . . the guy had a chest he coulda eaten lunch off of . . ."

"Yeah?"

"Yeah. Arms so big they looked like they had a heart and lungs of their own. He—"

"Could I get through, please? Could I . . . Look, I want by, I—"

Damn them! First Worden refused any help, now these lumbering mountains of muscle acted as if . . .

And just then one of them grabbed another around the middle from behind, the muscles of his arms ballooning with effort, and heaved the 250-pound man off the floor as if he were a ten-pound chair. With a great shout of laughter, he threw the other lifter right across the hall.

Right into Curt.

"Hey! Goddamn it, what are you—"

The momentarily vanquished warrior was not laughing. With a roar, he seized the nearest handy object to hurl back at the other man. This object chanced to be Curt.

But as the hamlike hands closed about his sport-jacket lapels, Curt's mind registered *choke hold* and his body already was responding as it had done thousands of times during hand-to-hand combat training. Reflexes, once highly conditioned at the First S.A.S. Camp at Kabrit on the Bitter Lakes in the Egyptian Sinai, and now stimulated by weeks of grueling weight-training, responded automatically.

His locked hands drove up between the opponent's oak-branch arms, tearing loose the iron grip on his lapels, then crashed back down at the bridge of the other's nose. Curt's timing was rusty enough so he smashed the lips and hit the upper plane of the chin instead, but it still brought the man's face down within knee-lift range.

Before he could connect, an arm of awesome power locked around his throat and jerked him back. Curt snapped his left arm across to clutch cloth at his attacker's right elbow, pulled down so his right hand could grip the other's right shoulder. At the same time he rammed his butt back, hard, into the other's belly, and jackknifed at the waist.

The man should have sailed over Curt's head, but instead twisted, spun about on Curt's back to break the hand holds, and came down on his feet facing Curt. "Halstead!" he yelled. "Cool it!"

Curt realized that it was Preston, and suddenly came back. "I'm sorry, Floyd, I . . . Christ, for a minute there I . . ."

A very large man with curly hair and a blood-smeared T-shirt was leaning against the wall with his hands over his mouth. When his eyes met Curt's, they were filled with respect instead of anger. "Hey, man," he mumbled, "you really did me."

Preston chuckled. "Vanucci, you'd better put cold water on that lip before you bleed all over the floor. I just waxed Sunday." He clapped a hand to Curt's shoulder. "C'mon inside, tiger, take a rest."

In the office, sharing the couch with stacked cans of protein powder, which Preston had been unpacking, Curt tried to apologize again.

Preston cut him off with a wave of the hand. "Man, it was beautiful! Where in hell did you get the training?"

Curt rubbed his face with his hands; his head ached in reaction to the sharp, hard action. "It was . . . well, during the Second World War, I was in one of those irregular warfare groups. Just . . .

just a kid then, actually, you think you've forgotten it all and then something sets you off, triggers those reflexes . . ." He switched directions abruptly. "How about you, Floyd? You didn't learn that shoulder-throw counter in any weight gym."

Preston grinned. "Same place you learned it—the service. I told you the other day that I'd been training cadre at Fort Leonard Wood during Korea. I showed aptitude during basic, so they made me a phys ed instructor first, and then a hand-to-hand combat instructor later. I trained guys in the techniques for over two years."

"Is that right . . ." Curt was getting the nucleus of an idea. "Say, then, I wonder if we couldn't start doing a little hand-to-hand practice at the end of my regular workouts? Nothing much, just a bit of fooling around over in the ladies' gym, say—since it isn't used in the afternoons and there are mats over there . . ."

Preston, leaning against the edge of his desk with his massive arms folded, was utterly still for a moment. Then he moved his arms. "So you've decided to go after them," he said softly.

"Not really," Curt began, then shrugged. "Yes."

Surprisingly, Preston remained thoughtful, almost quizzical. "Are you sure that's what you want to do, Curt?"

"Oh, I know that gangs like that can be damned dangerous," said Curt, remembering Worden's warning about punks with tire chains. "So I think if I can get some of my reflexes back, just for self-defense if I *would* catch up with them, I'd have a lot better chance."

"I was thinking of it the other way around," said Preston. "I . . ." Then he shrugged. "Okay, Curt, we'll start with a little session today."

At the Dutch doors, Curt was struck by another thought. "I almost forgot, Floyd. Do you know any private investigators?"

"Sure. Archie Matthews. He works out here at the gym, as a matter of fact. He's supposed to be good—at least he has all the work he can handle at fifty bucks a day. Why, do you want to—"

"Tell him I think I've a job for him," said Curt.

DEBBIE

FRIDAY, JULY 4TH–
MONDAY, AUGUST 25TH

CHAPTER 15

It was on the Fourth of July, when Ricky was driving her home to her folks' place in San Leandro, that Debbie realized she was in love. Really for keeps, not just for the summer. He had picked her up at the dorm that afternoon about one o'clock, to take her up to San Francisco for the fireworks display. She had been wearing her new pink slacks, the tight ones that made her want to blush, and a white blouse and sandals.

"We'll meet the gang over at Heavy's place," said Rick, "and—"

"The gang?" Something in her voice made him look over at her. She said defiantly, "I don't like them very much. *Any* of them."

"Well, they're *my* friends, Deb. No chick tells me who my friends ought to be."

Debbie bit back *What about Paula Halstead?* without saying it. She didn't *know* that Ricky had been doing things with the older woman. Someday, of course, she *would* know—even if she had to ask him about it right out. She said, almost timidly, "I know I don't *own* you or anything, Ricky . . ."

He broke the tension with a wide answering grin. "Don't call me 'Ricky' in front of the guys, Deb, or I'll belt you one in the mouth, I really will."

Yes, she thought, it had been a good day, a lovely sunshine-filled day, even after they'd switched cars at Heavy's place so she'd been riding between Heavy and Rick on the front seat of the old two-tone green station wagon. Champ and Julio were in back, and all the guys had beer cans down between their thighs, which they drank from after looking carefully about for possible "fuzz" who might "bust" them. She had a couple of guilty sips from Rick's beer, which made her feel rather daring.

"What if your folks would see you doing that?" asked Julio.

"My dad drinks at parties and things," she said almost defensively. Her folks were really cool, trusting her to never do anything she knew she shouldn't. "Mom can't, because of the doctor, so at parties she drinks this pink stuff with no alcohol in it—"

"A Shirley Temple," supplied Rick.

"Hey, *big* man!" exclaimed Julio, drawing out the second word.

"He learns from all the older women he runs around with," said Debbie with a giggle. The drive was turning out much more pleasant than she had expected.

Rick answered her with a wink, his voice casual. "Sure, kid, I drop you at the dorm and then go have a ball."

As he spoke, he covertly studied her profile. Christ, had she heard something about that waitress, Mary Davies, that he'd been banging for almost three weeks? No. She'd say something to him alone, not in front of the rest of them. She was just kidding around, was all.

But watching the back of Debbie's head, Julio Escobar felt his gut muscles knot up. She *knew!* Knew what had happened to the professor's wife that night! But how could he make Rick see the danger that Debbie posed? Rick would not listen now, just because Julio knew; Rick would have to be given proof. Julio would have to get it. Look at her today, hanging all over Rick, wearing those tight pants that told the rest of them, *see, see fellows, what you're missing?* Just as she'd done as a cheerleader, never let anyone touch her and then jumping around in those miniskirts and showing her legs all the way up on some of the yells she led. Well, she'd find out.

Heavy handled the station wagon like a scalpel, slicing from lane to lane through traffic at a steady eighty miles an hour. He left the freeway at Franklin, a one-way street that would take them up over

Pacific Heights and down to the Marina green on the other side, where the fireworks display would be held.

"I'd love to live up here," said Debbie. They were just at Broadway, where the houses were old and spacious, the apartment buildings new and dazzling. "Right here in Pacific Heights with a view of the Bay."

"Ah . . . how'dya know this is Pacific Heights?" marveled Champ. He never said much to Debbie, since she was Rick's woman, but when she turned and smiled at him he realized that he wanted to do some stuff to her no matter whose girl she was. Not that he would, of course.

"My dad used to bring me up here sometimes when we still lived on the Peninsula. He used to have some clients up here . . ."

Caliban, the blunt-nosed yellow cat her mom had named after a character in one of Shakespeare's plays, jumped up on the bed beside her. She rubbed him absently under the chin, and he strained back his head and purred like a refrigerator.

A good day? *The* day. The best day of her entire life.

Fifty thousand people had been on the strip of greensward between Marina Boulevard and the yacht anchorage, someone said. Out beyond the breakwater and rows of gleaming moored yachts was the Bay, with hundreds of flitting sailboats heeled over by the breeze. To the left was the red-orange arc of Golden Gate Bridge, leading to Marin County and unknown adventures. Behind her were the whitely glistening hills of the city, like something you saw in the movies.

Yes, she would love to live in San Francisco. She slid under the covers, and Caliban immediately flopped beside her hip with his chin on her thigh, still purring wildly. Motorboating, her mom called it. San Francisco. She and Ricky. All right, she was only nineteen, and her folks wanted her to finish college before she got married, but still . . .

As the light faded, a majestic freighter had slipped blackly under the bridge. On Marin County's sun-pinked hills the tiny fireflies had begun to gleam, as the residents had begun turning on their house lights.

She and Ricky sat on the seawall with the tide swirling a yard below their dangling feet. The fireworks were shot off from the end of the breakwater beyond the yacht anchorage. It had gotten chilly with dark, so they had a blanket around them, over their shoulders, and Ricky kept his arm around her waist with his hand cupped up under her breast. She hadn't made him take it away; she found it harder and harder to say no to him. It seemed so right with him, somehow. Each time a rocket faded to darkness, he kissed her.

And the end of this fairy-tale day had brought realization of her love for him. Lying in bed with Caliban beside her, she could remember lying back against the leathery-smelling bucket seat of the Triumph, her eyes shut against the lights of oncoming traffic on San Mateo Bridge, her thoughts drifting, so that the question just popped out unbidden.

"Ricky, how well did you *really* know Paula Halstead?"

"How well . . ." He licked his lips. "Debbie, where did you get the idea that . . . that I . . . uh . . ."

So she told it all to him: about not thinking a brush of fenders in a parking lot was his real reason for wanting to see Paula Halstead alone; about wondering at his reaction to news of Paula's death . . .

". . . of course, you don't have to tell me, Ricky, if the memories are too painful or . . . or anything . . ."

The oncoming lights cast his strong, handsome profile into bronze silhouette against the blackness flanking the bridge, and he didn't say anything for the longest time. Until they were off the bridge, actually, on the road to the Nimitz freeway. Gaps in the traffic cast Rick's face into alternate illumination and shadow here, and he spoke when no car was coming.

"I hadn't ever meant to tell you about it, Deb; that's why I made up that accident thing. It was just . . . something that happened.

We . . . met in this fancy cocktail lounge, by accident, sort of, and—"

"I knew it!" she exclaimed in soft triumph. "I *felt* it!"

"She . . . wasn't happy at home, her husband, that professor, he . . . didn't satisfy her. She took me over to her motel room, and we . . ."

When he trailed off, Debbie said, "Did you . . . more than once . . ."

"Never again, Deb." By the lights of an approaching car, his eyes were limpid with honesty. They took the on-ramp which shot them into the booming northbound traffic of the East Bay freeway. "But that wasn't the end of it, see? She wouldn't leave me alone. Kept calling me up at home, kept waiting around outside Jaycee . . . She was always after me to come over to her place on Friday nights when her husband was off teaching that seminar."

Debbie's face was tragic. "Then that Friday night you were going to go over there and—"

"—and tell her I didn't want her to bother me again. Ever. But *she* didn't know that's why I was coming, and I guess that when I had that flat tire and didn't show up, didn't call, she just. . . ."

And at that instant Debbie had known she was in love with Rick Dean. All the way in love, the marriage kind of love. He had been through so much pain. Parked in front of her folks' place, he had held her so tight that she could hardly breathe, for a long time wouldn't turn his face to her, so she bet that he'd been crying; and when he had raised his head, his eyes had been deadly serious.

"You've got to promise me, Deb, that you won't tell *anyone* what I've told you tonight—not *ever*. It would *kill* that professor to find out about her, I bet, and . . . I mean, she's dead and all, so . . ."

"I understand, darling. And I promise." She had turned toward him with her eyes shut and her face solemn. "And I love you, Ricky."

Yes, she thought, the happiest, most important day of her life.

With a contented sigh, Debbie slid lower and reached for the light switch.

As Debbie's bedside lamp went out, Rick pulled up in front of his folks' darkened house in Los Feliz. He cut lights and engine, sat behind the wheel without moving, going over it. He didn't feel now like going down to the oceanside cabin with his folks tomorrow, as he'd promised; but at least it would give him time to get alone on the beach and think. He really had to think, now.

Had he been convincing? He had just followed his instincts in fashioning the story for Debbie, instincts that had saved him from spankings by his ma ever since he'd been a little kid. A chick like Debbie, romantic-like, she wanted you to be wiping away that old furtive tear of tragedy. *I love you, Ricky*. Only a guy needed more than words.

Rick moved restlessly behind the wheel, fished out a cigarette, pushed in the lighter as he stuck it in his mouth. He wished it was a joint. He was all strung out; pot really helped with that feeling. Christ, he wished they'd been on pot instead of beer that night they'd shoved around that goddamn queer. Or if somebody was going to kill himself, why didn't *that* bastard do it? The lighter popped.

And just when everything seems safe, up comes Debbie. *How well did you really know Paula Halstead?* He didn't want to be answering that question for a judge, and he still thought he'd done the smart thing to make up the affair with Paula. This way, she wouldn't blurt out some dumb thing in front of somebody. Like Julio, for instance. That Julio, he was sort of paranoid about Debbie, or something, anyway. Julio didn't *understand* chicks, didn't know how to handle them like Rick did. Like he had handled Debbie, getting her to promise.

Rick grunted. Old Deb. Maybe she'd made another promise, to herself or something, about not letting Rick get into her pants.

Damn her. She was such choice stuff, was the trouble; and now he couldn't *afford* to just drop her. He hurled the half-smoked cigarette away.

Damnit, he needed . . . He looked at his watch. Mary Davies, the waitress, got off in an hour, at two-thirty. She'd put out for him that first time he'd picked her up. Taken him up to her apartment and let him start fooling around with her on the couch, with her roommate asleep in the bedroom just beyond, with the door wide open. After about twenty minutes she'd just stood up and said, "I must be nuts, with a kid your age," and had stripped down right there and had climbed right on top of him like a goddamn jockey getting on a horse or something.

Rick twisted the keys, jerked the starter decisively. Old Mary, some of the things she'd wanted to do had embarrassed him at first, had made him scared he'd hurt her, even. But then he'd found out she didn't care if he hurt her some, and he dug it all, now.

And she usually had pot at her place, too.

A few miles north, Julio Escobar was lying on the tattered sofa at his folks' place and watching the late show. Some of these old movies were really dogs, but he even did his homework in front of the TV. The noise, the sense of movement, made it easier to concentrate or something. Made him feel more *there*, you know? More real, solider. And tonight he had to concentrate.

That damned bitch, Debbie! He'd sat only two yards from her and Rick during the fireworks. He *knew* Rick had been getting tittie there, under the blanket; he probably was making it with her right now in that flashy Triumph. Hell, if Julio had a new car like that she'd put out for him, too, the same way. Probably the first time he got her alone.

And the hell of it was, she *knew*. About the Halstead woman, maybe even about Rockwell, too. Sure, they were safe as long as she was hot for Rick, but what happened to the rest of them if she and Rick had a fight? What then? He *had* to get enough on Debbie, enough proof that she couldn't be trusted, to make Rick listen to him. *Had* to, even if it meant following her around.

Then Rick would *have* to go along with the plan Julio had. Oh, that would shut her up, all right. It had *really* worked the once, it would work again—especially with a young chick like Debbie.

Just thinking about it made the TV movie fade, made him feel funny, made his palms get moist. He rubbed his hands along the fabric of the couch. Yes, when the time came, he would know what to do to her all right.

Cheap, teasing little bitch!

CHAPTER 16

Looking at his desk calendar, Curt realized disconsolately that July was half gone and he was no nearer to finding the predators than he had been a month before. Archie Matthews, the private investigator he had hired, had turned up nothing. Nothing at all.

Curt opened the center drawer, got out the folder containing a slim sheaf of reports that had taken five days of Matthews's investigation time. The detective had gotten no cooperation from the sheriff's office whatsoever, but despite that he had been thorough, damned thorough, Curt had to give him that. Checking the Los Feliz police department files for traffic citations issued on the night of the Rockwell assault to old Chevrolet station wagons. Negative. Negative also with the Highway Patrol. Negative on tows by the all-night garages.

Next, posting a reward notice in the all-night laundromat a short half-block from the railroad crossing. One woman had come forward; she had left the laundromat a bare five minutes before the attack had occurred. See nothing, hear nothing, left laundromat deserted.

Matthews had talked with the night people at the all-night restaurants and gas stations for ten miles north along El Camino: had four boys in a two-tone green Chevy stopped for food and/or gas that night? Nothing. Two months later, who remembered?

The night of Paula's death had offered even less to go on. He had repeated with the police, Highway Patrol, drive-ins and gas stations for that night, also, although there was no certainty about the direction from which they had come to Curt's isolated house. Negative. For those five evenings Matthews had drifted through the drive-ins, soda fountains, record stores, gas stations, and bars and beer halls, which he knew were not too careful about checking IDs. All the places where kids congregated. Looking (three station wagons observed that fit in color and age were unsuccessfully checked out), listening, talking, dropping the word that nobody, but nobody, had picked up.

When Curt had received, near the end of June, the detective's bill for services and cover letter withdrawing from the case, Curt had driven over to Matthews's office to talk to the man. It was a second-floor suite of rooms in a new anonymous glass and aluminum and cement building four blocks from the Los Feliz Civic Center. Through his windows they could see traffic on University beyond a municipal parking lot. Matthews had no secretary, merely an answering service.

"I'd like to see you catch up with those bastards myself, Mr. Halstead." He was a tall, well-built man with a stubby nose, cheerful blue eyes, curly hair, and a round face with a heavily cleft chin. He shrugged expressively. "But . . ."

"Then why are you quitting now? I'm willing to pay—"

"I've already cost you nearly three hundred dollars, counting expenses, and all I really did was go over what the police already have covered. I like a buck as well as the next man, but I not only can't guarantee results in this case—I can almost guarantee *no* results."

"Because Worden refuses to let us look into that file?"

Matthews took a turn around the room, oddly out of place in the starkly modern setting; he was an outdoorsy sort of person, with the weathered skin associated with yachtsmen. Perhaps, Curt thought, his six-two frame and guilelessly masculine good looks carried with them their own sort of anonymity.

"You've got Worden on the brain. There'll be nothing in that file we don't have, except for the name of that kid on the bicycle. Sure, I wish you could remember his name, and sure, I'd like to talk with him. But he was just a kid, ten years old or so, going by on his bike at night, in the dark, scared as hell and worried about a spanking from his ma for being late getting home." He turned from the window. "Hell, Mr. Halstead, if there was a handle in that file, Worden would have used it—no matter what he said to you about the D.A. not being able to prosecute even if they did turn up the gang. He's too good a cop *not* to use it."

Curt stood up with a deep sense of frustration. "Then . . . that's it? There's *nothing* else we can do?"

"Not unless or until we turn up a new witness, introduce a new factor, shift the equation around some way so we can see it from a different direction. Otherwise you're just wasting money and emotion."

Remembering it now, three weeks later, Curt experienced again the sense of baffled helplessness he had carried from Matthews's office. *Turn up a new witness, introduce a new factor, shift the equation around . . .*

What in the devil *had* that kid's name been? He had been through his memory of the meeting in Worden's office a thousand times, could *see* Worden as he said the kid's mother had called—but he could not see the name. It was gone, totally.

With an abrupt convulsive movement, Curt skidded back his chair by standing up, and went downstairs to the phone. It was the only thing he *hadn't* tried: going directly to the source. Well, indirectly, really.

He dialed, by chance caught Worden in the office and free.

"Curt Halstead here, Sergeant. I wondered if—"

"Curt who? Do I . . . oh. Yeah." Curt could almost see the disgust on the square, tough face. "What can I do for you, Professor?"

Curt's hand gripped the receiver, hard. "I was just wondering if you had heard anything about an accident happening to the boy on the bicycle." His stress on "accident" altered the word's meaning.

"Boy on the bicycle? I don't—"

"The witness who saw the station wagon by the golf course."

"Listen, Halstead," the sergeant burst out angrily, "I thought that you would have quit when that trained seal you hired gave up. If you've been messing around with that Anderson kid, I'll—"

Curt tried to keep the elation from his voice. "I've never laid eyes on the boy, Sergeant. It's just that I heard a rumor . . ."

"You heard wrong," Worden snapped. "Nothing happened to him and nothing *will* happen, because he doesn't know anything. Get me, Professor? *Nothing*. We could stand those four up in front of him with name tags on and he wouldn't be able to identify 'em." He paused, as if shaking his head almost sadly. "Leave it to the professionals, Professor. Like I said before, you start pokin' around teen-age hangouts and you're liable to wake up in a garbage pail some morning."

Curt hung up gently. *Anderson*. That was it, all right. *It seems a Mrs. Anderson called about her kid*. He could remember Worden saying it. Then his elation began draining away. The boy already was a dead lead as far as Worden and Matthews—the professionals—were concerned. And besides that, how did one go about finding a boy named Anderson?

Curt got out the telephone directory. A whole page, four columns, of ANDERSON listings for the county. So now what? Rehire Archie Matthews? *Hell, if there was a handle in that file, Worden would have used it*. All right, then, contact that hundred Andersons himself?

There had to be a way to narrow it down. State the problem.

Fine. Sears Lake was five miles away. The boy was late. He spotted the predators on Longacres Avenue Extension; at the Linda Vista T-junction, he would have had to turn either north or south.

South, he would have passed Curt's house, and south the university lay as a large block before the subdivisions beyond it. Unless the boy was a son of some member of the university faculty who lived on the campus itself or, like Curt, on its fringes. Curt could check that himself that afternoon at the Personnel Office.

North, he would be going toward the maze of small residential streets twined around Entrada Way. North seemed more logical. More houses closer to Curt's house. The boy had passed the predators at 8:00 P.M., the time he was supposed to be home. So, unless he had been *very* late, his home could not lie too far from that T-junction.

As Curt pulled on his shoes to head toward the university, he had to fight a sort of exhilaration. He had to keep telling himself that he had little hope either of finding the boy or of learning anything of value even if by some fluke he did find him.

But Curt also knew this was better than an endless, sterile, frustrating count of days marked only by inactivity.

The next day in training, Curt was successful for the first time in putting Preston on the mat with an over-the-shoulder throw. In the locker room, he found his weight was under 190 for the first time.

Preston, as they walked together down to the creamery for lunch, shook his head in mock wonderment. "You're getting too tough for an old man like me, tiger. You been into the wheat-germ oil again?"

"I'm back on the hunt." Curt was not aware of the strangeness in his image. "I have the name of the boy on the bicycle—tricked it out of Worden—and now . . ." Over sandwiches and milk, he outlined what he had done, finishing, ". . . and I think he went north, because the university lies between my place and any significant residential areas to the south."

"I disagree. Remember, Curt, she called the *sheriff's office*, not the city cops; but there's no built-up *county* land north of you."

"Maybe she called them because Sears Lake is on county land."

"Would you? If you were worried about your kid, you wouldn't sit down and figure out who has jurisdiction; you'd just call the law enforcement agency that serviced your home." Preston thought of something else. "Unless the kid's old man is on the university staff—"

"I spent yesterday checking that out. He isn't."

Preston nodded, and stood up. "That figures; on the campus she would have called the campus cops anyway. C'mon, I've got a big-scale county map up at the gym."

Two hours later Curt had his initial list of most likely Andersons. They had estimated the maximum distance that the boy should logically be living from Curt's house as five miles—unless he had been *very* late. So the list contained those Andersons in the phone book who lived south of Curt's home on county land.

There were four names.

CHAPTER 17

It was Friday, July 18th. Curt stopped in front of 5202 Seville Drive in Los Feliz county. It was the usual California ranch-style subdivision house: a curving drive flanked by shrubbery not watered enough, the surge, swish, and gurgle of a washing machine from the garage. A tricycle missing a wheel leaned in grumpy abandonment against the front of the house. Curt rang the bell.

After nearly a minute a very black woman who was a good two inches taller than Curt appeared. She wore bedroom slippers and a print dress stretched tight across her yard-wide hips.

"Woody ain't home," she said emphatically, in a true Dixie accent. She leaned forward to peer sharply at Curt. "This yere 'bout de car note?"

"Why . . ." Curt realized that ringing strange doorbells and talking to strangers was going to be like learning a new language. "Why, no. Are you Mrs. Anderson?"

She leaned against the door frame. Her laughter was rich. "I sho' ain't Mia Farrow, honey."

Curt could not help laughing with her. "The Mrs. Anderson I want has a son about ten years old, who—"

"Not *me*, honey." Then she roared with body-shaking laughter again. "Less'n dat Woody, he been messin' 'round 'thout tellin' me!"

Curt drove the VW into Josina Avenue before stopping to draw a line through *Anderson, Woody, 5202 Seville Drive.* He felt slightly guilty, because this was supposed to be a serious business and he had been vastly entertained by the ebullient Mrs. Anderson.

Anderson, Stanley, 2983 Montecito Court.

Montecito Court, despite the high house numbers, was a one-block street off Charleston Road. Curt could find no 2983. He finally settled for 2985, ringing the bell and then cupping his eyes to peer into the dim interior through a window. He was sweating from the bright sun.

A woman in her mid-fifties appeared, walking very carefully between the rather expensive pieces of living-room furniture.

"What can I do for you?" She spoke with care but clarity; her voice was golden with a very mellow Scotch.

"I'm looking for Stanley Anderson. He's supposed to live at 2983 Montecito Court, but I can't find that number. I wondered—"

"This's . . ." She stopped, frowning intently at Curt. She had the heavy drinker's blurred features. "This house b'longs to my daughter 'n' her husban', Frankie . . ." She belched, very delicately, said, "Shrimp cocktail," then added obscurely, "I'm from Seattle."

"Yes, ma'am," said Curt.

"Just visiting." She made a sweeping gesture that nearly carried her down the steps. "Try Mish . . . Mrs. Pershin' next door—2979. Neighborhood gossip, tell you anything you wanna know. M'daughter Maggie says she can tell you how many pimples on th' postman's fanny."

"Yes, ma'am." Curt was backing off, nodding and smiling like one of those little dogs with delicately balanced heads that nod in amiable idiocy from the rear windows of many automobiles. "Thank you, ma'am."

He paused to wipe his face before trying 2979, then realized that Mrs. Pershing already was on her front stoop, arms folded, head cocked toward 2985, her eyes glaring at the Seattle mother-in-law. She was in her sixties, with daintily coiffed bluish hair, a remarkably smooth complexion, and behind glasses her eyes were as bright and inquisitive as a mynah bird's.

Catching Curt's eye, she laughed. "Now that you've gotten the neighborhood bottleaxe report, come on up. Three weeks that woman's been visiting Frank and Margaret, and I've yet to see her sober, Mr.—"

"Halstead. Curt Halstead. I'm trying to find 2983, and . . ."

"That's Stanley. Actually, it's a cottage right behind us here. I'm his landlady; I hope Stan isn't in any trouble."

"Nothing like that." Curt remembered Worden's tactics. "Just routine, Mrs. Pershing."

"Come in and sit," she urged. "I've got some nice iced tea."

The living room was broad and spacious and cool, with a fireplace and a baby grand and a shelf of books that looked read. She bustled out to the kitchen, leaving Curt neatly immobilized in a comfortable chair. No doubt she would return to pick his brains with the skill of a Manchurian interrogator. She came back, he sipped tea.

"That's delicious, Mrs. Pershing."

She leaned forward with a quick and ruthless focusing of energies. "Must get tiring for a man out ringing doorbells on a hot day like this, Mr. Halstead . . ." Her delicate pause wore a question mark.

"Sure does. I'm . . . ah . . . with the California education system."

She nodded wisely. "Stanley's mother *is* a professor down south, UCLA, one of those places. I suppose that's why you've come. I look after Stan like he was one of my own, myself . . ."

Curt drew a mental line through *Anderson, Stanley,* asked his age.

"Oh, twenty-four, twenty-five. Has a *very* good job in electronics, but that little devil *still* makes me wait for my rent. Out chasing the girls in that little sports car of his . . ."

It took forty-five minutes, four evasions, and two outright lies before Curt could escape her inquisition to check on the next listed name.

Anderson, Kent, 438 San Benito Way.

The address was south and a bit west of the university, a long shot as far as Curt could see; there actually was a shorter way to the address, via Alicante Road, from Sears Lake than by Curt's house. But . . .

It was a one-story, garage-attached house, merely a permutation on the others he had visited. Frightening how many people *did* live in ticky-tacky boxes on uniformly curving streets. A new Olds was parked in the driveway; the lawn reflected pride of ownership. A man's home is his castle. The door was answered by a blond girl about seven, with straight-cut bangs and the hands of a mud-pie chef.

"Hello there. Is your mother home?"

"Mom 'n' Dad," she assured him seriously.

Curt waited until she returned with a small woman whose permanent frown suggested the need of new glasses.

"My name is Curt Halstead. I was wondering if you have a son about ten years old. I—"

"Why . . . yes, we do. Is . . . something the matter?"

"No, ma'am, I'd just like to talk to him for a minute or two."

"Kenny's around somewhere. I suppose it'd be all right if—"

"Talk to him about what?"

A short, pugnacious man had appeared behind her, wearing rumpled khakis, a white T-shirt, no shoes, and a two-day beard. He pushed his wife aside, roughly, and thrust his face into Curt's with all the belligerence so often displayed by a certain type of short man. "I don't like your looks, buddy. You tryna mix my kid up in a lawsuit or something? G'wan, get to hell outta here."

"Now, Kent . . ." his wife began as if it were a familiar scene.

"You, shut up. I know how to handle guys like this." He swung back to Curt with a semi-leer. "You still here? G'wan. Blow."

Anger boiled up sourly inside him, but Curt merely nodded grimly and turned away. It was the man's house, after all. Return the next day, or the one after, or whenever Mr. Kent Anderson might be gone, leaving only his gentle-faced wife to man the battlements.

Anderson, sensing victory, made a barefooted sortie down the walk behind him. "I gotta good mind to take a poke at you. I gotta good mind—"

"I doubt that," said Curt. On public property, he turned back in the slight defensive crouch made automatic by the months of training with Preston.

Curt's stance stopped Anderson's advance like a wall. "Yeah, well, you come around bothering my family when I ain't home," he muttered, "I'll have the sheriff on you."

"Ask for Sergeant Worden," Curt snapped without forethought.

The change in Anderson was remarkable. "You mean . . . well now, look, Sergeant, I didn't realize. I thought . . ."

So. Anderson hadn't heard Curt give his name. Was afraid of the cops, perhaps had a reputation as a troublemaker. Curt took advantage. "I want to know if your boy was riding his bike from Sears Lake past the university golf course on Friday evening, April twenty-third, at eight o'clock. Also, did your wife call the sheriff's office—"

"Wasn't Kenny," Anderson cut in eagerly. "Hell, I can't hardly get that kid offa his butt, let alone riding his bike all the hell way over to Sears Lake. Electronics, with him. Workshop's so damned full of wires and tubes and old radios . . ."

Curt thanked him and drove swiftly away, before Kent Anderson might begin wondering what a deputy sheriff was doing on a field call in a powder-blue VW sedan, sun-roof model.

Stopping a block away to draw a line through *Anderson, Kent,* Curt reflected again on the rather frightening isolation his profession had given him from what educators delighted in calling the total community. His social contacts over the years, by choice, had been limited mainly to those associated with the intellectual community; his vocational contacts, by necessity, had been limited almost totally to highly intelligent, well-motivated youth. Only now, ringing doorbells of a random sampling of people, did he begin to comprehend the staggering complexity of what was lumped together as The American Way of Life.

Anderson, Barbara, 1791 Edgewood.

Pulled over on a side street inside the university grounds, Curt consulted his map again. Edgewood was in a pocket of county land between El Camino and Linda Vista Road near the university Medical Center. In direct distance it was the address closest to Curt's house, separated only by the woods and San Luisa Creek; but the nearest access was all the way down University Way to the Medical Center, then cutting through from the rear of that facility to the subdivision. Almost beyond Curt's arbitrary five-mile limit.

It was a curving blacktop street lined with middle-income homes and littered with children's playthings. Down on El Camino the rush hour would be snarling like caged lions, but here the pre-supper hush of busy stoves and televisioned news prevailed. Curt rang the bell at 1791, looked about. Garage windows painted over, living-room drapes drawn; he could see nothing to indicate a child lived there. He rang again, was just turning away when a chain lock was withdrawn, a bolt was snapped, and the door was opened.

The woman had a mass of wavy brown hair with sun-lightened streaks, a pretty face as narrow as a fox's, and clear greenish eyes. The face was flushed, the hair-tips steam-dampened; her terry-cloth robe was of pink and Chinese vermilion in intricate pattern, and huge fluffy pink slippers peeked from under the floor-length hem.

"I'm looking for a Barbara Anderson, ma'am," Curt began.

"I'm *a* Barbara Anderson," she said and smiled. She was in her early thirties, old enough to have a son ten years old. Her mouth was small, with laughter dimples at the corners, and her chin was delicate and narrow.

"My name is Curt Halstead. I'm looking for a boy, named Anderson, who saw four men getting out of an old station wagon one evening last April. His mother reported the incident to the sheriff, and . . ."

He stopped because Barbara Anderson was shaking her head. She drew the robe closer about her as if belatedly chilled from her bath. Her eyes were totally expressionless. Her hands, well-shaped yet strong-looking, were without rings. Her voice was high and a little flat. "I guess you want a different Barbara Anderson, Mr. Halstead. I'm not married and I have no son. I'm sorry."

"Well, I'm sorry to interrupt your bath. I . . ."

He stopped again, this time because she had shut the door firmly in his face. He heard the bolt snap into place, and grimaced. No real need for her to be so abrupt. Not, of course, that he could really blame her, living there alone. Rather strange that she was, actually.

Curt started the VW with a little jerk because his mind was on things other than driving. Probably divorced, obviously childless, had gotten the house as part of the settlement, perhaps. He wondered if she worked, or lived on alimony, or what. A damned attractive woman.

After turning into Westpoint Drive, toward the Medical Center, Curt remembered and pulled over long enough to draw a line through *Anderson, Barbara* on his list of possibles.

CHAPTER 18

Curt ate a solitary Sunday breakfast, staring, without really seeing, out the kitchen window into the live oaks behind the house. In one tree was a vireo, in another a pair of wood warblers. Carrying his dishes to the sink, he saw the calendar. August 10th. Almost a month since he had begun looking for the Anderson boy, and summer vacation was drawing to a close. Fall term raised feelings of active distaste, probably because teaching meant a curtailment of his search.

But what further could he do? Advertise? He not only had exhausted all possible phone-book Andersons; he had, at Archie Matthews's suggestion, gotten further names from the *Polk Directory* and the voter registration rolls at the County Courthouse. In all, sixty-seven Andersons.

Curt ran water over his dishes. To hell with it. Today he would try to forget it, the whole thing. Take a walk, maybe. This morning, right now, before the day got too hot. He thrust aside the insistent memory of planning a similar hike with Paula on the Friday night he had driven home to find her dead, and put on soft-soled shoes, sunglasses, a polo shirt. At the foot of the driveway, he paused: north or south? Had the boy on the bike gone north or . . . damnit, stop it. South he would go, toward the university.

He crossed Linda Vista to be facing traffic, started past the old green phone booth, which stood with open door, inviting confidences. Curt had none to impart, but he did stop, and in an untoward lightness of mood, pulled down the coin return. He chuckled aloud. A dime. He could buy two thirds of a cup of coffee with it somewhere.

Striding along in the growing heat, Curt tried to feel enthusiasm for the resumption of classes. No use. Looked at coldly from the shoulder of a country road, the whole concept of graduate study seemed artificial somehow. Perhaps it was because you could never admit error: not to your department, nor to your students, nor, given enough years of enforced infallibility, to yourself. Curt had always stressed, for instance, that environment determined behavior; yet could he really swallow that the predators were merely determined puppets, no more responsible for the destruction strewn in their wake than a hurricane that savaged the Florida coast before swinging blindly back to sea? No. Curt knew he couldn't buy that. *Wouldn't* buy it. Unless men were responsible, all of their actions were without meaning.

A quarter of a mile beyond the phone booth, Curt came across a narrow footpath beaten down through the high weeds of the ditch. He turned off into it, after a few steps found his trousers dotted with the thistles from August-ripened weeds. The narrow path was iron-hard from lack of rain; it probably had been worn by venturesome small-fry on long school-less summer days.

San Luisa Creek was dry, raggedly edged with blackberry bushes, mugwort, and the telltale red leaves of poison oak. The path rose beyond it, plunged abruptly into a thicket of elderberries and ceanothus and then under the shade of a stand of sycamore. It was much cooler under the trees; a flash of white wing patch and a glimpse of iridescent tail marked the passage of a yellow-billed magpie, and a squirrel scolded from a low branch. Curt topped the slight rise, could see the white siding of a house through the thinning undergrowth.

Beyond the trees was a strip of dusty straggled weeds, a shallow ditch littered with paper, and a loop of blacktop. Across it were tract houses. Curt shook his head. A few years ago there had been no path, no subdivision at the end of it. He crossed the ditch, turned left, downhill toward an intersection a hundred yards away. The cross street was Westpoint, he found; he had been walking on Edgewood Drive.

Aptly named, Edgewood. Wait a minute. Edgewood. Was that . . .

It came back in a rush. Barbara Anderson, 1791 Edgewood Drive. One of his first four prime possibilities. An attractive brown-haired woman in a red robe whom he had disturbed in the middle of a bath. He lengthened his stride until he was nearly trotting. A boy living on Edgewood, late home, would have walked his bike through those woods, along that path. Five minutes.

But she had said she was unmarried, had no children.

Women had lied before. When Curt got to 1791, he was sure she had lied, and felt a little sick to the stomach with frustration. The lawn was shaggy and yellowing, the neighborhood shopping papers distributed free were yellowing in a messy heap on the porch. Planted in the middle of the sere grass was a small neat FOR SALE sign. *She* had been the one, unless he accepted it all—path, precipitous move from the neighborhood, proximity to Curt's house—as a series of coincidences.

Curt looked about almost wildly. Neighbors. Find out if she had a son. Find out where she had gone if she did.

Directly across the street was an open garage door with a car parked in the drive. A man was dragging a green plastic garden hose from the garage. He wore a Giants baseball cap, a white T-shirt, and Bermuda shorts shoved down under his stomach, so the ends of the legs covered his knees.

Curt crossed the street. "I'm looking for Barbara Anderson, sir. Could you tell me if—"

"She moved." He scratched his nose reflectively. "Just about three weeks ago, real sudden like. One week talking about her lawn, next week just . . . packed up and gone, bag and baggage."

Three weeks. Almost immediately after Curt had talked with her. A three-week head start. "Is she a Mrs. Anderson, or a Miss?"

"Missus. Well, you know, divorced. Thought at first she'd gone back to Charlie, but the next week here comes the realtor's sign up."

Curt nodded. "Funny she'd just move out that way, with the boy and all . . . I guess he'd be about ten now, wouldn't he?"

"Jimmy? Yep."

The man started to turn away, when Curt had a sudden inspiration. "Say, do you remember if anyone else was around asking about her? Say . . . sometime last spring, maybe?"

"Nope." Then he frowned, and rested a foot on the front bumper of his car. "But now you mention it, a kid about high school age come around one Sunday morning, musta been in May, just about this time of the day, right after Barb took the boy off to church. Said he was looking for some other Anderson, I disremember the name—remember the kid 'cause he looked sorta Mexican. You know, dark skin, black curly hair—oh, and a long nose. I remember that nose, all right."

Somehow they find out where the boy lives, talk to the neighbors to get the right name, then make a threat, probably by phone. A virulent threat, Curt thought, if he was right: because it had made Barbara Anderson and her son disappear just because Curt had dropped around to ask a casual question. Yes, it fit. Door bolted, night chain on in the middle of the afternoon. A tottery theory on a shaky framework, but . . .

"You . . . don't know where I could reach Barbara now, do you?"

"Sure don't, mister. Like I said, just moved out sudden. She didn't leave no new address, not even a phone number. Not that I guess you'll have much trouble finding her."

"How's that?" asked Curt quickly.

The man jerked a calloused thumb. "Realtor. Or Charlie, even."

Curt arrived home fifteen minutes later, sweaty-faced and branch-lashed from his hurried return through the woods. Before going up to shower and shave, he dialed the Heritage Realty Company, 2101 Armando Road, to see if they were open on Sunday. They were. When he came back downstairs in fresh slacks and sport shirt, he paused at the phone again. There was no listing for Barbara Anderson, but there was for Charles. Homestead Avenue,

Mountain View. Curt dialed, got an answer on the sixth ring from a voice full of Sunday morning phlegm.

Curt said, "Sorry to disturb you this way, Mr. Anderson, but I'm trying to get in touch with Barbara. She—"

"It's in the phone book, for Chrissake! 1791 Edgewood Drive . . ."

"She moved from there about a month ago, Mr. Anderson."

"Look, buddy," he said flatly, "we got divorced two goddamn years ago. She got the works: house, bank account, everything but my left nut, see? I don't have anything to do with her, don't wanna, beyond the support payments—which go to her P.O. box. I ain't seen her or the kid, either of 'em, for half a year. She owes you money, look somewhere else for it." He slammed down the receiver with a curse.

Heritage Realty was a small place sharing a new but cheaply constructed building with a doughnut shop. The walls were covered with diagrams, mocked-up house-plan blueprints, and faded Polaroids of uninspiring tract houses. Behind a redwood-faced counter were four desks littered with papers; at the second desk, on the telephone, was a rather suet-faced woman with dark hair. Her name plate announced MRS. PINNEO to a waiting world. When she hung up, Curt asked his question.

"1791 Edgewood Drive? A lovely property, sir. Three bedroom, two bath, patio, electric kitchen, built-in barbecue, new—"

"I'm just trying to get in touch with the owner."

She had dark piercing eyes, her best feature, a small pursed mouth as if she were drinking cold coffee, and pads of flesh over her cheekbones, which gave her a squirrel-faced look. Her smile got soft around the edges at Curt's remark. "We are fully authorized to act as Mrs. Anderson's agents."

"Yes, I'm sure. This is personal, however. Her address would—"

"Quite impossible." The smile had thawed, and a frown was freezing quickly into place. She tapped her pencil impatiently on the desk. "We cannot give you any information whatsoever regarding Mrs. Anderson."

"Well, then, just a phone number. I can call—"

"That number is unlisted, sir. Good day."

"But I—"

"I said good day, sir."

Curt stopped outside the door, blinking in the glaring midday sunshine. So. No closer to Barbara Anderson, perhaps; but morally certain that she was the one he wanted. She was, after all, obviously secluding herself and her son from someone or something. Curt didn't doubt for a moment that it was the predators by whom she felt threatened. And didn't that mean there was a good chance that she, or her son, knew something Curt didn't? Something the police didn't? That Worden didn't?

It was time for Archie Matthews again, because this was it: the new factor in the equation. Barbara Anderson. And Jimmy.

CHAPTER 19

"Floyd tells me you're about ready to qualify for the private investigator's exam," Archie Matthews said with a grin.

"He oversold the product," said Curt gloomily. "I'm pretty sure that Barbara Anderson is the mother of the boy I want, but it doesn't do much good if I can't find her. When your answering service said on Sunday that you wouldn't be available until today, I got her P.O. box number from her husband and sent her a letter. But she didn't answer."

It was Wednesday, and Curt was in Matthews's anonymously modern office again. The private investigator had been working a case in the East Bay, had just gotten off it two hours before, and was yawning.

"What about the realty office?" he asked Curt. "They have to be able to reach her in case they get a firm offer on the house."

"I tried them Sunday. The woman wouldn't tell me a damned thing."

Matthews yawned again. "Sounds like this chick has covered herself pretty well. Probably took an apartment with utilities included—which means the connection still would be in the landlord's name, and my contacts with the gas and electric people wouldn't be able to help." He sat down at the desk and reached for the phone book. "Let's try it the easy way. What's the name of the woman at the realty company?"

"A Mrs. . . ." Curt squinted, thinking hard. "Mrs. Pinneo."

Matthews dialed Heritage Realty, leaning back in his expensive leather swivel chair and gazing at the ceiling with bloodshot eyes. Curt got the feeling that countless hours of Matthews's life had been spent in just this way, patiently, emptily—and a line from Eliot's *Prufrock*, popped into his head: *I have measured out my life with coffee spoons*. Or, in Matthews's case, phone calls.

Matthews leaned forward abruptly. "Yes, Mrs. Pinneo, please." His voice had thickened and harshened. "Mrs. Pinneo? This is Charles Anderson. I drove by to see Barbara today, and found your *For Sale* sign on the Edgewood Drive house."

The phone made squawking noises. Although Matthews's tired face remained bland, almost cherubic, his voice became positively biting. "And just why the hell wasn't I contacted? If my ex- had bothered to show you a copy of the divorce decree, you'd know that I retain a one-fourth interest in . . . what? Don't give me that crap, lady. I gave *nobody* any permission . . ."

He broke off for more squawks, caught Curt's eye, winked, and then went on in a nearly apoplectic voice. "You go right ahead. I'd contact her myself if I had her new address and—say, you'd better give me that, now I think of it, I—*what?* What the hell do you mean, you don't . . . oh. Well, address, phone number, what the hell's the difference? After three o'clock, huh?"

He listened a final time, scribbled on the back of an envelope, dropped the receiver back on the hooks, and gave the envelope to Curt. "She can be reached there, 982-7764, any time after three P.M. It's probably unlisted, but she might have gotten cute and given a work number. Just let me check . . ." He got the phone company service rep on the number, asked for the registration on it, and after thirty seconds of waiting, listened, nodded, and hung up. "What I thought. Unlisted. That makes it tougher, because Ma Bell is a bitch with employees who dish out unlisted numbers." He shot a look at the wall clock. "We've got until three o'clock to wait."

Curt said, "You're damned tired, Archie; I didn't mean that you should do this today, without sleep . . ."

Matthews yawned again, rasped his hand over his stubbled chin. "Yeah, I just came in today to check the mail; was just on my way to the gym when you caught me. What say you meet me there at three o'clock and—"

"Only if you let me pay you for a full day's work."

The detective shook his head. "To hell with that, Curt. I cost you three yards without turning a damned thing, and here you find the kid all by yourself. For my professional pride I've got to do you *some* good. Tell you what. Buy me and the mirror athlete a good lunch, and we'll call it square."

Over lunch with Preston and the detective, Curt realized that Matthews, like Preston, was another of a type that was coming to interest him more and more. A doer, not a talker. Not a cynic, but a bleakly hard-nosed realist, accepting human nature as he found it, not attempting to explain evil, merely accepting its existence. *Hell, Curt, my profession is the deadbeats, the dropouts, and the cop-outs. Those who aren't making it or want to make it all at once.* He sounded remarkably like Monty Worden, that professional prober in the soft underbelly of society. *There's just two kinds of people in my book, mister: the worms and the human beings. Law-breakers and law-keepers.* Even Preston, whom Curt had come to regard as a professional man, lived by the philosophy: *If a guy wants trouble, hit him first.*

And were they so wrong? If Curt found the predators, would it make any difference to him if they were products of slums or broken homes or racial minorities? Had it made any difference to Paula? Or to Rockwell? The only difference between a "disadvantaged" boy and a Yale student swinging a tire chain was that the disadvantaged boy would probably be a hell of a lot more accurate.

They got back to the gym at 2:55, and Matthews sat down at the desk to begin laboring over a sheet of scratch paper. "Working out my cover story," he explained. "The most important part of skip-tracing is to never let them ask a question you can't answer."

When he finally dialed the phone, Curt found himself taut as a cable; he had come to feel that Barbara Anderson and her son somehow would furnish the key to all his questions.

"Yeah, hello," said Matthews in a bored voice, "are you still having trouble with your phone?" He listened then, nodding unconsciously. "I see. Still humming sometimes, huh? And this *is* 982-7764? Mmm-hmm. Thought so. You see, I dialed 362-4872. That's right. It's what we call at the phone company an 'electronic inversion'—caused by faulty wiring, insulation rubbing away, or sometimes just by a misconnected circuit. Beg pardon? No, not all the time, that's what makes it so rough. That means we have to trace it all through each time it happens . . ."

Despite his offhanded tone of voice, a sheen of sweat had appeared on Matthews's face; he was working, and working hard.

"Yes, ma'am, that's right, Lineman Chester Drumm, ID card 384, Telephone Repair Service. Yes. What I'll have to do is trace right through from your main relay box." A drop of sweat fell from the end of his nose with the strain of keeping all strain out of his voice. "Do you have a one-family dwelling or an apartment? And what's that number? Twelve? That's fine ma'am, I'll be out in an hour if that's convenient for . . . oh, I almost forgot, I'd better get the street address, hadn't I?" He chuckled. "No, ma'am, in repair service we're never given more than just the phone numbers themselves, as a safeguard for the subscribers. Some people have unlisted phones, and . . ."

Curt held his breath as Matthews broke off, but the detective was nodding again and writing on his scratch paper. He finally thanked the woman and hung up and expelled a long whistling breath.

"It's always damned touchy when they're on the run," he said. "Let's hope she's not just ducking a bill collector."

"The only thing that bothers me," said Preston, "is how the hell you knew she'd been having phone trouble?"

Matthews laughed and stood up. "I didn't—and I doubt if she has been having phone trouble. It's just that everyone always *thinks* there's something wrong with his phone, if he's asked about it." He handed the paper to Curt. "Arroyo Towers, apartment twelve, 1482 Robles Drive in San Mateo. She says that if a white Ford is parked in her stall, she's home. If the car's gone, she'll be down at the supermarket and you should wait. I'd make sure the car is there before you ring her bell, just on the off-chance she'd be coming back and get a look at you before you want her to."

CHAPTER 20

Because of the rush hour, Curt's fourteen-mile drive to the Arroyo Towers took until 4:35 P.M. He noted the white Ford in the correct stall, checked mailboxes, and found *Occupied* in the name slot for apartment twelve. When he pushed the plastic button above the box, the gleaming aluminum-and-glass door clicked open to admit him to the lobby of the modernistic apartment building.

The elevator moved with maddening deliberation; in the carpeted hallway, Curt paused to wipe his palms down his trouser legs. It was like staring from the jump door of the Lockheed, with empty sky whipping by outside at 120 miles an hour, your hands gripping the metal edges of the door, knowing that when the lights flashed red and then green, and the jump master bellowed in your ear, you could only go forward.

Curt rang the bell of apartment twelve.

Barbara Anderson opened the door. "Mr. Drumm? I—oh!"

"Curt Halstead. I wrote you a letter earlier this week . . ."

She had started to slam the door, but had paused indecisively when Curt made no move to stop her. Her orange dress had a starched white apron over it that couldn't conceal the excellence of her figure; the smell of baking brownies had followed her to the door.

"I . . . got your letter." Her clear greenish eyes held his, but her voice shook just a little. "I didn't answer it because I . . . because my son is not the boy you are trying to get in touch with. He . . ."

"We both know that isn't so, Mrs. Anderson," said Curt reasonably.

Then he stepped forward, through the still-open door, so she had to give way before him in a parody of hospitality. Joe Louis once said that if he *saw* the opening in another fighter's guard, it already was too late to exploit it. Before Curt really registered that the woman was staring blindly at his face with true terror in her eyes, and was going to scream, he already was flopping down in the nearest easy chair.

"I could do with a cup of tea" he said conversationally. As if on cue, a sharp *ding!* came from the archway to the kitchen. "And I think your brownies are ready to come out for cooling."

"I . . ." The blindness was fading from her eyes; the muscles along her delicate jaw were relaxing. She had a fine-boned face, a wide generous mouth, without lipstick, heavy eyebrows and lashes. She ducked her head under his relaxed scrutiny. "I . . . of course. Brownies."

From his easy chair, Curt watched her disappear into the kitchen, then prowled the room with his eyes. The apartment was new, soulless, its rug a pale acrylic fiber, its walls prefabricated, its glass sliding door in the far wall opening on an iron-railed balcony all of three feet wide. Even the picture over the sofa had come with the apartment. Instant decorating, like instant coffee; quick, but obviously ersatz.

"What sort of work do you do, Mrs. Anderson?" he called through to the kitchen.

"I'm a . . . I work in a hospital. A registered nurse."

That explained the three o'clock return: shift work, probably arranged so she could pick Jimmy up after classes during the school year.

Five minutes later Barbara Anderson reappeared with a tray of tea things. She also had renewed lipstick and rouge on a face that had gone pallid when she had seen him in the hallway. Curt decided that she was probably a self-reliant woman, as Paula had been—which would have helped destroy her marriage if her husband was actually as weak as he had sounded on the phone. Curt got started.

"As I explained in my letter, Mrs. Anderson, I am a professor at Los Feliz University and live off Linda Vista Road—just across the golf course from where your son saw the four men in the station wagon."

Barbara Anderson made a small impatient gesture. "I *know*—now—who you are; I called the university after receiving your letter. But who were those men? And if they're so important, why did the sheriff's investigators say it was just a 'routine investigation'?" She gestured again, again impatiently. "They *didn't* molest Jimmy in any way, you know; he barely saw them as anything more than shadows. He overdramatized it because . . . well, because he's good at that, Mr. Halstead."

Curt poured tea, was pleased that it was very strong and black. Adding his usual milk and sugar, he was reminded of Alice's mad tea party. Their polite sparring over whether he would, or would not, get to speak with Jimmy Anderson observed the social amenities—like colonial administrators dressing for dinner in the bush while their empires crashed in ruins about their ears—but did little to relax tensions.

He said mildly, "Could we make that 'Curt'?"

After a moment's hesitation she nodded. "All right. And Barbara. And you still haven't answered any of my questions, Curt."

"I'll have to start by asking another. Do you remember, last April, when a man named Rockwell was attacked by a teenage gang?"

"I don't really . . . Oh, of course!" she suddenly exclaimed. "I wasn't working up here at County General then, but . . ." A look of disquiet darkened her face. "Wasn't he disfigured or . . . or blinded?"

"Blinded. By accident, I think, I'll give them that much. Anyway, my wife had been up to the San Francisco Spring Opera and so had

Rockwell. They got off the bus together and . . ." By the time he led her up to Matthews's call that afternoon, Curt was sweating. The necessity of putting the whole sequence together in logical order had evoked memories more bitter than he had been prepared for. Barbara's face was ashen when he stopped talking and reached for his teacup.

"So if Jimmy could *identify* those men he saw . . ." She shook her head. "And of course that explains the terrible phone call I got. When my husband and I were divorced, two years ago, I went back to work at the Los Feliz Med Center—just a few blocks from home. After the phone call I made Jimmy quit his paper route, and got a job up here at County General because I couldn't get a shift at the Med Center that would let me pick Jimmy up after school. When you came around asking questions, I was afraid you were one of them, so I put the house up for sale and got this apartment right close to County General Hospital."

"I should think I'd be pretty hard to mistake for a teenager."

"The one who called sounded like a mature man, not a boy. Except for what he said . . ." She paused, and a shudder ran through her, raising gooseflesh on her bare arms. "My dad was a longshoreman on the San Francisco docks, and I've been a nurse for years—I thought I'd heard all the obscenities. But that call . . . It was a Tuesday—May twenty-seventh. The call was worse than obscene, it was . . . moronic."

"Do you think he was serious, or just . . . fantasizing?"

A look of true revulsion made her face momentarily ugly. "He meant them." She gave a rueful little laugh, half-giggle, that Curt found somehow enchanting. "That's why, when you rang the bell here . . ."

Curt thought back over the long weeks of careful chipping—like a paleontologist chipping stone from the fossil of a pithecoid jawbone—that had brought him to this place at this moment in time.

"I don't think you have to worry about the predators finding you," he said.

"Predators?"

Curt heard his voice become slightly defensive. "It's . . . just a tag I've used for them, the gang, in my own mind."

"It's a good one. It . . . They sound so dangerous, and sick, and totally vicious. Are you sure you want to . . ."

The doorbell rang. She looked at her watch, and stood up. "That'll be Jimmy; he's been down by the pool."

Then her clear jade eyes sought Curt's brown ones; their gazes, their wills met and locked. They stared at one another wordlessly. Curt cursed himself, his weakness, silently. He shouldn't have seen her first, shouldn't have talked it all through with her. Now he knew he really couldn't ask her to let him question the boy; she had been through too much already, too much fear, too many sleepless nights. And Curt knew himself too soft to question the boy without telling her.

Barbara finally lowered her gaze. The bell rang again. She said, "I'd like you to stay for supper, Curt. Just potluck, but then you can bring up that night casually, in conversation—which might make him remember something he forgot to tell the sheriff's deputies."

Curt released an unconsciously long-pent breath, and wondered if his silly fatuous relief and gratitude showed on his face.

The supper was indeed potluck: the end of a canned ham butt, eggs scrambled with canned mushrooms, fried potatoes. But Curt hadn't enjoyed a meal so thoroughly in months; in fact, since . . .

Jimmy was a slender boy with straight dark hair always in his eyes, his mother's enchanting smile, and fey, slightly tilted eyes of the same greenish color as hers. He had come in with the rush and flurry that belongs so peculiarly to youth, had gone shy at the presence of a stranger, then had expanded, during supper, under the male attention. Curt introduced the four men by the golf course casually, easily.

"*Those* guys?" Jimmy was scornful. "*I* wasn't scared of 'em, not really. I just said I was, 'cause . . . 'cause . . ." His voice slowed as he realized where his tongue was leading him, and he cast a quick sideways glance at his mother.

"Go right ahead, young man," Barbara said. "I know perfectly well that you wanted to make me think that *they* had made you late."

"Ma can't spank hard enough to hurt *me* anyway," Jimmy bragged, recovering. "I didn't see anything, really, 'cept the Chevy wagon."

That was all until dessert, which was ice cream and the freshly baked brownies. Curt described the "Mexican-looking" boy who had been seen on Edgewood Drive, but Jimmy didn't react. Worden had been right; it was hopeless. They went into the living room, leaving Barbara to stack the dishes, and Jimmy leaned forward confidentially.

"I was gonna call Ma from that phone booth there by the golf course an' tell her my bike had a flat tire," he admitted. "You won't tell her, will ya? I know that woulda been lyin', but I didn't really do it . . ."

"Between us men, strictly," said Curt with a straight face. The phone booth, he decided, must have been the one across Linda Vista, where he had found his lucky dime. "Why didn't you call, Jimmy?"

Barbara called from the kitchen, "Dish washer or dish dryer, Curt?"

"Uh? Washer, I guess." He stood up.

Jimmy was going on. "I couldn't call 'cause there was this girl sittin' in the booth."

Something in what the boy said stopped Curt dead; he felt the hairs prickle on the back of his neck. But what? What was so odd about a girl making a phone call? Then he realized that the oddness was in Jimmy's phrase. Not making a phone call; sitting in a phone booth.

"You mean that the girl was using the phone, Jimmy?"

The boy shook his head. "She didn't even have the receiver off the hook or nothing. Just sittin' in there with the door open an' her feet sorta stickin' out—"

"But it was dark, Jimmy. How could you see that clearly?"

"I'd walked right up to the booth, see, wheeling my bike, and this car was coming by and I seen—saw her, plain as anything."

"And you didn't tell the man from the sheriff's office about her?"

"*Him?* He acted like I was eight years old or somethin'," the boy said scornfully.

Eight. Instead of ten. That figured; boys straining for those fabulous teens resented being called younger than they were. And Curt had his fact that Worden didn't have. Why would a girl be merely sitting in that particular phonebooth on that particular night, in the dark, not using the phone, not doing anything? Like a lookout, or something.

A lookout.

Almost not daring to breathe for fear of tensing the boy up, hoping desperately that Barbara would not choose that instant to call again from the kitchen, he said, "Ah . . . you wouldn't remember anything much about this girl, I guess, huh, Jimmy?"

"She was just a . . . uh, girl, you know. Older, sorta. Not *real* old, like Ma, but, uh, nineteen or twenty or somethin'." He chewed his lip, then brightened suddenly. "Her dad's name is Marsden, 'cause I used to deliver papers to him before they moved away." His mouth was hanging slightly open as he looked into his own brief past. "Big white house with a stone front on it, on the right-hand side of Glenn Way. The daily an' the Sunday, both. Her dad gave me a baseball once."

Curt's drive home was a kaleidoscopic whirl of half-formed questions and bits of sensual image: the faint remembered fragrance of Barbara's perfume, the way she had seemed to bend toward him as she had said good night, the fervor of her demand that he call her with whatever he might uncover about the predators. And the questions. A lookout? But how? Why? What sort of girl helped a gang rape an innocent woman?

He walked across the road to the booth, sat in the little metal seat, leaned out to stare up and down Linda Vista. Yes. Across the road he could see the dull gleam of his VW's chrome at the bottom of his drive; higher, he could see fragments of light from his own house gleaming through the foliage.

A lookout. They *would* have set sentries—a sentry, anyway. And even on a black night such as this he could have seen anyone walking up the driveway toward the house. Or driving, of course.

From the front porch, he stared down toward the invisible booth. How would such a lookout communicate with those inside the house? A phone call? Feasible, of course, but subject to dialing error . . .

A car whipped by down on Linda Vista, its headlights showing for a moment the empty booth, the open door, even the metal seat inside.

Of course. A lookout down below, a relay on the porch.

Curt walked down the drive, crossed the blacktop, shut the door of the booth, and returned to the porch. Perfect. And in April the foliage would not have been as full as it was now, in high summer. In April a relay lookout couldn't help seeing the girl in the booth if she stood up, pulled shut the door to make the light go on, and pretended to dial. The relay merely opened the front door, shouted . . .

But . . . a *girl?*

There were such women, of course, consorts of motorcycle gangs in leather jackets and stomping boots and Nazi helmets, but . . .

But who cared what sort? Not an individual girl, a human being at all, to Curt. Just . . . one of the predators. Tomorrow it would begin. The new search. No need of Archie Matthews now. Just find Glenn Way, start looking. Asking questions. Her folks had moved away previous to last April? Well, she hadn't. Not just a street, not just a stone-faced house he had, but a name. Marsden. No first name, but again, who cared? He would learn it, would find her, would ask questions.

As he started up the stairs toward the bedroom, a momentary worry stopped him. What if she were innocent, not one of the gang, just a girl who had been out with a fresh date, had slapped a face, had begun walking home and had stopped at the phone booth to sit down and rest?

Curt shook it off. Too much coincidence. And besides, how had the predators known where to find Jimmy Anderson, if not through the girl in the phone booth? He had recognized her, it was reasonable to assume that she also had recognized him. Tomorrow . . .

Only when he was in bed with the lights out did Curt think again of Barbara Anderson, and then she returned to his memory with a warm rush of vaguely realized excitement. Sun-frosted brown hair, steady jade eyes, rounded mature curve of breast and hip and thigh as she moved between sink and cabinet with the dried dishes.

And she had asked him to call her—had almost demanded that he call her, in fact. Nothing more than a very natural desire to know about the predators who had threatened her and her child; and yet . . .

Perhaps just some tiny part of it personal, also? Some tiny part of it just between her and Curt? Some spark of emotion, perhaps?

CHAPTER 21

Debbie left her French exam and started back toward the dorm. As of right now, summer school was over; and summer itself rapidly was drawing to a close. But Debbie felt none of the sadness attributed by pops songwriters to that passing, because a path of joy, beginning tonight, stretched down the years for her and Rick. In half an hour he would pick her up and they would drive down to his folks' cabin on the coast for the weekend. Just the two of them. It bothered her a little that she'd had to lie to her parents, tell them she was going to be staying at Cynthia's place in San Jose—but it was so *right* with Rick!

Walking along she felt flushed, almost feverish, but knew that it was just excitement. Tonight . . . Cynthia said it wasn't too bad, even the first time, if the boy was gentle. And Ricky would be gentle.

Up in her room, drifting on her dream, Debbie packed her Lady Baltimore train case with cosmetics and swim suit and the half-used card of C-Quens she had gotten from Cynthia, whose father was a druggist. She had been taking them for ten days, ever since deciding that she would give in to Rick's entreaties and go to the cabin with him.

She snapped down the catches on the train case, picked it up, and saw for the first time a note that the house mother had put on her pillow. Debbie caught her breath. What if Ricky couldn't . . . If she didn't go through with it now, she wasn't sure she could ever get herself steeled to say yes again.

But it was a university extension number. Whew. Probably just something to do with the French exam, or the glee club during the upcoming fall term, or maybe even with the student newspaper. It could wait until Monday when she got back and . . .

But she'd be rushed on Monday, clearing out her room to go stay with her folks until the new term started. Better call now, Ricky wasn't here yet anyway. She went downstairs to the pay phone in the little alcove off the wood-paneled common room, dialed the university central switchboard and asked for the proper extension.

"Anthropology Department, Miss Reeves."

Anthropology? She didn't have any anthropology courses. "This is Debbie Marsden. I'm returning a call to your number that—"

"Oh yes," said the flatly efficient voice, "I'll connect you."

"But . . ." But the key already was flicked. Anthropology? Who . . .

The line opened, a heavy voice said, "There you are, Miss Marsden. Curt Halstead here. I'm sorry I left no name on my message, but I wasn't sure you would return my call in that case."

"Not . . . return your call?" Debbie asked faintly. Professor *Halstead?* Whose wife had slept with Ricky and then had killed herself when Ricky didn't show up that Friday night? But he *couldn't* want to talk to her about that. He just *couldn't.* She'd just *die* if he said anything . . .

He didn't. "Why, yes, Miss Marsden, you don't know me, never had me for a class, I was afraid you would just ignore the call." The voice seemed heavy, faintly sarcastic, not at all like the man she vaguely remembered from the faculty-freshman tea as big and loosely built and with a nice smile. "You see, I recently lost my wife . . ."

"I . . . yes, I heard, I . . ." Debbie clung to the receiver, pressing her shoulder hard against the wall to keep from sitting down suddenly. Her face felt chalky.

"Well, then," said the voice, with heavy joviality that was somehow menacing, "can I expect you at my house this afternoon? I checked your schedule, your last exam is finished—"

To his house? Why? How? *This afternoon?* "But I . . . Professor, I . . . this weekend, I . . ."

"Tied up? All right then, Miss Marsden, I'll expect you for tea on Monday afternoon. But . . . let's make it early, say . . . two P.M.?"

"But I . . . I don't . . ."

"That's fine, Miss Marsden. I expect you know the way."

She leaned against the wall, thankful for the cold steel of the partition against her forehead, idiotically clutching the dead receiver to her ear as if it would tell her more. Her heart was pounding. What in God's name could he want? She made herself straighten up. More pertinently, what was the matter with her? What had she to feel guilty about? Granted, it had been an odd conversation, but . . . not a conversation where phone booths, or Friday nights, or even suicide had come up. The trouble, of course, was that she knew of Paula Halstead's infidelity and Professor Halstead didn't. And now that Paula was dead, wouldn't he be happier with his memories of his wife intact?

Up in her room, Debbie sat down on her bed to await Rick's arrival. She would tell him of the phone call; he would know what she should do. He . . . but no. This was her problem, she wouldn't say anything until after she had seen the professor. She would feel really silly if she got there on Monday and it was something about the newspaper or fall classes or something like that. She wasn't going to let it ruin her weekend with Rick. Not *this* weekend, when everything belonged just to the two of them. Nothing must intrude, and most especially nothing that might remind Ricky of Paula Halstead.

She realized the red Triumph was stopped at the end of the walk, horn tootling. She picked up her train case and went out. Downstairs, she tossed it into the back of the car, hopped in beside Rick, and shyly stretched over to kiss him. The butterflies were back in her stomach. As they pulled out, neither noticed the green

Rambler, parked a short block down Dormitory Row, which started up behind them.

At the wheel, grim-faced, was Julio Escobar.

The cabin was perched at the bottom V of a deep wooded ravine, enclosed by jagged coastal bluffs and backed by a thick stand of Douglas fir and tideland spruce. There were two small bedrooms, a living room dominated by a cast-iron wood stove, and a tiny kitchen with a butane cook stove. On the roof was a rain-filled water tank to gravity-feed the kitchen sink, toilet, and shower. The front of the cabin, the living room, looked out over the beach, and the front door opened on a flight of fifteen rough wooden steps terminating on the sand dunes that rimmed the beach. This was a V of white sand, not over a hundred yards wide at the water's edge, that faced a mirror-image V of water. It foamed in from the open sea between enclosing black blades of granite that dropped down from the bluffs flanking the ravine.

Debbie clapped her hands in excitement. "Oh, Ricky, we've got our own private beach!"

Rick came up behind her and put his arms around her waist. She turned in the circle of his arms and kissed him briefly, then broke loose with a nervous little laugh.

"Whoa!" she exclaimed. For an instant she had felt a giddy touch of near-terror: in a few hours, when darkness came, she was committed to surrender everything to him. "Can . . . we go swimming, Ricky?"

"Sure, nude if you want to!" he mock-leered. But she heard his voice quaver a little, and then it was all right. He was nervous too! "They can't even see this cove from the highway; in all the years my old man's had this place, nobody's ever come down here."

"I'll wear my suit, thanks. What if your *folks* came down?"

"I told you, Deb, they *won't*. Hell, they think the other guys are down here with me. They know we wouldn't want 'em hanging around."

His slap across her backside made her yelp. "Let's get our suits."

Debbie stripped in the left-hand bedroom. She had shut the door behind her, and the window was filled with the dark green branches of a fir tree close behind the house, so she studied her nude body in the full-length mirror on the inside of the door. Long and slender legs, without any excess flesh inside the thighs, where so many girls jiggled when they walked. Waist tight and firm, breasts thrusting and well-formed, without a woman's mature fullness yet to draw them down.

A tiny scratching from the window made her spin about with a muffled *yip*, trying ineffectually to cover her groin and both breasts with only two hands; then she giggled and sank down on the bed. A chipmunk peered in at her intently, one paw up with a single tiny claw hooked through the screen. He jerked his head twice, a comic's double-take, and was gone with a flirt of the tail, so instantaneously that Debbie could not be totally sure he ever had been there at all.

What a cutie he was! She'd put out nut meats for him later.

She got into her bikini quickly, the funny hollow feeling back from having seen herself nude; in a few hours Ricky would have explored every secret place of that body . . .

"Hey, quit gawking in the mirror and c'mon," he called.

"I wasn't gawking," she said as she emerged. "This chipmunk . . ."

Her voice trailed off. She wore just the skimpy halter and abbreviated trunks of the most daring bikini she'd been able to find in Los Feliz, and Rick's avid stare, hot and frank and wanting, made her blush furiously. He'd never even seen her in shorts before, and now he could see almost all of her.

"I . . . I'll race you to the water!" she exclaimed, avoiding his gaze, frightened again by his nearly nude, very male body.

They splashed in almost together, with yells from Rick and squeals of despair from Debbie at the fifty-degree temperature; then it was a water fight and finally a thorough ducking despite Debbie's pleadings and shrieks. Rick finally desisted; they kissed hurriedly, then ran back up the sand to the dry, sun-warmed beach below the dunes, where they flopped out on their towels out of the wind.

Julio, no longer able to see them from his place of concealment in the conifers by the foot of the gravel drive, gritted his teeth and turned away. He climbed up the narrow track, went over the locked gate, and trudged back to the Rambler parked in the view-area two hundred yards beyond.

Lying bastard, pretending he wasn't making it with Debbie! For all Julio knew, he was balling her right there on the beach right now. He'd go make sure, if he could be sure they wouldn't see him. It was all right that he'd been following Debbie, off and on, since the Fourth of July, looking for proof that she might betray their identity to someone as the attackers of Paula Halstead; but he had no excuse for having followed her and Rick today.

He got in the Rambler, U-turned back toward San Conrado, the nearest town, some ten miles north. Yeah, it was a sort of sick scene, following them today. Especially when he knew he would come back after dark, try to actually see them making out. It was like a goddamn fever or something, which had gotten worse the more he followed her. He had seen no signs of treachery, but he had learned every turn of her head, every expression of her face, all the movements and graces and occasional coltish awkwardness of her body. He had fed upon her, had even considered picking her up and just taking what she was giving to Rick.

Anything, in fact, to put out the fire that raged in his guts.

At sundown they went in and shut the windows and got a fire started in the wood stove. Debbie made steaks and baked potatoes and salad and warmed the French bread; they sat cross-legged on the living room rug to eat, facing one another.

Debbie felt herself getting tense again whenever Rick, dark and handsome and intense by the reddish flickering glow from the stove, caught her eye. Finally they were finished eating, and then

Rick took her Coke out of her hand, set it aside, and gently pushed her down on her back. They were still in their swim suits. He started kissing her, then put his hand in the hot V between her breasts, his fingers curving around her breast under the halter.

She tore loose suddenly, and started sobbing. "I'm sor . . . sorry, Ricky. I just . . . I . . . please, be patient . . ."

"*Patient?* What the hell . . ." He was sitting up, panting, his eyes glowing angrily. Then he took a deep breath and nodded. He stood up. "Okay, Deb," he said. "I'll be right back."

In the kitchen he poured out orange juice from the old refrigerator into two glasses, then added vodka from the bottle his old man kept under the sink. He saw his hands were shaking. Goddamn her! Then he told himself to take it easy. She was a goddamn virgin, had to remember that. Big deal for her. Mustn't blow it by coming on too hard, scaring her so she froze up. He'd never gotten a virgin, and he wanted to, real bad. Like one of those old kings or something in history class, take anyone in the kingdom they wanted. Always a virgin.

He went back in with their drinks, and made his voice cheerful. "Screwdrivers, they call them, kid. Just orange juice and vodka. You won't even taste it, but it'll make you relax."

"I'm sorry," she said humbly. "I tried, I really did, I—"

"That's okay, baby." His eyes gleamed. "Just relax . . ."

And with three screwdrivers warming her stomach, revolving in her head, she did, letting her body take over, make its own responses to his mouth and hands. She kissed the back of his neck a little dizzily as he unsnapped her halter, and clung to his brown, muscular back as his mouth sought her bared breasts.

Then they were in the bedroom, and for the first time in her life she was gripped by that ancient urgency far older than the brief human species of which she was but a momentary spark. Her legs parted; when he entered her she cried out once, sharply, then moaned, and whispered his name again and again, fiercely, a talisman to carry her beyond the pain to the pleasure that sex education courses had promised her.

As she clung to him, whispering her love to him, Rick, above her, grunted and thrust and finally pumped, careless of her stifled outcries, the biggest man in the world, making it, balling a virgin, getting his.

When it was over they lay side by side, Debbie crying proudly into the hollow of his neck, by some miracle knowing that the strange urgency would grip her again in a few minutes' time, and Rick, staring up into the darkness, complacent at having made his first virgin. Old Deb, she hadn't been much this first time, but he dug being the first one, dug knowing he had hurt her and had made her like it. A whole different thing than with Mary, who you couldn't get to even by hurting because she dug every sort of weird scene you could dream up.

But it had been sort of like getting Paula Halstead, all over again. Goddamn her! He wished that it was her next to him, not Debbie. He'd show her some things that would take that pitiless contempt from her eyes—that look he'd never been able to change or forget.

Thinking of Paula got him going again, and he turned toward Debbie as the chipmunk, that she'd seen outside the window earlier, scrabbled getting those silly damned walnuts or whatever the hell it was that she'd left out for him. Debbie heard it, too, but didn't react. There was nothing in the world for her just then but Ricky.

Outside, Julio slipped off through the darkened woods, unaware of the city-bred noises he was making. Not that he would have cared even if he had been aware of his clumsiness in the undergrowth. He was half-blind with frustration and desire and hatred.

Dirty goddamn whorish bitch. Oh, she'd get hers. When the time came, and it wasn't far off, she'd get plenty.

CHAPTER 22

It was 2:03 on Monday afternoon when Debbie rang Curt's doorbell. Waiting, she straightened to draw in her already flat stomach and thus thrust her breasts a little more noticeably forward. I'm a woman now, she thought a little complacently. Ricky has made me a woman. As a woman, she knew, with a woman's weapons, she had nothing to fear from Professor Curtis Halstead, even if it would be something about his wife.

The door opened, and Curt was looking at her.

"Miss Marsden? Come in, please." He shut the door behind her; she was totally unlike anything he might have imagined. "Would you like some tea, or coffee?"

"I . . . tea would be fine."

She's nervous as a cat, Curt thought. He said, "I'll just be a moment, Miss Marsden. Or may I call you Debbie?"

"Debbie is fine, sir."

She sat primly on the couch, feet in their flat shoes flat on the floor, knees held tightly together. She watched him disappear through the double doors into the dark-paneled dining room. He was nothing at all like her vague remembrance from the faculty tea; he must be as old as her dad, maybe, but he moved the way that Ricky moved. She felt a momentary stab of uneasiness; he looked like a man who might be proof against the woman's weapons she had thought to rely on.

Curt returned with the tea service on a tray, and was reminded vividly of that first morning with Monty Worden. But this girl was so young, so pathetically young. But he had to get those names from her. The names of the predators.

"The water will boil in a moment." Then he added, in the same conversational voice, "What time did you leave the phone booth that night? The night that Paula killed herself?"

"I . . . what do you mean, I . . . don't understand . . ."

"The paper boy has identified you, Debbie. You *must* recall him."

Debbie realized that she had half risen, made herself sit back down. Then she realized she was staring at her fingers, intertwined in her lap, so she quickly dropped her hands to the sofa. The paper boy! She remembered him, all right. But how had the professor found out about him? And . . . And . . . She mustn't admit being there; she had promised Ricky she would never tell about him and Paula Halstead and . . .

She heard her own voice, like the voice of a stranger speaking from a great distance, saying, "I . . . about nine-thirty. I . . ."

"Paula killed herself just a few minutes before my return at about eleven forty-five. If I had returned directly following the end of my seminar, she still would be alive." He said it entirely without visible emotion. The teapot began whistling thinly, and Curt stood up. He started for the kitchen, then whirled abruptly: Worden had taught him the value of shock tactics. "What were you *doing* in the phone booth?"

Startled, Debbie tried to counter weakly with, "What . . . does one usually do in a phone booth?"

"One usually makes a phone call—which you didn't."

Then he was gone, leaving her staring numbly after him. She fought an urge to bolt out the front door. She mustn't tell. Mustn't mustn't mustn't. Remember: if his old wife had left Ricky alone, none of this would have happened. It was *her* fault, not Debbie's or Rick's.

Curt returned, poured tea, added milk and sugar to his as Debbie added lemon and sugar to hers. Was it possible, just barely possible, that she had been there innocently? But her hands, holding the cup, were shaking slightly, and her eyes would not meet his.

He snapped at her, "Well? What *were* you doing in that booth?"

Debbie's hands jerked, spilling tea; she felt her control slipping, knew she would start sniveling in a moment like a high school kid. He was watching her as if she were something from under a stone.

"I . . . Ri . . . a friend asked me to . . . to . . . Please, don't look at me like that, I . . . it was . . . your wife's fault. If she'd left . . . left him alone . . ."

Curt dropped, "Indeed?" into the silence. He moved over to the fireplace, leaned an elbow on the mantle. From here he could see the clean even line of her hair parting. "Left whom alone?"

Debbie just shook her head, eyes squeezed tight shut to keep the tears inside. She mustn't tell.

Curt, sensing the resistance in that direction, swung off at right angles. "Here. Use my handkerchief. What did Paula do to him?"

"All right!" she flared, red-eyed and hating it, but now able to hide her face behind his handkerchief, at least. "All right! Your precious wife picked him up in a motel bar and took him to her room and . . . *seduced* him! He's not even twenty yet and she was . . . was . . ."

"Thirty-six." All right, old, to nineteen. He said, "What motel was it? What month? What day?"

"I don't know any of that." Debbie found herself a little put out, through her tears, that she didn't. Ricky had left her woefully unprepared to defend herself against this hateful accusing man who hadn't really accused anyone of anything yet; but then, she thought, it wasn't Ricky's fault. She hadn't told him about Professor Halstead's call. She went on, controlling her tears now, "But that wasn't all. She kept calling him at home, waiting around for him outside Jay . . . outside where he . . . works. She wouldn't leave him alone. She was . . . was *insatiable*."

As she used the damning word she watched his face, waiting for it to crumble under the impact of his wife's infidelity; but he just stood there quietly, gravely attentive. None of the wrenching pain that she would feel if Ricky were to . . . But maybe when you got old, your emotions didn't touch you anymore. Or maybe it was no surprise to him.

"You were in the phone booth because of your friend?"

Now that the bad part was past, Debbie didn't mind talking. She nodded almost eagerly. "Ri . . . he planned to see her that Friday night and tell her to leave him alone, but then he had a flat tire and . . ."

"And so Paula, in despair, killed herself."

Curt supplied the ending almost absently. Unless this girl was a consummate actress, she knew nothing at all about the vicious attack on Paula. Her boyfriend, call him X, had been damned clever, using Debbie's love—whatever love meant at nineteen—by telling her a story she would *want* to believe, a tragic story that would give him stature in her eyes. Too sophisticated for nineteen? No. Not if you assume a doting mother, say, to spend a boyhood practicing on, a sister or two, perhaps, to study and observe as he grew up.

"You were his lookout, right, Debbie? So he wouldn't be surprised here with her, and be . . . compromised?"

She nodded eagerly. "Except he was worried about *her* reputation, not his own."

Curt nodded almost benignly, as an icy anger began to grip him. "One little thing that puzzles me, Debbie. If he was here because Paula wanted him to be, why would he need a lookout? If anyone rang the bell, she needed only not answer it."

"I . . . don't . . ." Debbie was momentarily stricken by the implications of the question. "Maybe . . . he was afraid you'd come home . . ."

"Have you ever heard of a man named Harold Rockwell?"

"I . . . no, sir." She seemed genuinely confused. "Is he another of her . . . I mean . . ."

"Another of Paula's lovers?" Curt felt grimly amused and a bit sick at the same time. X had done his work well. "No. Harold Rockwell was assaulted on a downtown street and beaten so viciously that he went blind, one week before my wife's suicide. Four teen-agers did it, Debbie. Driving a two-tone green Chevrolet station wagon, a fifty-five or fifty-six model."

He was watching her closely; the station wagon had sunk in, all right. It had meant something to her. But she tossed her head almost nervously, like a thoroughbred mare; still spirit in her.

"I don't see what this has to do with . . . with anything."

"Paula was a witness to that assault—the *only* witness. Because Rockwell was blind, only she could identify the attackers. One week later, on the Friday night Paula killed herself, my home was invaded by four teenagers. Four predators, if you will. Just at eight o'clock, when you were in that phone booth, they parked a two-tone green fifty-five or fifty-six Chevrolet station wagon north of the golf course, walked down the fairway to the fourteenth green. You had the phone booth door open, the all-clear signal, so they came up to the house—"

"*No!*" she exclaimed, catching the implications for the first time.

"When Paula opened the door they hit her in the stomach, and then dragged her into the reading room . . ." He pointed toward the back hall. "Through there, just a few steps. There's a daybed in there."

Debbie was drawing her face from side to side in negation, eyes tight shut, as if already aware of what was coming. Curt knew he should stop now, but he couldn't; he had reconstructed it too often in the silence of his mind to stop now.

"And then they raped her, one after the other. Maybe they even had seconds because she was such prime stuff. But always one of them would be on the porch to watch the phone booth through the trees."

"Stop it," she sobbed. "Please stop . . ."

"An hour, two hours after they left—we aren't sure just what time that was—Paula went upstairs and very carefully and almost ceremoniously slit her wrist and bled to death." He moved in on her, haunted by Worden's coarse, unfeeling remark four months before. "Why do you think she did that, Debbie? Do you suppose she found out she *liked* it?"

He had come to a stop standing over her, breathing hard, sweat pouring down his face, shirt sodden. Debbie was huddled on the couch with her arms folded under her breasts, each white-fingered hand gripping the opposite elbow.

When she raised her face there was true horror and revulsion in it. "And you think that *I* . . . that I would *help* somebody . . . do . . ."

Curt backed off, shook his head; he felt sick. He said gently, "No, Debbie, I don't think that. I think you were used, unwittingly."

But he had lost her. He had lost control, pushed too hard, put her into a corner she had to get out of at any cost to logic or thought.

"I . . ." Her lips were so dry that she had to stop and wet them, but her chin thrust stubbornly and her eyes were almost transfigured. "Do you really expect me to believe that *Ri* . . . that my . . . that he would do something like that to anyone? I . . . *know* him. I . . ."

Curt knew she was just fighting back, that her mind was simply refusing the monstrous, the unacceptable, but it still momentarily shook him. What if he *was* wrong? What if it all just had been a series of grotesque and terrible coincidences? What if Paula *had* been having an affair with Debbie's nineteen-year-old boyfriend?

He sighed. "It happened, Debbie, pretty much as I've told it. If you're so convinced that your friend isn't involved, give me his name. Let me talk with him, let *me* be convinced, too." Even as he said it, he knew it was useless.

Debbie stood up on legs that she seemed to find tottery. "I want to go away now, please."

"I'll drive you back to school."

"I'd rather walk."

As she started for the door, Curt, on sudden impulse, picked up from the mantlepiece the envelope with Paula's suicide note in it. The words had long since been burned indelibly into his brain. At the door, he thrust it into her hands. She met his eyes almost blindly, not understanding, still bewildered by lingering shock and emotion.

"Read it," he said. "It's her suicide note—Paula's note. If it raises any questions in your mind, call me. Give me a name. Just one name is all I need. And tell your friend that he doesn't have to worry about trouble with the police; the law can't touch him if he had anything to do with it or not."

Debbie somehow got away, down the steps, down the driveway, the envelope clutched in one hand. Walking jerkily back toward school on Linda Vista, she took out the note and read it. It shook her.

I am doing this because of something intolerable in myself . . .

Debbie's steps slowed, then quickened triumphantly again. Of course. Paula had been an old woman; she hadn't been able to face life without Ricky. *Something intolerable in myself*. Yes, shame had driven her on. You read about it all the time. The older women, seeking the younger and younger lovers, finally killing themselves from shame.

As for the rest of it, that Harold Rockwell thing, she was sure that had happened the way the professor had said it had, but that didn't mean Rick or any of the others were mixed up in it—even though it was the sort of thing it wouldn't surprise her to hear about that icky Julio doing. Julio, whose eyes always undressed her when he looked at her. She felt a faint disgust with herself. To have even for an instant felt any doubt of Ricky, after this past weekend together! She wouldn't say anything to him about today; it would be too much like questioning his actions. Their love was still too new, too fragile and wonderful, to risk that way.

Curt stood on the front porch, watching the girl go down the driveway toward the blacktop. She soon was lost to his view behind the trees and undergrowth, but he continued to stand there abstractedly. So it went on. Talking with her dormitory house mother, talking with her parents—not that they necessarily would know who Debbie's special boyfriend was. Parents or school authorities seldom did these days. Failing there, talking with her special girl friends among the students. Maybe, if necessary, putting Archie Matthews back on it.

He stared unseeingly at a green Rambler that dawdled on Linda Vista toward the university, in the direction Debbie had gone. In his brief glimpses through the foliage, Curt could not see the driver.

The trouble was he had handled it wrong. Pushed too hard, too fast. Left her no way to turn, so she *had* to deny to herself that her boyfriend could be involved. It also bothered him that she had believed so strongly. Maybe he *was* wrong; he had to be *sure* before he moved against anyone. At least he had the threat against Jimmy Anderson; he hadn't told Debbie about that. He still had that as a lever.

RICK

TUESDAY, AUGUST 26TH–
FRIDAY, AUGUST 29TH

CHAPTER 23

Rick drew on his cigarette, and the glowing tip cast a faintly theatrical glow over the angles of his face. He and Julio wore swim trunks but neither had been in the water; it was just that nothing said out here by the pool could be heard except from the kitchen windows, and they were closed.

"Not Debbie," he repeated doggedly. "I know her, Julio."

"Yes, man, Debbie." Julio's voice was low and intense. "I followed her out there, and waited down the road until she came out again."

"What the hell are you doing following her anyway?"

Julio's face was just a blur in the gathering darkness. "Remember the Fourth of July? She said something about you and older women? That showed that she knew about Paula Halstead, so I have followed her ever since, waiting for her to show that she is dangerous." Then as if sensing Rick's unasked question, he laughed harshly. The laughter seemed to congeal in his throat. "Yes, last weekend, too. To the cabin. Did you think Julio so dumb as to believe you were not making her? Will the others be so dumb as to believe you when you say she is not a danger?"

The redwood fence blocked off the evening breeze, but Rick still seemed to find the evening getting chilly. He shivered. He'd told Debbie that Paula Halstead had been in love with him, and here was Debbie going to Halstead's house. Could she be wiggy enough to *tell* Halstead that story Rick had made up? For the first time he felt things closing in about him. Debbie. Halstead. The rest of the guys. Julio.

If. He looked over at Julio, just a pale blob on the cement beside him now, as the darkness thickened.

If Julio wasn't making it all up because he was paranoid or something about getting his hands on Debbie. Now that he thought of it, what the hell was Julio following Debbie around for when she was with *Rick?* Was Julio maybe thinking that Rick should no longer be the moving force of the group? This was Rick's problem, Rick Dean would handle it. It was time for him to regain the offensive.

"Well, what do you think?" demanded Julio impatiently. "Do you not think the others will agree with my idea that we should—"

"I think you're full of shit," said Rick viciously.

Julio's mouth sagged in surprise. It was always that way: Rick would switch moods, change gears, and neatly be in command again. Rick was going on, his facile imagination working smoothly.

"I told Debbie to talk with Halstead—pretend to be interviewing him for the first fall-term edition of the student newspaper—about his wife's death." His lips curved in self-satisfaction as he put it into Julio, watched the bastard squirm. "You know the way Deb is with me, Julio, I didn't give her any reason why I wanted her to ask. I never have to give Deb reasons. She does anything I say. *Anything*. But, since you're so damned chicken—"

"I am not chicken," denied Julio thickly.

"I said, since you are so chicken," Rick went on, "I'll ask her what she found out. Just for you, so you can sleep at night. I have a date with her tomorrow night, in San Leandro. I'll ask her then."

Once Julio was gone, however, Rick sat down in one of the canvas deck chairs and thoughtfully lighted another cigarette. It was all very well to say to Julio that he was on top of things, but *he* knew he hadn't told Debbie to go see Halstead. It was that Julio didn't know how to handle chicks. He came on too hard with them.

Chicks took everything personal, you had to make them think that they somehow had injured you.

He drew on the cigarette, watched the tip glow. Tomorrow was Wednesday, the twenty-seventh. He really had to find out what was going on, before things went sour. The real danger was that fruiter, Rockwell. So he'd screwed Halstead's wife, hell, she'd begged for it; and now she was dead, they couldn't prove a thing there. But Rockwell still was around. Christ, Rick's old man would *freak* if he was arrested for *that*. He still could feel that queer's face grinding into the gravel, almost.

Caliban jumped up on the couch beside Rick, regarded him warily from quarter-sized eyes. Caliban's throat was achingly white and the tip of his nose was pink; he weighed thirteen pounds. Rick ran a hand down his back and then, because Debbie was still out in the kitchen telling her ma about the movie, shoved Caliban on the shoulder, hard, trying to knock him on the floor. The cat merely yielded with the push, like a boxer slipping a punch, gave a single indignant *rowhr!* and jumped off the sofa with wounded dignity. Dogs were okay, wagging their tails and everything, but a cat wouldn't even *purr* unless he wanted to.

Debbie came in, looking really sexy in a turquoise thing with a short swirly skirt and a tight top that really showed her jugs. Man, he had to get her down to the cabin for a repeat real soon.

"Mom went up to bed," Debbie said.

Rick grunted. "My old lady, she'd stay up and keep thinking of reasons why she had to walk through the room or something, where we were."

Debbie sat down beside him, up close beside him, but all he did was take her hand. It was time to find out. He cleared his throat. "Listen, Deb, Julio was driving out Linda Vista Road on Monday and he . . . ah . . . thought he saw you going into that Professor Halstead's house."

Debbie pulled the hand away. "He just *happened* to be driving by? In that green Rambler he borrows from Heavy all the time?

Rick, he gives me the creeps, he really does. I keep seeing him on the campus at the U. Whenever he looks at me, I feel like I don't have any clothes on." Then she shook her head. "The only one I like is Champ."

Rick remembered Champ on the phone with that snoopy little bastard's mother; if Debbie only knew! He said, "*Did* you go see Halstead?"

"He called me up on Friday, and I went to see him Monday." She met his eyes steadily. "Have you heard of a man named Harold Rockwell?"

Rick felt as if he had been hit in the stomach; but somehow he kept his face and his voice even. "Rockwell? Isn't he some real square old cat who paints these real square pictures or something?"

"That's *Norman* Rockwell, silly." But Rick could hear the faint thread of relief in her voice. How the hell much had Halstead told her, for God's sake? How the hell much did Halstead know? Debbie went on, "He was beaten up, this Rockwell, one night way last spring in Los Feliz, and Mrs. Halstead was the only witness . . ."

Goddamn it, what were they going to do? How much had he told her, for Christ sake? "You mean, Deb, that you thought *I* had some—"

"No, silly," said Debbie almost gaily, fears allayed, "but the station wagon they used to attack Rockwell was . . . well, sort of like that one of Heavy's, and I thought . . . I mean, maybe you weren't with them . . . it was the week before Paula Halstead died . . . And then Professor Halstead said that the same station wagon was parked by the golf course that night, and that his wife was . . . was *raped* and everything before she killed herself, and . . ."

"Aw c'mon, Deb, I was *with* Julio that night, remember? And I think we were all to a drive-in movie the Friday before." He was squirming inwardly, but made himself seem nonchalant. "That professor must really be wiggy. What else did he tell you?"

Listening to her, he felt a ball of lead growing in his belly. Jesus, Jesus, worse than he'd thought. The worst it could be. All summer they're sitting around on their butts, and that bastard is tracking them down. But who would have thought . . . I mean, a goddamn *teacher* . . . And he had *all* of it: the station wagon, the kid on the bike, even using the phone booth light as a signal.

". . . and so I *had* to tell him about you and his wife, Ricky, even though I promised you . . ."

Even that, Halstead had. Oh, that bastard was *smart*. He cleared his throat. "Ah . . . what did he want to do about all this?"

"He wanted your name, wanted to meet you. He said . . ." She thought carefully, trying to remember things heard through the haze of her shock. "He said that even if you were one of them, you didn't have to be afraid, because the police couldn't touch any of them anyway . . ."

Oh yeah, smart, that bastard. Tricky. Just what Rick would have said in his place. Rick stood, began pacing theatrically. With chicks, you had to get their sympathy.

"This is bad, Debbie. I mean, really *terrible!* We're just kids, except Champ—and he's hardly bright enough to do that gardening work of his. So us being kids, who would the cops believe if this Halstead creep went to 'em and claimed we'd attacked his wife or some stupid thing?"

"But, Ricky—you haven't *done* anything!" she cried.

"So what? I mean, Deb, now he knows his wife picked me up in a motel and went to *bed* with me. What do you think he'll try and do to me if he ever finds out who I am? How do you even know his wife was raped and all that stuff he told you? Was it ever in the papers?"

"No." Then Debbie's face crumpled, and she started to cry as the enormity of what she had done struck her. "Oh, Ricky, honey, I'm so sorry! I didn't mean to . . . I . . . I didn't think . . ."

So that was all right. He'd shut her up for the time being, so she wouldn't go to Halstead again until Rick was ready for her to go. And that would take some planning, because Halstead was a tricky cat.

As quickly as he could, Rick disentangled himself from Debbie's tearful remorse, and headed back across the bridge toward Los Feliz. God, everything was a real mess: it was all crumbling in on top of him. *Him*, not anyone else. *He* had blinded that goddamn queer, had gone after Paula Halstead, had gotten her so hot to put out for them; *his* was the great danger, and there was chicken Julio yelling about *his* danger!

From Debbie, yet. The real danger was Halstead. They'd cooled everything else, and meanwhile there was Halstead, spending the whole damned summer fitting everything together like a damned puzzle or something, until he'd gotten to Debbie. And if Halstead could get to Debbie, the cops could. Halstead. Asking for his name, wanting to see him.

See him, huh? Rick paid the toll on the San Mateo side of the bridge, drove on, hunched over the wheel in concentration. Well, if that smooth snoopy bastard wanted to see him, maybe Rick would let him. On Rick's terms. At a place *he* chose.

The cabin. It was perfect. Isolated. No interruptions.

Rick turned over in his mind what he knew was necessary, curiously, like a chimpanzee turning over a mirror found in its cage. Funny, the idea didn't scare him as it would have a few months ago. Halstead was the one who was pushing. *They* hadn't killed his goddamn wife, had they? All they'd done was give it to her, just the way she'd wanted. So why didn't he just let it drop? Oh no. Not him. Not Halstead. So they had to do it to him.

He got on Bayshore south, toward Los Feliz. There still was a lot of traffic, even though it was midnight.

And that left Debbie.

No problem, actually, until Halstead . . . disappeared. But then . . . Hell, they would have to use Debbie to get Halstead down to the cabin, alone, the way they wanted him. And, he thought with a touch of odd pride in her, once Debbie realized what had happened to Paula, and then to Halstead, she'd go to the cops. Or she would unless . . .

Unless he used Julio's idea.

Julio was right, there. It would work. It had worked before. But . . . Debbie? Well, hell, still, if he had to choose between Debbie getting hurt some, and him going to prison for a long time, with his folks and everybody he knew finding out about Rockwell and all . . .

It wasn't like she was some untouchable virgin or something. Now that he thought of it, how could he be sure she had been a virgin before last weekend, down at the cabin? She'd sure let him, easy enough, after a little bit of playing the game there until he'd given her a couple of drinks. Hell, chicks always played the game, the young ones like her. And look how far she'd let him go last year, out by Sears Lake.

He swung into the street his house was on, from the freeway access road, and then braked in the closed and darkened gas station on the corner. Getting out of the Triumph, he felt saddened. It was like in the war movies that he dug so: those in command were the ones who had to make sacrifices. And, after all, *he* was the leader. The other guys depended on him to get them out of this.

He dialed Julio's number, late as it was.

CHAPTER 24

Curt's watch read 7:39 when he pushed the buzzer on Barbara Anderson's door. It hadn't started out to be a date; he merely had called to report his progress in searching for the predators. She had, after all, urged him to keep in touch. But she had been so interested in getting the details in person that they had ended up with a mutual decision to go out for a drink together.

The door opened and Barbara smiled up almost shyly at him. Seeing her, the clean-lined beauty of her face, the now strangely tranquil jade eyes, Curt felt a stab of almost adolescent excitement. Which was silly and, he felt, somehow disloyal to Paula's memory; but the feeling persisted.

"You look lovely, Barbara."

She made a small mock bow, standing aside to let him by. She wore a navy-blue dress with a short flaring skirt to emphasize the excellence of her legs. "Thanks for them few kind words, sir. I only spent four hours getting ready. How about a drink before we go? I have Scotch, or Scotch."

"Scotch is fine." Curt grinned. They were both a little keyed-up and tense, and a drink would help with that.

They stood on the narrow balcony, looking out over the swimming pool, softly lit and empty and very blue and lonely-looking.

Curt tinkled the ice cubes in his glass. "What happens to Jimmy while we're out?"

"He's used to it; I sometimes have to work an extra shift at the hospital. We take the TV into his room, and he watches until eight-thirty—that's what he's doing now. Then, lights out. He has the manager's phone number, the police number, and the fire department number. Plus, once we get wherever we're going I'll call and give him the number there." She wrinkled her nose at him. "Enough?"

Curt held up his hands defensively. "Sorry I asked."

Yes, vaguely sparring, like teenagers on a first date. They drove slowly south on El Camino, finally choosing an anonymous cocktail lounge with big vinyl booths that successfully isolated them from the other patrons. A bar waitress in black mesh stockings took their orders, rather wearily, as if her feet hurt.

Barbara made her phone call, then returned, lit a cigarette, and looked at Curt through the wisping smoke. "Filthy habit, wish I could break it. And now I want to hear all the details about what you've found out."

"Well, I still haven't found my predators," Curt said a bit ruefully, "but I think I'm darned close. You remember Jimmy told me that the girl's folks were named Marsden and lived in a big white house with a stone front on Glenn Way. That turned out to be a four-block street in the Hillcrest Development, and there were only two houses that fit."

In one house he had found a childless couple named Moyes who had been living there for eight years. That left the other, in which lived a family named Tucker, and they had been there just about a year. They didn't know who had lived in the house before they got it.

"But, then, it seems you were no better off than before," said Barbara. "If you wanted the Marsdens . . ."

Looking across the table at her, Curt felt that vaguely disquieting touch of excitement again. She was more animated than she had been before, her eyes alight, her face rapt. He had a rather absurd urge to reach across the table and take her hand, but he didn't. It was too much like someone in a darkened unfamiliar room, holding out a tentative hand because he was afraid of running into something sharp or unpleasant.

"It's amazing how much neighbors know about other people," Curt said. "I just went to those on either side of the Tucker house."

The Marsdens were well remembered; they had lived in the subdivision for years, until moving to San Leandro the previous year. The Marsdens had a nineteen-year-old daughter named Deborah. Curt had called San Leandro Information, gotten their new address, and had driven across the Bay to talk with the girl's parents.

"Did you tell them why you wanted to talk with her?" Barbara's lips were half parted; Curt could see a pulse beating in the hollow of her throat above the scoop neck of her dress as she leaned forward.

"No. Her folks are very fine people, and I didn't want to . . . well, until I was sure I had the right girl. And what they told me made it seem even less likely that she would be a lookout for a—a gang of rapists. Debbie, they said, was an honors student but was currently attending summer classes at a certain Los Feliz University—which also boasts on the faculty a certain professor named Curtis Halstead—"

"Oh, Curt!" Barbara exclaimed. "Right in your own back yard! If you only had known. All those weeks of looking . . ."

"Until I talked with Jimmy, remember, I had no idea that a girl might be involved."

"*Is* she involved?"

Curt grimaced, and signaled the waitress for refills. "That's where it starts to get sticky," he said.

He told of checking the school records, finding which class the girl was in, what dorm she lived in, what classes she was attending, and of leaving his number for her to call. The setting up of the meeting for the following Monday, because the girl was busy on the weekend.

Barbara sampled her drink. "If you ever want to quit teaching, Curt, you could get a job as a private investigator."

"Maybe I ought to. This past summer I've learned more about

people, and human nature, than I learned in twenty years of university life. But"—he shook his head—"I still don't have the predators."

"Debbie didn't show up on Monday?"

"Oh, she showed up, all right." He described the encounter with the girl, ending up with his impulsive handing to her of Paula's suicide note as Debbie went out the door. "I was hoping it would break her down. You see, I believe her, Barbara. She knew nothing of what went on that night, and just thought she was there to help the one—I call him X—who's supposed to have had an affair with Paula."

"Do you think he did?" Seeing Curt's blank look, Barbara added, "Have an affair with Paula, I mean."

Curt felt his face coloring up.

Barbara laid a hand on his arm. "I'm sorry, Curt," she said simply. "That was really a sort of rotten question to ask."

"It doesn't bother me, Barbara—really." As he said it, Curt was surprised to realize that it didn't. Paula was gone: how could it affect, one way or the other, what their relationship had been? He went on, rather pleased with the discovery, "The hell of it is that Paula *could* have, I suppose. We each lived our own lives, after all. I don't believe it for a minute, but . . . this Debbie was very persuasive in her belief in her boyfriend's innocence of any violence."

"But she won't give you his name. You know, Curt, kids—even kids who are nearly adults—can delude themselves so completely when they think they're in love. If . . . if it's so important to you to . . . go on with this, give Debbie my phone number. Tell her to call me, I'll tell her just what was threatened on that phone call to me."

The same thought had occurred to Curt: using Jimmy and Barbara as a lever to pry information from Debbie. But now he realized that he didn't want to do that. Barbara seemed somehow to identify his problem as her own, but he found it distasteful to think of putting her or her son into possible further jeopardy from the predators.

"I couldn't let you do that, Barbara," he said flatly.

"But, Curt, my number is unlisted; even if they got it from her, they couldn't get my address. And I want to help you if—"

"I said no, Barbara." He looked at his watch. "It's almost ten o'-clock. We'd better be going."

She looked at the stubborn set of his face. "All right, Curt."

He drove north toward the Arroyo Towers. When he parked the VW in an empty slot just two stalls from the apartment building's front door, Barbara turned toward him on the seat. "What will you do now, Curt?"

"I suppose I'll have to start asking questions again—of her folks, her teachers, her house mother, her friends. Find out some way who her boyfriend is—or boyfriends are. Then, check them out."

"No police, anywhere along the line?"

Curt's lip curled. "So they can tell me to be a good boy and go home and do nothing? No police."

"What if classes start before you find your . . . predators, Curt?"

"Then they start without me. I'm committed to this, Barbara."

Her eyes were troubled in the dimness of the car. "Have you ever thought what's going to happen if you find them, Curt? You're a college professor, not a . . . a professional fighter or anything. They're a vicious gang, probably sick or disturbed. They—"

"I wasn't always a teacher," Curt began tightly, then was disgusted by the cheap dramatic overtones of his own remark. He turned to face her, talking intently. "All right, sure, Barbara, the world is full of people today who maim and destroy, who get their kicks doing it. Old traditions are breaking down, and the new ones haven't filled the gaps. In some ways our society seems to be falling to pieces—there seem to be predators all over, striking indiscriminately. I've heard all the arguments, that we have police to cope with them, that it is an inescapable product of swiftly changing mores. But *these* predators struck at *me. My* home, *my* wife. Maybe I'm weaker than other people, maybe I feel frightened or . . . or threatened because this could happen to me without some punishment coming to those who did it. I don't know. But I do know that

I have to try and find this particular gang. Find them, and break them, so they don't ever do it to anyone else."

In the darkness, Barbara gave a little shiver. "So . . . now I know." She tried for lightness, but wasn't successful. "A dedicated man, no less. But . . . take care of yourself, Curt. Don't . . . let yourself do things with consequences you can't foresee. Don't change—you."

She came forward into his arms, pressed her mouth against his for a long moment. Her lips were almost feverish. Then she was out of the car, looking in at him through the window.

"If it's any help, Curt, I . . . feel threatened, too . . ."

CHAPTER 25

Rick swung into the gas station he had selected for the call. It had a broad blacktopped lot beside it, with four phone booths along one edge. When he stopped the Triumph, Debbie turned to face him on the seat, not even aware of her short beige skirt riding halfway up her thighs as she did.

"Ricky, I *still* don't see why we have to be so sneaky about it."

"I told you, Deb. If he thinks the cabin is a place that a bunch of chicks have rented for a week, he won't check up who owns it."

"But if I just tell him you'll be there to talk to him, he—"

"—he'd probably have half the sheriff's deputies in the county down there with him. And then what good would *my* word be, against a college prof's? I gotta have it so that if he *won't* believe me, I've got time to get away without him stopping me or finding out who I am."

He got out, went around to open her door, the tension whining inside him like a wire drawn too tight. Debbie went down to the end booth and went in and closed the door. Rick stood directly outside but with his back to the booth, so he wasn't watching her. He went over it all in his mind: if the professor was home, everything went into motion, set for the next night. Well, the next day, really.

Inside the booth, Debbie thought, I'm glad he's not watching. She knew it would make her even more nervous if he were watching. She made herself drop her dime resolutely, but hoped down inside that the professor wouldn't be home. It was all happening so fast. The trouble was that by being stupid she had put Ricky into terrible danger; somehow she had to make up to him for that, make sure of his safety.

On the fourth ring, the professor picked up the phone.

"Professor Halstead? This is—"

Curt's voice was pleasant and relaxed. "I'm glad you called, Debbie. Have you something to tell me?"

"I . . . yes, sir. Well, that is, I want you to meet me somewhere. D'you have a pencil and paper there?" Curt said he did. "All right, then, do you know where San Conrado is?"

"A little town south of Half Moon Bay, isn't it?"

"Yes, sir." She had begun breathing easier; it wasn't so bad after all. And her charade really was *helping* Professor Halstead in his search, because it would get him off the false trail of Ricky and the others. "Just about ten miles south of San Conrado, on the Coast Highway, is a small gravel drive leading off to the right—down a ravine. It's got a big heavy wooden gate across it, and a big padlock on the gate. Down the gravel road, about a quarter of a mile, is—"

"Will the gate be locked or open?"

She shut her eyes, trying to visualize the gate. "Locked. I guess you can just park in front of it and walk down. Can you meet me there at eight o'clock tomorrow night?"

"Yes, surely. But why tomorrow? Why there? And why at night?"

Rick had rehearsed her on this. "Because I don't want my folks to know that I'm still going out with . . . with my friend. They don't like him. A bunch of us girls have rented the cabin for a week before school starts—we're going down tomorrow, and tomorrow night the rest of them are going to a movie in Santa Cruz. I'll say I've got a headache, so I can be there alone at eight o'clock."

"I see," said Curt. "Will your friend be there with you?"

"I don't know. I'm going to *try* and get him there . . ." She almost giggled on that one; Ricky was so smart to have foreseen the professor's asking about him! "He'd *like* to come, but he's scared you won't believe him, no matter what he says, and that you'll try to get his name and get the police after him because of . . . of what your wife did with him. He says—*Oh!*" she exclaimed suddenly, the way Rick had told her to. "My mom just came in the front door. Tomorrow night, eight. 'Bye."

She hung up quickly, pushed open the door of the stuffy booth. Her green sleeveless blouse was sticking to her back, not entirely from the heat in the airless booth. She felt pride in having done it right, and a great sense of relief that it was over. She hated lying.

"It worked, honey! He'll be there tomorrow night at eight."

"That's groovy, Deb." So, the plan was on. That meant that from now on, Debbie had to be kept away from phones, away from her family, away from everyone until after tomorrow night. Rick had come up with the greatest idea for that, one that took care of everything at once. "So we've gotta wait until tomorrow night, so what are you doing tonight?"

She smiled raptly up into his face. "Going out with you, I hope?"

"Let's make it the whole day, Deb. And night. Go back down to the cabin, right now—just the two of us, just like last weekend. We've got our swim suits in the car, and—"

"Oh, Ricky, do you think we *dare?*" But her eyes already were alight with the idea. "I could . . . I could call the folks and tell them that I'm getting a bus down to Cynthia's place and . . ."

". . . and that you'll be back tomorrow afternoon, or—wait a minute—tell them it's for the weekend." Debbie wouldn't be at the cabin tomorrow night, Rick knew, but she couldn't know that now. He'd come up with an excuse to bring her back up to Los Feliz in the morning; that would be easy. He had to remember to check up that his old man's pistol and shells were still in back of the bottom bureau drawer. "We'll have a ball today, honey . . ."

Getting into the car, Rick felt a twinge of guilt about the velvet night ahead, when tomorrow . . . But there just wasn't any other way. He looked over at her, excited and happy beside him. Sacrifice: the leader always had to sacrifice. It was her or them, once Halstead . . .

Of course, Halstead, tomorrow night, would be easy. Tricky he might be, but he was just a college prof and real old besides. Deb had said he was over forty. It would be easy to take care of an old cat like that.

CHAPTER 26

After he had hung up, Curt stood with his hand on the receiver for a good thirty seconds. It didn't make sense. A cabin, down by the ocean, thirty miles away—so she wanted to shield her boyfriend in case Curt tried to put the police on him, still . . .

On his large-scale county map, Curt checked the area south of San Conrado. Just at the place she had indicated was a small cove, with a narrow entrance between headlands that were probably spines of rock reaching down from the precipitous, irregular bluffs.

It looked isolated. It looked, in fact, like a trap.

So? So Curt had better go down there right now, today, to make a recon of the area, because he was operating on a set of assumptions.

One. Debbie was not trying to trap him, she was sincere.

Two. She was being manipulated, however, by the unknown X, if he indeed was one of the predators who had attacked Rockwell and Paula.

Three. If X and his cronies were the guilty ones, they now would be seeing Curt as a mortal peril to their liberty.

Four. A cabin clinging to the bottom of a remote ravine by the Pacific was much more reasonable for an assault than a consultation.

Five. The assault might well be fatal.

But then, he thought, what about Debbie? What did they plan to do about her once Curt disappeared? That was the hell of it, of course. He was dealing with teenagers: explosively immature human beings in grown-up bodies who were probably unstable teenagers to begin with. Who the devil ever knew what kids were going to do? Half the time they seemed not to know themselves from one minute to the next. Dealing with this gang, if they were the predators, would be like handling plastic explosives. Which didn't alter the fact that he had to reconnoiter.

Curt looked at his watch. So what was he waiting for? This was the confrontation he had striven for weeks and months to bring about, wasn't it? Then into his memory came Barbara's strained, frightened face the night before. *You're a college professor, not a professional fighter or anything. They're a vicious gang, probably sick or disturbed . . .*

Curt snorted at himself, and went out to the car.

He drove via La Honda Road to California 84, which he then took through the thick stands of redwood and conifers to San Conrado. En route, he realized that in all of his planning he had forgotten to allow for his own emotions. He was scared. Whoever they were, the predators had acted viciously, without hesitation or compunction, each time they had felt themselves threatened. If Debbie's boyfriend was one of them, probably their leader, then tomorrow evening . . .

Who would be broken in body and spirit? Who would do the maiming? Even big, rugged Monty Worden professed fear at the idea of being dragged down by a pack of frenzied punks.

From San Conrado he went south along the twisting blacktop of the Coast Highway. In places it ran along the very edge of the bluffs; elsewhere it clung to the face of the cliffs themselves. After nine miles by the speedometer, Curt began watching for the gravel driveway. Another problem: Debbie's absolute certainty that he was wrong about her boyfriend. But as Barbara had said, the young in love could delude themselves to a terrifying degree; and to accept Debbie's beliefs meant to accept a dizzying series of coincidences, concluded by a fortuitous blowout on that Friday night of Paula's suicide.

Curt braked suddenly, seeing the padlocked wooden gate on the right-hand side, but then went on by. Two hundred yards beyond, the road swung right to the edge of the fall and a dusty view-area, well out of sight of the gate. Curt got out, went back afoot along the inside edge of the highway, where it was flanked by an immediate rise of bluff. On the ocean, the gate side of the road, was a steep fall covered with evergreens that effectively screened any glimpse of the ravine, cabin, or cove below. In the fog, this stretch of highway would be dangerous.

The gate bore a sign PRIVATE ROAD—NO TRESPASSING. Curt went over quickly, ducked into the heavy cover beyond it. Deep ditches beside the steeply slanting drive would carry off water during the rains; on either side rose the wooded, brush-tangled sides of the ravine. A good place for a sniper with a rifle.

Curt descended in short rushes, even though he doubted if anyone would be at the cabin today. At the bottom, under cover of a large spruce tree, he waited for his heart to quit pounding. It didn't. He grinned to himself; he had the wind up for sure. Well, he always had gone into combat scared green; it gave an edge to the reactions. He hoped.

He studied the cup that held the apparently deserted cabin. On Curt's left, the Douglas fir and tideland spruce of the ravine thinned into a strip of heavy tangled shrubs and small trees, mainly wax myrtles, judging by their smooth gray bark and dark green glossy leaves. They fringed the base of the cliff nearly to the edge of the dunes, where they phased into coarse reeds. To his right, the conifer forest extended around beside the cabin.

Under cover of the myrtles, Curt worked his way left along the cliff base to the plant-topped dunes that shielded the narrow V of beach. Deserted. Beyond the mouth of the cove, Curt could see the foaming swells of the Pacific and the jumbled smoothness that marked the presence of a large kelp bed.

As a trap, the cup was a damned good one. The cliffs probably could be scaled—it even looked like a ledge about forty feet up that might allow one to get back to the ravine—and a good swimmer might be able to enter the cove from the next beach south, depending on the width of the headland. But the normal, unsuspecting man's approach would be down the ravine, where a man in good cover with a rifle . . .

Curt dropped down on the beach, under cover of the dunes' three-foot lip, worked his way up to the cabin. Yes, deserted. He prowled about for another ten minutes, looking in uncurtained windows, checking the position of the electric fuse box. Then he went back up the drive, over the gate, and walked to his car. Leaning against the fender of the VW, he checked the width of the spine of rock that formed the left-hand side of the cove he just had left, and the right-hand side of the beach below the view-area. A man could probably scramble down to the water here; equipped with wet suit, snorkle, fins and face mask, he then could swim around to the cove. Curt, after all, had done some amphib operational training in S.A.S., rubber rafts and all that lot.

But it would be down the gravel for him tomorrow night, he supposed. Risky, but . . .

Unless he had a second man to cover him.

Curt suddenly felt better. He probably could hire Archie Matthews to—but wait a minute. Matthews, with a license to protect and knowing Curt planned a direct assault on the gang if the predators were there, probably would refuse. But what about Floyd Preston? Preston, as an old clandestine operation teacher, would do it for a lark.

Driving back past the gate, he didn't see the fresh tire tracks of Rick's Triumph, overlaid on his own footprints in the dust beside the road. Rick and Debbie had missed him by a bare five minutes.

"I think it's a setup," said Preston.

Curt had just spent half an hour detailing the physical layout by the cabin. "I can't be sure, Floyd, that's the hell of it. If I go down there tomorrow night, I might find Debbie waiting there alone—"

"—or you might find a bullet in your spine when you get halfway down the road. A guy in the woods, with a good rifle—"

"Not if I'm covered by a second man," said Curt.

Preston ignored the suggestion. In tightly pegged gray slacks and form-fitting T-shirt clinging to his lithe, tremendously muscular torso, he looked like every boy's dream of Tarzan.

"Don't go, Curt," he said. "Or if you do, take that Sergeant Worden with you."

"Hell, Floyd," Curt burst out, "he's already told me where the law stands on this: since there's nothing they can do, I'd better not do anything on my own or I'll be in trouble. No, all we need is you and me. You can act as my cover, to see I'm not shot in the back, and—" He faltered, for Preston's Indian-featured face wore an oddly startled expression, as if realizing what he was about to say was a shock to himself.

"Well, you see, Curt, I couldn't go down there with you."

"But . . . I thought . . ." Curt felt the blood rising in his face. "I mean, I thought . . . you used to . . ."

"You see, Curt," said Preston equably, "it just isn't worth it to me. If this *is* the gang, they'll be playing for keeps. Someone's liable to be hurt, or even killed. You've got a hard-on against them, but I don't. I've got a business to run, and getting mixed up in something like this . . ." He slowly shook his head. "I've got a wet suit and mask and flippers you can use, if you decide to go in from the ocean side, but as far as my coming along . . ."

Swallowing all the angry phrases trembling on his tongue, Curt turned and walked from the office. He tried to hang on to the anger on the drive home, but by the time he was parking the VW beside the porch he had realized how naïve his expectations had been. Why the hell *should* Preston help him in a private vendetta? The trouble was that as the anger dissolved, it left only his knot of fear behind.

It was the old problem of the *Hand-to-Hand Manual* all over again. In the *Manual* you threw people around, stabbed them to death, and it all was clean and tidy as a sheet of print in a book. Reality was the gasping, clawing sentry, the stink of fear and sweat and loosened bladder. Finding and disabling and breaking the predators in theory had a clear and terrible clarity about it; but reality was a frightened man, forty-three years old, facing alone a moment of truth for which he was not prepared. Alone. That too had a clear and terrible clarity about it.

Curt went out into the kitchen and poured himself a glass of red wine. It was the first since the weekend of Paula's death. He returned with it to the living room, sipped at it, stared out the window at the slanting golden late afternoon sunlight on the golf course.

What was his alternative? Give up, as Preston had suggested. Was there any *real* reason he had to go the next day? No. Nobody except himself wanted or expected him to go on with the search. He could call Debbie Marsden next week, say—oh, say he had found evidence pointing elsewhere than her boyfriend. That would end it, that easily. No one further would be involved, no one else hurt; if a trap was planned at the cabin tomorrow, it would just be forgotten by all concerned.

And tonight? Call Barbara, let her tell him he was making the right decision. Well, no, he wouldn't do that; but Curt knew he would not be going the next evening. Feeling better, he carried the nearly untouched wine to the kitchen and poured it down the sink.

CHAPTER 27

Julio pulled shut the double doors of the garage and dropped the old-fashioned wooden bar into place. To eyes still dazzled by the outside brilliance, the artificial light seemed flat and weak.

Heavy looked up from the mechanical depths of the stripped-down Ford that was hoodless in the center of the garage over a great black puddle of oil. As he wiped his hands on a greasy rag, his skull-and-crossbones ring glinted dully. Champ straightened up from his stool in front of the workbench, his pectoral muscles jumping like a frog activated by electric shock.

"They are coming," said Julio.

Then they listened. The crunch of gravel as Rick's Triumph turned into the drive, growl of motor as it drew up outside the double doors, a single tiny squeak of brake drum as it stopped. A door slammed with a heavy mechanical sound, then another. Debbie's voice spoke indistinguishable words as it approached the side door. The knob rattled.

Light burst upon them. Debbie exclaimed, "Oh, it's dark in here!"

She wore her clothes of the previous day: beige miniskirt, green sleeveless blouse, sandals on bare feet. Rick still was dressed in his chinos, short-sleeved sport shirt, and desert boots. His voice was alive with excitement or nerves. "Gentlemen: I give you Miss Deborah Marsden!"

"Silly," chided Debbie, giggling, "I know them all."

Rick insisted. "On my right, by the tool bench, Mr. Ernest "Champ" Mather, who features the biggest arms and smallest brain in Northern California. Champ, make a muscle for the lady."

Julio had explained it all to him, but Champ still couldn't get over the feeling that Debbie was Rick's girl. Still . . . He grinned hungrily at her, his flawed, deep-set eyes moving over her; then his biceps jumped out under his short sleeves like grapefruits.

"That is not a can of Crisco by the Ford, but Delmer "Heavy" Gander. His father owns this fine establishment, but he's fishing this weekend on the Delta. Heavy, take a bow."

Instead Heavy, smelling strongly of sweat, emitted a terrific belch. Julio went off into a paroxysm of high, almost hysterical laughter. Rick pointed at him like a ref calling a foul on a basketball court.

"Finally is Julio Escobar, who claims to be the only boy in Los Feliz High who didn't get to make out with you under the bleachers while you were a cheerleader. He says—"

"Why, Rick, that's not *true!* I—" Debbie stopped, her face scarlet. It was a put-on, she realized, Ricky's idea of a joke. But then she saw that a fine sheen of sweat covered his face, and she was uneasy, almost frightened, so she said, "Hadn't you better get the tool you needed from here and we'd better . . . I mean, if you and I are going back down to the cabin this . . . afternoon . . ."

Her voice trailed into puzzled silence, and Rick put an oddly gentle hand on her arm, detaining her as she turned toward the door. His voice sounded funny, as if he were sick or something.

"You'd better wait a minute, Deb," he said.

"But . . . why?" She looked from face to face, uncomprehendingly.

"Because of your friend, Professor Halstead!" exclaimed Julio, darting forward. "Because you have betrayed us into very great danger!"

"I . . . betrayed into great . . . but . . ." She was truly frightened: maybe they were all high on speed or hair spray or something, like some of the girls in the dorm bragged about sometimes. Then it struck her, full force, and she cried at Julio, "*You!* You mean that you three, you and Heavy and Champ, you . . . you *raped* her? Like the professor—"

"We *had* to do it, Debbie." But the voice that spoke was Rick's, not Julio's; and for an instant the two of them were frozen, face to face, outside time together, isolated from the others. Seeing the expression in Debbie's eyes, Rick cried, "She *saw* me, when I was stomping that queer. And that other night, she . . . she *begged* for it . . ."

Debbie ran for the door, catching them enough by surprise so that she had thrust an arm and shoulder out, her mouth opened to scream, before hands dragged her back and smothered her cries.

The hands that had snatched her from safety were Rick's.

"See?" hissed Julio. "You see what she would do? Now you know why it is necessary to teach her to keep her mouth shut."

Debbie stared into Rick's face; his eyes were bloodshot but a stony finality dwelt there also. The whole fabric of her existence dissolved like cloth in acid. Then Rick, with a convulsive, almost blind movement, thrust her at Champ. His hands circled her arms like articulated steel straps.

"Ricky . . ." she pleaded. "Oh, God, please, Ricky, don't—"

"You'd better . . . gag her first." His face was stark white; he had aged a dozen years in as many seconds. "And make sure you tie her up when you're . . . through. I'll . . . meet you down at the cabin."

Heavy's hand closed hotly over Debbie's mouth, mashing her lips against her teeth. Her eyes rolled wildly, like a fire-trapped mare's, as Julio dragged an old mattress out from behind the workbench. He dropped it by the Ford, and began fumbling at his pants.

"I got seconds," Champ said hoarsely from somewhere above her.

She heard the door shut quietly behind Rick.

Hands jerked her roughly forward, flipped her over on the grease-stained mattress so a wad of oily rag could be thrust into her mouth. Other, eager hands plucked at the waistband of her trim beige skirt, then jerked at her panties. Then, for a long time, there was only the continuing nightmare of sweat and thrusting pain and the lesser abrasions of the mattress cover against her back. Finally there was nothing.

Curt awoke feeling hollow, drained, without purpose. He tried to tell himself that this evening he would be going down to the cabin to meet Debbie and possibly her boyfriend, or else to face the predators; but he knew it was a fraud. He knew he wouldn't be going. Perhaps, he told himself, he lacked the necessary edge of hatred or of anger. Or perhaps it was just that the years had taken too much out of him. But if even Preston was afraid to go . . .

Classes would start, Curt would return to teaching, and would, in time, recapture his enthusiasm for it. Perhaps he would start once again on his book. Perhaps . . .

The phone rang. It was 1:47 P.M.

"Curt Halstead here."

"Don't go! Don't . . . they'll be waiting for you, all of them!"

Curt recognized the weak and anguished voice immediately; he leaned forward tensely. "Debbie, what have they done to you? Where . . ."

"They wouldn't . . . stop . . ." The hysteria in her voice brought sweat to his face. It ran down his chin and stung where he had shaved his neck too close. "There was a mattress . . . they took turns . . ."

He tried to make his voice even, conversational. "Debbie, everything is going to be all right, you're doing fine, just tell me where—"

"Ricky just . . . left me alone with them. He just . . ." She suddenly whimpered, "Please, please . . . help me . . ."

Curt dashed the sweat from his eyes, reached for the phone book to balance it on his knee. "Debbie, *where are you?*"

"I . . . Heavy's place. They . . . they wouldn't stop."

"You're doing fine, Debbie. Heavy what? What's his last name?"

"Heavy." Her voice seemed farther away, abstracted. She gave a long sigh, then said very distinctly, "Heavy Gander. Please help me."

"Gander." Curt leafed through the G's, ran his finger down a column. Only one. Gander, Charles. "Debbie, is the address three-eight-seven Cuesta Avenue?"

There was no response.

"Debbie, honey, is it on Cuesta Avenue?"

No answer.

He made a decision. He set the receiver down beside the phone, so the connection still was open, tossed aside the phone book, and ran for the car. Check the map. Cuesta. North. He raced the VW up to Entrada, over to El Camino, north again. Only one Gander in the book, had to be the right one. Had to . . . But if it wasn't, the phone connection still was open—unless Debbie would come out of it and hang up. God. They just had repeated—he even could understand their thinking. The last time, the woman had killed herself. It sure as hell would work to make Debbie keep her mouth shut.

And have a little fun in the bargain. A little innocent fun.

God. Curt had triggered this; now he couldn't let things drop. Was it just last night he had been so naïve as to think he could just walk away from it, and no one hurt? And no Debbie . . .

He was nearly to the Fifth Avenue turnoff that would take him to Cuesta before he even thought of stopping to call an ambulance, or the police. Hadn't he done enough already? It was time for the professionals now, he had the predators where he wanted them: a chargeable offense, with an assault victim who could and probably would identify.

Curt didn't even slow down. What had Worden said? *The D.A.'d be damned lucky to get 'em on probation and remanded to the custody of their parents for a year*. Harold Rockwell. *Blind*. Paula. *Dead*. Barbara. *Terrorized*. Debbie. *Raped*. Whoever they were, whatever they were, Curt wanted vengeance. Personal vengeance. On their bodies.

It was an indifferently kept-up bungalow on a weed-choked half-acre. Curt left the VW in the driveway with the door hanging open, ran across the untended yard to the front door. Locked.

He ran down beside the house, poked an arm through the kitchen screen door, flipped up the hook. Inside he saw a broom; he picked it up and with a wrench of powerful forearms broke the handle in half. A compelling weapon, a jagged-tipped broom handle, when jabbed at eyes or throat. He crossed a kitchen where green-bellied flies buzzed around a sinkful of unwashed dishes. Wife either dead or divorced, man and his son batching it. Charles Gander and his son Heavy. The father off for the weekend, maybe . . .

But the house was empty. Plenty of disorder, except that it was the continuing disorder of careless living, not of violence.

He went back outside. The wrong Gander? But . . .

Garage. Double doors closed. He was running again, carrying his broomstick. The doors were barred, so he went around to the side. Would they have a phone extension in the garage? Well . . . He laid an ear to the side door and called her name.

No answer. And the windows were painted black inside, so he could not see in. He rammed the broomstick through a pane. Still too dark to see anything; so he stepped back and smashed out the whole window. He could see a stripped-down Ford in the middle of the garage, and beside it, flopped carelessly beside the puddle of oil under the car, a greasy old mattress. *There was a mattress . . . they took turns . . .*

Debbie was crouched in the angle of the farthest corner of the garage, half hidden by a workbench. She still held the receiver of Heavy's bootlegged phone in her hand, but her eyes were merely dark, empty pools in the shadowy garage.

"Debbie?" She didn't even turn her head to Curt's call.

He unlocked the window, pushed up the glassless frame, wriggled through. Debbie's naked breasts were rising and falling shallowly and rapidly, her only sign of life; her ankles were tied. At some time, perhaps before she had called him, she had pulled her stained and bloodied miniskirt up into her lap in a terribly forlorn attempt at modesty. She seemed beyond any of that now. There were a few smears of blood on the mattress, not very many, and dark stains on the cement floor where she had dragged herself to the telephone on the edge of the workbench. There were also heavy dark stains on her forearms and wrists.

Curt uttered a short exclamation, starting forward with the terrible fear constricting his chest that she was bleeding to death, as Paula had. Then he checked himself.

The dark stains were oil. Oil to make her wrists slippery, let her slip off the ropes tying her arms, pull free from her mouth the filthy rag that probably had been used to gag her. A lot of guts, a lot of determination for a girl on the edge of hysteria. How long had it taken her to figure a way to get loose? How long to get to the phone and dial Curt's number?

Curt was damned glad he hadn't stopped to call the police. If she had wanted the cops, she would have called them, not Curt.

"Debbie," he said gently, "I'm going to take the phone. I'll just touch that, I won't touch you. Okay?"

Her eyes, those dark shadowed wells without any sign of recognition or comprehension, didn't react; but when Curt gently took hold of the receiver, her fingers released it immediately. Her hand dropped laxly to the twist of ruined cloth that covered her womanhood.

Moving slowly, like a man trying not to startle a wild animal, Curt carried the phone to the far end of the workbench. He got the number from the operator, and dialed, watching Debbie the whole time.

"County General Hospital."

"Barbara Anderson, please. She's an R.N. on duty until three o'-clock, I don't know the floor or section. It is an extreme emergency involving Mrs. Anderson personally."

The switchboard girl was either very bright or very efficient; in less than thirty seconds he heard Barbara's voice, tight and high with tension, demanding to know what had happened to Jimmy.

"Nothing. This is Curt. I can only tell you this once, Barbara, so take down what you need. They've raped another girl, the one I told you about. Debbie Marsden. In the garage behind three-eight-seven Cuesta Avenue, C-u-e-s-t-a. She's alive and conscious, but she's catatonic, very pale, her respiration light and fast. I didn't want to touch her to check the pulse. There's been some bleeding, I'd guess internally, but I'd guess not very much unless they used something on her besides themselves. She'll need—"

"The ambulance will be on its way directly." Her voice was crisp.

"Right." Curt was still looking at Debbie, his mouth a tight thin line. "Can you keep the police away from her until tomorrow?"

There was a pause. "If she's in the state you describe, the doctor probably will put her under anyway. But . . ."

"I need tonight. I know where they are; they're going to be waiting for me. I don't want to disappoint them."

"Oh." She was silent for what seemed a long time. "You feel you—"

"That's right."

Curt could picture her, seemed to look into those remarkably clear green eyes.

She said, "I'll manage. Come back to me, Curt."

"Right," he said again. Then he hung up.

He opened the double doors, waited until he heard the first far whisper of siren, and walked down to his VW. As the ambulance wheeled into Cuesta, he pulled sedately away from the curb. He drove north to Preston's house in Redwood City, stuck an elbow through the glass of the kitchen door, and spent eight minutes finding Preston's skindiving gear.

Back home, he waterproofed a flashlight with electrician's tape, rummaged through his old foot locker in the study until he found the black commando knife he had carried all through the war, and spent fifteen minutes on it with an oil stone. It had a needle point, double-edged blade. He needed it to butcher them, one by one, as befit the unspeakable pigs they were. Tonight they would die, or he would.

Finally he studied moon, tide, and sunset tables for that night, Friday, August 29th. Planning strategy, all fear burned away.

It was eighteen weeks to the day since Paula's suicide.

CHAPTER 28

Champ Mather stood up and stretched his massive body in the deep shadows under the trees just beside the cabin, delighting in the tight powerful play of muscle. By the luminous hands of his watch, 8:45. That guy, that Halstead, he was almost an hour late. Pretty soon it'd be too dark to see him if he did come down the drive. That was too bad, because old Rick had fixed it up real smart. Champ here; Julio up beside the gate; and Heavy inside to answer Halstead's knock.

But he sure was late, that guy.

A faint scuff of shoe on gravel dropped Champ back into his crouch. Through the gloom he could just make out, beyond the muted gleam of the Triumph, the lighter strip of gravel that marked the drive. That sure was smart of Rick, too, leaving the Triumph right out in plain sight while the wagon was hidden behind the cabin.

That Halstead would think Debbie and Rick were alone in there, would walk right up to the cabin. Once he was inside, they'd do him.

Champ licked his lips in delighted memory. Debbie'd been better than that old woman last spring, because she'd had that look in her eyes. Like a rabbit's eyes when the back legs are busted with a bad shot, so you can take hold of its head and twist, slow-like, and feel the fibers letting go one at a time while it kicked and thrashed.

That Debbie, she wouldn't walk with her legs together for a week, he bet. Champ snorted aloud with delight. He'd gone four times, himself. Julio only went the once on her. Heavy, he went twice, like to flattened her just getting on top of her.

"Some lookout *you* are," said Julio, from right on top of him.

Wow! Remembering, he'd forgot about watching. He said, "Hey, Julio, how come that professor ain't showed yet?"

"I don't think he's coming. What were you laughing at, Champ?"

"I was remembering how we done Debbie today."

"Oh." Julio's voice was subdued. "Let's go inside. It's so dark he'd have to use a flashlight now if he came."

"Gonna be some moon pretty soon, Julio."

Julio led the way around the cabin to the kitchen door. Remembering how they done Debbie. He shuddered in the dark, felt an urge to cross himself. He would never forget that. That terrible mistake. He envied Champ, in a way. Champ would probably get as much fun out of using a knothole, except that a knothole couldn't feel pain.

He knocked at the door; after a moment Heavy's fat, frightened face looked out. Grease gleamed in the corners of his mouth; bread, mayonnaise, processed cheese, and canned corned beef were laid out for sandwiches. "Oh, it's you guys." His voice was relieved. "Guess he ain't coming, huh?"

"That ought to make you happy," said Julio wearily.

He went through the doorway into the living room, sickened by the remembered image of Heavy's white balloon buttocks flexing sluggishly between Debbie's knees. Rick was standing up against the wall beside the door, the automatic clubbed in his hand. Smash the butt down on Halstead's head, then carry him unconscious down to the cove and drown him. Better than shooting. Rick and Heavy, the good swimmers, would then carry the body out to the mouth of the cove and let it go. If he was ever found, he'd be accepted as someone who'd fallen off the bluffs, or something, like you read about all the time in the newspapers. So simple. Except Halstead hadn't come, and it all had been wasted.

"Why did you both come in?" demanded Rick in a thin sharp voice.

Maybe, Julio thought, giving him Paula Halstead's suicide note after finding it in Debbie's handbag had been a mistake. "Hell, Rick, he isn't coming. Not now. And if he does, we—"

"He's got to come!" cried Rick almost petulantly. "It's all set up for him to come."

Julio shrugged wearily. "So he's chicken. We can get him some other way, Rick."

"He's got to come tonight!" Rick raised his voice. "Champ! Go back outside where you were."

Champ stuck a head and massive shoulder around the doorjamb. "Okay, Rick. I'll just get me a sammidge, and then—"

"Right now! Heavy can bring you out a sandwich later."

"Okay." Champ didn't mind being ordered around by Rick; he knew that Rick was a lot smarter than he was.

Julio, in the doorway, watched Rick sit down on the couch and put the .32 Colt automatic on the cushion beside him. Rick brought out the suicide note Paula had written, unfolded it, and began reading it again. An intense worm of fear wriggled in Julio's stomach: Why hadn't he just left it alone with Debbie? Or why had the others listened to him? What if she went nuts or something, all tied up and gagged and everything, her eyes like in one of those horror movies where they wall somebody up alive in a chimney or something?

He cleared his throat. "Ah, Rick, ah, if this Halstead doesn't show up pretty soon, hadn't one of us better drive back up to Los Feliz and let Debbie loose? I mean, she won't tell anybody, and—"

"Debbie?" Rick seemed to have walled his knowledge of Debbie away, not in a chimney, but in a corner of his mind that he did not intend to enter again. "We made a mistake about Debbie."

"That's what I was saying, Rick, we ought to—"

One of Rick's legs had begun jiggling nervously. He said, "It was a mistake to leave her in the garage. We should have brought her down here and drowned her, along with Halstead."

"Drow . . ." Julio realized he was shaking his head dazedly. "Wow, man, what . . . what are we turning into? I mean, everything we do seems to shove us along further, instead of—"

The lights went out.

The sudden blackness behind him jerked Champ's head around, brought him erect in the screening bushes. What the hell? How come they had killed the lights all of a sudden? Should he wait here? But if Halstead somehow had gotten by him, was at the house, Champ didn't want to miss all the fun. Maybe . . .

A dark shape flitted past the corner of the cabin and ran swiftly and silently out across the open area toward the Triumph, quite visible under the wan light of the rising half-moon. Just short of the car he seemed to tumble over, sort of, and disappeared into the black shadow.

"Rick?" Champ called softly. No response. "Julio? Hey . . ."

Still no response. He flexed his powerful hands with indecision, like a cat yawning when it doesn't know what to do. It sure as hell hadn't been Heavy; Heavy couldn't run that fast. Not Rick, or Julio.

That left Halstead. He flexed his hands again, then walked out into the vague moonlight toward the car, not rushing, not trying to be quiet, moving stolidly forward like a tank across open terrain. If it was Halstead, Champ would do him. Do him good.

But when he got to the car, nobody was there. Couldn't nobody have got inside with him watching, anyway, but he checked to be sure. Then he bent to look underneath, and his mouth dropped open in surprise. All four tires were flat. What the hell . . . And *where* the hell . . .

A rustle of foliage over across the clearing jerked his head around toward the cliff. Into that foliage a dark shape was just disappearing. Champ ran a few steps in that direction, then stopped. How the hell had Halstead gotten over there? Champ hadda keep him from working his way back to the gravel drive, and getting away; but he hadda warn Rick, too. Standing in the moonlight, he bawled Rick's name.

"Hey, Rick! Hey! Outside here! I seen him! C'mon!"

Then he turned and ran heavily across the clearing toward the bluffs. He crashed into the foliage, then stopped to listen.

Inside the cabin, Heavy, who had been telling Rick and Julio that it was just a blown fuse, stopped in mid-word. He already had lit the old-fashioned kerosene lamp, so they could see one another. At Champ's shout, Rick's face went white, and he whirled on Heavy.

"You goddamn fool!" he cried in a high voice. "You and your goddamn fuse box! It was *him! Halstead!*"

"Let's go!" shouted Julio. "We have to help Champ!"

But when they got outside, into the open beside the Triumph, they could see no Champ. They could see quite well by the gibbous moon now hanging above the banked clouds; they could hear the incessant surf baying angrily at the fence of rocks that protected the cove; but they could neither see nor hear anything human.

Rick, flashlight in one hand and .32 in the other, made a short crablike rush to get under the cover of the car. "Get into the shadows!" he yelped. "Don't give him a clear target to shoot at."

Crouched beside him, Julio said, "How do you know he's armed?"

"If you were him, would *you* come down here without a gun?"

Heavy grunted. "There he is! I see him! On the cliff!"

A dark shape indeed was swarming nimbly up the rough stone face of the bluff, already a good twenty feet above the bushes. Rick ran into the open, raised the .32 to jerk off a shot. Nothing happened. He brought the gun down, looked at it blankly, then thumbed off the safety and raised the gun to try again. He jerked the trigger as fast as he could, so the light gun bucked and spat in his hand, eight times. Then Julio caught his arm.

"For Chris' sake, man, cool it! Champ is going up after him!"

The clip was empty anyway. Rick realized that the smaller shape had disappeared into an irregular strip of shadow, about forty feet up the cliff, which seemed to be cast by an overhang of some sort. Below he could see Champ's heavier, slower shape moving cautiously upward.

"C'mon! We can go up and help—"

"No!" Rick's voice rapped out to still Julio's. He hefted the .32 in his hand. "The clip's empty. We'll load up first, and then—"

"But we can't let Champ go up against him alone—"

"—and we can't afford to get picked off one by one, either."

"We oughta check the cars," Heavy cut in. Sweat stippled his moon face. "I mean, if he did something to the cars . . ."

"First we reload," Rick said with finality.

"But what about *Champ!*" Julio almost yelled. "He's up there . . ."

Fifty feet above, Champ's iron fingers had found a ledge. With a leg-up and a lithe twist, he was lying on a narrow path. End of the line for Halstead: But was he to the right or to the left?

Champ held his breath, listening. Nothing. Far below, in the moon-touched clearing, he could see the others arguing about something, because he could hear their raised voices if not the words. As he watched, they turned toward the auto. Pride welled up in Champ.

They were going to let him take Halstead alone! They trusted him not to foul it up! Rick sure knew how to make a guy feel good.

From his left came a very cautious scraping sound, and a single pebble was flicked off into space by an incautious foot beyond a concealing outjut of rock. It was not repeated, but it was enough. Halstead! His head drawn down between his shoulders like that of a wild animal on the stalk, Champ began inching silently forward, toward the bulge of rock that concealed his unsuspecting prey from view.

CHAPTER 29

Curt had come in through the narrow neck of the cove at dusk, so the last rays of the sun, glinting yellow-white off the water, would dazzle any observer on the beach. The swim from the adjoining beach to the south had been hampered by the kelp beds, for these huge leathery sea plants formed a thick layer of stems and foliage at the surface that reeked of iodine and often forced Curt to swim underwater. Without Preston's mask and snorkel and flippers, it would have been impossible. The rubber suit had insulated him against the mid-fifties water.

As it developed, there were no observers on the beach. Curt covered the thirty yards to the dunes by wriggling on his belly, even though no heads appeared at the lighted cabin windows. Once in the reeds, he stripped off the wet-suit, put on the clothing he had carried in a small waterproof bag he also had taken at Preston's: black turtleneck sweater, black Frisko jeans, steel-toed climbing boots, his commando knife stuck through his belt in the small of his back.

He worked his way silently through the myrtle trees toward the drive, one foot at a time, all senses alive in the near-darkness. By the drive he squatted down. One: locate the enemy snipers, which already worried him. Why hadn't they been watching the beach? It suggested either that they'd already spotted him, or that they had an incredible lack of respect for the terrain. That worry aside, once the sentries were located, he had to disable the Triumph parked so invitingly out in the open and then find and disable the second car that would be parked somewhere behind the house.

An incautious scuff of city-bred shoe on gravel froze him into immobility while Julio's dark shape passed close enough for Curt to reach out a hand and trip him up. He didn't. Instead he listened to Julio and Champ talking, gritting his teeth over Champ's delight at "doing" Debbie. Now he knew not only who they all were—Rick and Heavy and Julio and Champ—he also knew *where* they were. And then Julio and Champ disappeared around the corner of the cabin, giving him the Triumph.

He raced silently across the open to the car; as the kitchen door closed behind them, he already was sawing through the tough black rubber of one tire. He slashed all four, was into the clump of bushes the two sentries had quit within two minutes of their departure. He kept right on, around the corner of the house opposite the one they had used, and into the evergreens shrouding the bedroom windows. Here he found the station wagon, which he cautiously hooded to slash and jerk every wire he could reach. He also smeared grease on his face to darken it.

Unless Rick, the apparent leader, was totally ignorant, a sentry would be back out directly. Curt was right. He heard the kitchen door open just as he lowered the Chevy's hood. From the rear corner of the cabin, he watched Champ's dark form return to its vigil in the bushes. Curt could have slit his throat right there, but the plan called for the lights next.

He moved back past the bedroom windows, around the front of the cabin under the living-room windows, up tight against the siding so he could not be seen from above. At the fuse box he inched the small metal door open, then paused for a full sixty seconds while he mentally rehearsed his sequence of moves. The moon, rimming the cloud banks with silver, soon would burst from behind them; he wanted to be in cover then.

Knife gripped gingerly between his teeth, he pocketed the two spare fuses from the box. He set one hand on each of the connected fuses, then quickly twisted them out. Darkness inside, voices inside raised in question. Curt jammed the fuses into his pockets, and with the knife slashed out a two-foot section of now-dead wire above the box.

A fast sprint, right down the side of the cabin past the kitchen door, right out across the open to the Triumph. Two yards from the car he dove in a front-shoulder roll that brought him up in a crouch in front of the car, out of sight of Champ. Without a pause he ran right on, silently, in a crouch, with the car between him and Champ. He darted into the myrtle bushes, threw away the fuses, squatted to watch.

It took Champ a full sixty seconds to make his decision, to loom up very big in the moonlight beside the car and begin snuffling around it like a dog by a hydrant. It appeared that the predators were not at their best in open terrain. Curt had to actually shake the bushes to attract Champ's attention. Once he had it, he went to the base of the cliffs. Yes. It looked like an easy ascent. He heard Champ's yelling for Rick, and started up. A little dicey, maybe, if they had a gun, but he knew how tricky shooting in the moonlight was. And he had to entice them after him, had to make them come to him.

Curt was nearly to the ledge when Rick started firing. Eight shots, .32-caliber by the sound of them, none even close. On the ledge, he looked down: the one with the pistol had been firing from the far side of the clearing, wildly, at a range of better than fifty yards. No wonder the slugs all had been impossibly wide!

Curt looked down. Only one coming now. The big one called Champ. Four minutes, about. The others, in a dark group, started back toward the cabin, incredibly enough—unless they were going to reload the pistol—then detoured to the Triumph. Actually flashed their light at the flattened tires, thus destroying their night vision.

Curt shifted a little uncomfortably on the ledge. Predators? He had come after leopards, had found hyenas. Of course, dangerous in the aggregate or when trapped, but . . . predators? Scavengers, rather. Not that it made any difference, he told himself uneasily. He would take them one by one, so they would know it was coming and would have to wait for it, tasting their fear like the taste of a brass bullet casing.

Two thirds of the way along the ledge was a jutting shoulder of rock that narrowed the path to just a bit wider than a foot. To get beyond it, Curt had to edge around with his back to the rock. Perfect.

He followed Champ's progress by purportedly cautious sounds: the scrape of a shoe on rock, panting, a muttered curse. Did Champ really think he was making a silent approach, so he could take Curt by surprise? Or was he so confident he didn't give a damn if Curt heard him? Finally the noises showed that Champ was on the ledge, was waiting for Curt to betray himself. So Champ thought he was undetected! Curt let him wait for two minutes, then scuffed his boot, once, to knock a single pebble off the path.

Then he waited.

Two minutes later Champ's left hand and arm came gradually into view around the knob of rock, as he edged along with his back to the cliff face just as Curt had done.

Now.

Curt kicked with his right leg, jackknifing in the middle for added balance and power, shattering Champ's elbow with the steel-shod tip of his boot. It was a beautifully delivered kick, which would have sent any normal opponent hurtling into space by mere reflex action.

But Champ's reflexes were those of an animal, for he sprang not out, but sideways, yelling with shock and pain but still sideways right past Curt, so they were facing one another on the ledge a mere yard wide.

"You . . . you busted my arm!" exclaimed Champ in amazement.

Then he sprang. Curt, still unnerved by his opponent's agility and strength, was driven back into the rock before he could set for a defense. His head slammed into the stone; he went woozy for a moment. Champ's head came up under his chin, forcing his head back, arching his back, at the same time that Champ's right arm circled Curt's waist and his clenched right fist dug into the small of Curt's back.

Legs wide-spread, Champ turned their locked bodies, inexorably, so Curt's back was to the drop. Still dizzy from his head striking the rock, Curt found his left arm pinned in the terrible strength of Champ's bear hug; his right hand was free but had no ready place to strike, since Champ's head was drawn down between his giant trapezius muscles like that of a turtle into its shell. Curt groaned. He was strained so far back that his face was pointed skyward, his shoulders actually were over the chasm. There was a muted double pop, and pain tore through his chest as two ribs cracked.

The pain snapped him back. All finished, was he? Not quite yet.

Curt drove his left knee up between Champ's legs. The big man shuddered, squirmed, tried to shield his testicles from the second blow he knew would come—but he didn't slacken his grip.

Again. Champ moaned. He turned his head to the left, grinding his skull harder against Curt's jaw. But he also exposed his face. Curt locked his right hand into a judo fist, second knuckle of the middle finger protruding, and drove it with all his strength into the place that he hoped Champ's left eye would be.

It was.

Champ screamed, twisting away and back, clawing his right hand at the injured eye. Curt teetered for a second on the edge, almost gone, then got his balance just as Champ lurched toward him, yelling, all fighting sense gone in rage and pain. With almost surgical precision, Curt used his steel-shod right foot again, but driving it this time into Champ's crotch. The big man collapsed, going down onto his knees like a heart-shot buffalo, and Curt smashed the knife edge of his right hand in a backhand blow at the exposed neck vertebrae to crush them. He struck three inches too low, across the back of the shoulders, but the force of the blow knocked Champ forward, right over the edge.

Curt was dragged to his knees by the ragged knife-blade of pain between his ribs. He dragged in shallow half-breaths, choking still from that awesome bear hug. He looked over the edge.

Champ had slid headfirst for the first few feet, had clutched a protrusion of rock with his right hand, had clung desperately as his body slid by into space. His fingers had held on even under the shock of the full weight of his body; now he swung over emptiness by just that one hand, his broken left arm dangling uselessly at his side.

When Curt looked over, he stared right into the fear-stricken face.

"I . . ." Terror thickened Champ's voice. "Mister . . . *please* . . ."

Debbie moaning on the phone—*please*. Curt watched, unblinking, as the clawed fingers began to very gradually straighten.

"*Please* . . ."

He couldn't do it. Curt went down gingerly on his belly, stretched an arm down, was able to close his fingers around Champ's wrist. "Try to chin yourself," Curt began. "Try to pull up where I can get—"

Champ's fingers straightened, his full weight, held only by Curt's grip, fell free and slammed Curt down against the rough stone ledge.

Curt yelled and realized that the weight was gone. His own hand had popped open under that scourge of pain.

Champ fell backward, shoulders hunched, legs windmilling above his head, right hand clawing empty air. He made no outcry. His heavy body plummeted through the undergrowth and smashed on the jagged unseen rocks at the base of the cliff with a sickening thud.

Silence. Mutter of distant surf.

Curt struggled to his feet, leaned against the rock, face ashen. Predators? Well, he had learned something about himself then. Not in cold blood could he do it. His victory was bitter in his thoughts. As for the others . . .

There were no preliminary whimperings—just sudden open-throated shrieks of pain, like the ululating wails of mating panthers. Curt jerked his head around, stared horror-stricken into the shadows below. After a fall like that, the man couldn't live, couldn't . . .

Once in the desert they had been pinned down for two days by enemy air and a man in a perimeter position had been hit and had yelled for nine hours without pause, so that three men were killed trying to get to him and they finally just had left him there, screaming until he died . . .

Curt had to find a way down. Had to *do* something. But . . . no way down. Not for a man with broken ribs. Up, then? Impossible. One way: work obliquely along the face of the cliff toward the edge of the ravine, try to find a way off the cliff face and into the trees. Then down the gravel drive to the man dying below him.

Curt started to move, then paused. His eyes swept the clearing below, and a chill of realization ran through him. The others had not appeared! The pale glow of a kerosene lamp shone against the curtained windows he could see from there. They must have heard the body falling; they must be hearing the screams. But none of them had emerged. Even if they thought it was Curt, not their buddy Champ . . .

Curt shuddered again; that callous disregard was the worst thing they had done. Then he started edging his way painfully along.

CHAPTER 30

They were in the living room when the heavy body smashed down through the foliage to stop with an abrupt thud on the rocks. Rick came to his feet with the darkly blued .32 Colt automatic clutched in his right hand, his face very pale.

"What was that?" he demanded in a hoarse whisper.

Heavy also was on his feet, rosy-cheeked face beaming. "Champ got him!" he exclaimed happily. "Champ knocked him off the cliff!"

Julio was halfway to the kitchen door when Rick called him back in a flat, almost deadly voice. "If that *was* Halstead falling, we'll know when Champ comes back."

"But what if it was Champ? What if—"

"Then we can do nothing for him anyway."

To hell with that, thought Julio. Ever since the rape of Debbie, he seemed to have been waking by painful degrees from some sort of bad dream that had begun last April with the attack on Rockwell. A dream in which he did not what he wished, but what seemed dictated by something outside himself. Well, he was through following Rick's lead.

He started again for the door, but behind him the safety clicked off. He looked back: the pistol was trained on him, and the look in Rick's eyes, almost a madness, brought him back to his chair.

Then the screams started.

Julio's lips drew back and his eyes started from his face as if he were being throttled. "That's *Champ's* voice! He is hurt, he—"

"It might be a trick."

The gun didn't waver. Julio sat still. Fifteen minutes passed, while the cries continued. Heavy sat on the couch like a fat white grub, eating a corned beef sandwich; Rick sat in the easy chair beside the cold potbellied stove, with his right leg over the arm of the chair so he could rest the butt of the .32 on his knee.

"Rick, please, listen to that . . . that noise. Champ—"

"Shut up."

The cries continued for the next hour intermittently, as if the injured man were undergoing surgery without anesthesia. Heavy, who had made a whole loaf of bread into cheese and corned beef sandwiches before the lights had gone out, was very steadily and surely eating his way to the bottom of the stack.

Julio spoke to him suddenly. "Will you come with me? I can't stand that sound anymore."

Heavy stared at him with piggish eyes, and then gave a great raucous belch. His cheeks were pouched with half-chewed bread; the white melting fat of the corned beef ran down his chins. Around his mouthful he managed, "Ca . . . do it, Jul . . . Ri . . . gotta wait . . ."

"Empty your mouth, for Chris' sake, you pig!" stormed Julio.

Heavy chewed, swallowed, belched. "Rick says we gotta wait." He shot a look over at Rick, who had Paula's suicide note open in his lap again. "I ain't chicken, no matter what anybody says, but I ain't dumb, either. The Triumph's screwed up, an' I bet the Chevy is, too, and I ain't about to try an' fix 'em in the dark. So we can't get outta here: So what's the use of goin' outside?"

Julio began pacing, roaming the room like a caged animal, quivering each time that another of Champ's screams tore at his nerves. A flash of hatred almost palpable in intensity shot through him. Halstead had done that to Champ; had done something to Rick, changed him some way so they were stuck in here, while outside, Champ . . .

What had happened to Rick? To all of them? Rick wasn't yellow like Heavy, but tonight he had just sort of flipped. Sat there staring at the dead woman's note to her husband. Julio checked in his pacing. Rick's face that morning when he had turned Debbie over to them—maybe that had started it. Or maybe it had started months ago, with Rockwell. Then they had been a group, a unit, a whole bigger and stronger than all its parts. But Rockwell, and then Paula Halstead, and Debbie, and . . .

It was like being on one of those fun-house things that go around and around, faster and faster, and no matter how you try to hang on to one another in the middle of it, you are finally flung off, sliding and clutching impotently, to the periphery.

He had to get out of here. He stopped in front of Rick.

"You sit there and swing your leg and pretend to yourself that you are not afraid. But you are. You are even afraid to shoot." He turned and walked unsteadily to the kitchen door, where he paused and looked back. "Even me. Even in the back."

He turned deliberately, and went across the kitchen toward the back door. Face white, lips bloodless, Rick slowly lowered the gun butt back to his knee again. His left leg began a slight uncontrollable twitching.

Heavy reached for another sandwich.

The moon was lower and the fog banks were building up to engulf it; in the air was a bone-deep chill that helped steady Julio. He had expected a slug in the back, he really had, but he hadn't been able to stop himself. Funny, he felt almost sad about Rick. For this, they were all destroyed. Now that it was too late, he knew that if they had stopped, before any particular piece of violence, they could have ended it. But they had gone on, and now it was too late. For them. For Debbie. For Paula Halstead and Harold Rockwell. For Champ.

Champ cried again, with a broken gagging note like the sound of some animal or something in those doggy jungle movies on TV.

Julio left the shadows of the house, walked out across the open toward the base of the bluffs where he knew he would find poor, dumb, busted-up Champ. But not Halstead. That bastard would be long gone.

But as he came under the bushes he heard a voice speaking a bare five yards away. Halstead! Trapped here, under the cliffs! Julio went into a tense crouch, switchblade suddenly open in his hand, and went on.

"Easy, son," Curt was saying in the voice of a man gentling a horse. "I had a tough time getting down from that cliff. Now I—"

Julio went in like a ferret from behind, his knife sweeping up in a short vicious loop at Curt's kidneys. But he was too eager, or he uttered a sound of anticipation, or the failing moonlight was deceptive. Curt rolled forward and up and around, facing him, and Julio's blade stabbed only air.

But Halstead still was trapped in this small clearing, and Julio's teeth showed in a grin by the dim, filtered moonlight. He began sliding forward.

Curt spoke in a voice oddly steady. "Your friend is very badly hurt. I think his back is broken. But he may survive if I can get help here in time. Let's—"

Julio laughed outright. Afraid of the steel, Halstead was; truly, the knife made a giant of he who had it. Champ, on the ground two yards away, moaned fitfully. A ragged wisp of cloud deadened the moonlight even more. Julio heard Champ, had heard Curt's words, but none of it was even registering. All that registered was that Curt was still backing away from him, and to Julio, that meant fear.

"I am going to kill you," Julio hissed.

A change took place in the grease-smeared face facing him, but it was not the change he had expected. Terror did not enter it, but instead a . . . well, almost a sort of pleasure. Halstead's right hand went behind him, reappeared with a deadly-looking twin-edged blade, dull black so it caught no moonlight.

"Don't try it, son. I forgot about it with your friend here, up on the cliff, but I was fighting with this knife before you were born."

A tiny finger, almost of fear, touched the back of Julio's neck; but then he leaped forward, slashing up and across and back with the half-clumsy technique of the street fighter who has seldom faced another man's knife, and who has fought only with others as unskilled as he. Curt whipped his blade at the boy's knuckles, to cut the tendons and disarm him. But the moonlight was almost extinguished by the fog, and he wasn't sure where he had connected. Probably just a superficial cut.

Julio fetched up beside Champ, turning back toward Curt with an almost wooden expression on his face. "Hey, what . . ." he began.

"Look," said Curt, "I can take you, kid, and I will. Stop . . ."

Julio took one step toward him and fell face-forward to the ground. Curt waited, making sure it wasn't a trick. Actually, it *had* to be a trick; the most he had done was slash, not stick. But Julio gave no hint of movement. Then the fitful moon emerged for a second, and Curt saw that Julio's switchblade lay a yard from his curled fingers.

With a muttered exclamation, Curt went in, dropped to a knee, turned the boy over. Dark sightless eyes stared far beyond his—as Paula's had at the dressing table, as the sentry's had in his nightmares, as many men's had during the war. He sighed wearily, and stood up. He wiped his blade on his sweater, and put it away.

He had missed the knuckles but had gotten the wrist, where the radial artery is a bare quarter-inch below the skin. Julio had been unconscious in thirty seconds, dead in two minutes. But even as Curt felt the shock and revulsion at this senseless death, the thought came through his mind, unbidden: *For an old sod, Halstead, you haven't lost too much of the old speed, have you?*

It was gone as soon as it had come, but it left behind it a taste in the mouth like vomit. He looked down at the two victims: the dead and the maimed. Madness. And two more to go? he thought furiously to himself. No. This was the end, the finish. Predators? If only he had arrived a few seconds earlier the night of Rockwell's blinding, or had been there when they had come for Paula, none of this . . .

But perhaps, he realized, only on the long tortuous road he had traveled since her death had he learned that threat and force and fear could only be met by similar threat and force and fear. As Curtis Halstead, professor, he would have temporized, appeased, reasoned—and would have been destroyed. Perhaps only as Curtis Halstead whose roots reached back to the violence of the desert campaign was he able to . . .

He shook off the thoughts. It was over now, finished; leave the other two to Monty Worden's ministrations, or to whatever private demons they might carry within them. If any. He removed his heavy sweater, laid it over Champ, and felt his pulse. Light and fast from shock, but steady. He might make it, if Curt could get help in time.

Only when he stood beside the VW in the fog, which now swirled thickly and made everything ghostly and dark and wet, did he realize he had lost his car keys. Now what? He didn't know how to cross ignition wires to start a car, had no way of knowing where or when the keys had gone. Only one thing for it.

He started trudging slowly through the fog toward San Conrado, ten miles distant, his cracked ribs stabbing at every breath, shivering with the cold now that his sweater was gone. And with the fog, there was a good chance, he knew, that he would have to walk the entire distance.

CHAPTER 31

Sagging the ancient couch beneath his bulk, Heavy wondered how long Julio had been gone. Sure, the screams had stopped, but the silence was even more scary in its way. As long as there were screams, that meant somebody was alive out there. *Alive.* His moon face puckered; a great racking belch snored up from his belly. "Ah, Rick, how long you figure before Julio comes back?"

Rick slowly turned to look at the fat boy. His eyes were hooded, and his left leg, still outthrust in its pathetic pose of nonchalance, jerked as steadily as a heartbeat. His laugh was a caricature. "You know as well as I do that he's dead, Heavy."

Heavy shifted uneasily, belched again. He reached for a sandwich but the platter was empty. Julio dead? Or up on the Coast Highway right now, thumbing a ride? "Ah . . . I'm gonna make some sandwiches, Rick. You want one?"

Rick watched Heavy lever his bulk up off the couch; his lip curled. "Go ahead, stuff your belly. He can't get at us in here."

Heavy waddled into the kitchen, by the light of two candles busied himself over the bread board. What the hell gave with Rick? He'd thought Rick was going to shoot Julio, he really had. He mayonnaised bread thickly, opened a can of Spam, salivating slightly at the spiced aroma of the meat. If only it were light out, he could cannibalize the Triumph to get the wagon started. Or if he were up on the highway, even afoot, or swimming out of the cove to the next beach to the south . . .

He stopped for a moment, meat knife in hand; then he went back to the front room. "Hey, Rick, I bet I know how that Halstead got by Julio and Champ. I bet he just swam out around the rocks from the next beach south and in through the cove—it'd only be about half a mile . . ."

"Shut up!" Rick snarled. "He came by *them*, down the driveway. The stupid, yellow bastards . . ."

Under Rick's fury, Heavy retreated to the kitchen. Man, that Rick sure was getting strange. He went back to his sandwiches. He wished that he had a gun like Rick did, to go up to the highway . . . Then he thought of that long steep narrow driveway, flanked by concealing black trees. Well, maybe he wouldn't. But he bet that if he were down on the beach right now, he'd swim for it. Only, the door was locked and the key was in Rick's pocket. Of course, a window could be pulled open, but . . .

He stopped again, considering. The fog would hide him from Rick once he was on the beach, or even from Halstead if he was there. Roll out the window quick, down to the water, swim out of the cove. Go down to Mexico somewhere, nobody could find him . . . His old man wouldn't miss him anyway, and . . .

Heavy clambered laboriously up on the sink, with a quick frightened look over his shoulder toward the living room where Rick sat, out of sight, and jerked up the window. A blast of cold air swept through, snuffing one of the candles.

"Heavy! What the hell are you—*Heavy!*"

Grunting, he dove in head-first panic, hit in a totally graceless front roll, so his pants ripped all the way up the seat with a great snoring sound. Then he was running. The .32 splatted, three times, but he was already down behind the lip of the dunes in the thick ropy fog. Crouching, he ran about thirty feet, then thrust his head up cautiously. Yeah. Rick already was pulling the window back down. Safe.

The fog goosebumped his flesh, and the ripped trousers admitted a shocking amount of cold air to play across his backside. He trotted straight down to the water, ponderously hippo-like, shoes full of sand and nostrils full of the wet iodine odor of beached kelp. His belly swayed almost sedately as he moved.

At the water, Heavy paused. It seemed so damned *lonely* out there in the darkness where unseen breakers smashed themselves to foam on black rocks; he would rather be up on the highway, where the fog would stop traffic so he could maybe get a ride. But death—*his* death, the finish of the entity called Heavy—might he that way.

He kicked off his shoes and socks, shuddering when his feet touched the icy sand. God, it was cold. He dropped his pants, removed his shirt, stood elephantine in skivvies and T-shirt. He made a bundle of the clothes, with the shoes inside, set the bundle on top of his head, and fastened it there with his belt buckled under his chin. He would want those dry clothes when he reached the next beach.

Wading in was like being progressively paralyzed from the feet up. His teeth started chattering and he went numb. When he was in up to his neck, he began stroking out into the fog. Instantly he was isolated in a world of gray-black iciness that muted even his own splashings. He swam awkwardly, holding his head up to keep the clothing dry. At first only the growing roar of the waves guided him toward the entrance, but then he could see the occasional gray turn of a breaker on black rock. Helped by the ebbing tide, he entered the turbulence near the entrance within a few minutes.

Careful now. Don't get swept up on the rocks . . .

A heavy wave hammered him against black granite rendered invisible by darkness. His face went under; he was dragged bumping and scraping along the rock face for a few agonizing seconds, his flesh shredded by sharp-edged barnacles. *Kick free! Kick free!*

He was off the rocks, but somewhere in that struggle his clothing had gone; only the belt hanging around his neck remained. He pulled it off, finally glad of the numbness from the icy water, which kept him from feeling the pain of the dozens of superficial gashes he had suffered.

Don't panic, he told himself. *Go back. You can't make it.*

A breaker smashed over him, filling his unprepared and gaping mouth with salt-bitter water. He gulped, belched, momentarily panicked, got control. Back. He had to go back, he . . .

The backwash of waves off the narrow neck of the cove struck him, spun him, and suddenly he was out beyond the cove and into the open ocean. *All right. Don't panic. Go on then, you're through now, go . . .*

He churned wildly, fighting for his life, for his legs had been gripped by the slimy tentacles of . . . of . . .

Kelp.

Wow. Just kelp. He rode with the lift of the next wave, was free. But panic still nibbled at him as he thought of the huge leathery sea plants rising up from the ocean floor below him. Underneath him lay perhaps half a hundred feet of icy night ocean, filled with kelp like dead fingers, clutching like unknown sea beasts . . .

Thrashing, he was in it again, enwrapping foliage gripping him, dragging him down. He fought in blind terror against it, and then the first cramp hit him.

It was a giant fist that struck his churning stomach an unbelievable blow and jerked every muscle of his flaccid body with agony. He went down, was suddenly clear of the kelp except for the nude brushing of smooth stems; he caught one, hung on, dragged himself upward. But as he pushed his head free, to gulp air, another wave washed over, filling his mouth with water.

Another cramp struck him. He sank again, gasping, choking, getting more water into his lungs, flailing with arms and legs that sent out erratic shock waves. Heavy was drowning.

Blood from his abraded hide filled the water, attracting a lean torpedo shape from the open sea. It arced in toward the kelp, drawn by blood and those erratic movements that, to a shark, always mean that something is in trouble and hence is potentially food. It would not attack yet, of course, despite that deliciously maddening scent of blood. Despite the viciousness of its attacks, the shark is a cautious predator. It is thus that it has survived, unchanged, for 350 million years.

Eventually, of course, it would move in to feed.

In the cabin, Rick thought: Who needs them? Of course, he had to get up from his chair every few minutes to check each window, carefully, automatic in hand. But it was worth it to have no more worries about which one would betray him next. No loyalty, no guts, that had been the trouble with them all along. If he'd had the proper backing from that first night with Rockwell, none of this would have happened. Not that he was to blame for what had happened to Rockwell.

No, the real trouble all went back to Paula Halstead.

His dark, troubled eyes went over her note again. Goddamn that Julio! If he hadn't given Rick the suicide note from Debbie's purse—hell, if he hadn't insisted on getting his hands on Debbie . . . Not Rick's fault, what had happened to Debbie. None of it his fault.

please understand that I am doing this because of something intolerable in myself

See? In herself. Nothing about it being because of what had happened with Rick. No, she'd fallen for Rick the second she had seen him. That had happened, she had come, only because of Rick. Nothing else. That look of self-loathing he'd remembered from her face, that hadn't really been there. She'd *wanted* it, man. From Rick. He'd turned her on, like he did Debbie and Mary and . . . and all the chicks.

But still, somehow, it seemed all to go back to Paula Halstead, to the note in his lap addressed to her husband. Back to Paula, and forward to him. For it all ended with Curt Halstead.

Rick made his round of the windows again. He was glad Halstead had gotten the others. Oh, Rick had the gun, once it was light he would make out okay, but he was glad about the others. Champ, last one you'd think was yellow, was the first one to break. Pretending to be chasing Halstead when really he'd been trying to get away.

Then Julio, yellow spic bastard. Going to run away, up the ravine, knowing that Rick wouldn't shoot him. Only, Halstead had been waiting for him, in the darkness and the swirling fog.

And finally Heavy. Going to swim for it, he bet, after trying to foul Rick up with all that crazy talk about Halstead swimming in. Who the hell had he been trying to kid? That would have meant that a lookout posted along the beach would have warned them of Halstead's arrival; it meant that Halstead had outmaneuvered Rick at tactics. That was wiggy, man. No damn teacher was better at tactics than Rick Dean. Sure, better at sneaking around in the woods, maybe, but . . .

But anyway, Heavy was gone. Halstead would have him by now.

That made it neat, tidy for Rick. Everybody gone except Debbie. Well, *he* hadn't had anything to do with what happened to Debbie. No matter what she might claim, all he had done was walk out and leave her with the fellows. How could he have known what they would do to her? Besides, she'd put out for anyone; he bet she hadn't even fought it.

After four. Dawn soon. Time to make his move. He stood up, shivered—it had gotten cold in the cabin, that was it—and went to the back door. Very silently he turned the key in the lock, eased the door ajar a hairline. Speed. Surprise. Catch Halstead unawares.

Rick found he was trembling again: the damned cold fog! He put the automatic under his left arm, wiped his sweaty palms down trouser legs that were crumpled from his all-night vigil, took the gun again. He patted his hip pocket. Yes. The loaded spare clip was there.

He kicked open the door, skidded through, fell on the wet cement, screaming in terror and firing at Halstead's shadowy lurking form behind the Triumph.

No return fire. Just the gently whisping fog, moisture dripping from the cabin eaves. The air smelled of the dawn and of the sea.

He scrambled to his feet, raced, dodging and weaving, to the

Triumph where he could crouch behind the bullet-starred hood. He panted raggedly. *Okay, okay, so you made me waste two. You don't know I've got the spare clip.* He licked his lips: the bad one now, across the open to the foot of the drive. Halstead might be ambushed there . . .

Now . . .

Racing across slippery grass in the misty dawn, then his soles spurning gravel. Sharp air knifing lungs as he slid to his knees against the rough bark of a fir tree. Chest full of razor blades, head full of wraiths, but safe here. Apart from the distant mutter of surf, silence utter and complete. Swirling fog. Shadowy trees . . .

He flipped himself sideways, rolling, into the gravel roadway, pumping bullets up into the fir tree where Halstead had shaken a branch above his head, showering him with dew.

A mountain jay arrowed away raucously into the fog. *Nerves, Rick baby. Four used, five left in the clip. He's working on your nerves, baby, doesn't know about that spare clip. Once you make the blacktop with that spare clip of bullets, you're safe. Got to make the blacktop.*

Go, man!

Legs pumping, he ran head down, arms working, toes digging into the sharply rising gravel. He was the hero of every war movie he had ever seen, running through enemy sniper fire unscathed; during that short burst of speed he felt no wounds, received medals, was present at his own hero's funeral to receive the plaudits of the mourners.

Rick was up and over the gate, whirling in the safety of the highway, free from the masking bushes. His mouth was full of cotton, his chest was heaving, his knees were wobbly; but his gun muzzle pointed unwaveringly at the gate. Halstead would have to come over that to get him. He had made it, won free!

"I'm ready for you!" he cried menacingly into the fog.

He hoped now that the bastard *would* try it. He'd shoot him where he wouldn't die right away, in the crotch, say; he'd grind the bastard's face into the blacktop, he'd gouge out his eyes . . .

The gray fog swirled about him, wetly caressing him, hampering his vision, so when it swirled away . . . Was that a shadow straddling the gate? Rick stood with a foot on either side of the white center line of the highway, making his stand. If that was . . .

Halstead!

He went into a half-crouch and fired again and again, flashes of muzzle gas lighting the grayness. The gun clicked, he jerked the trigger again, nothing, not even a click, empty, clip used up.

Rick made a sick whining sound in his throat and broke his fingernails scrabbling at the empty clip, hunched over it furiously like a mad alchemist, unable to get the catch to release the spent clip into his hand. Ah! He hurled away the dead clip, dug in his pocket for the second, eyes on the gate.

A muffled growl, *behind* him, made him whirl. A monstrous shape loomed up from around the bend of the highway, yellow eyes fog-dimmed, Christmas-festooned with the red and yellow lights worn by the big semi-truck-trailer rigs that roamed the Coast Highway like unleashed animals. Air brakes hissed; wheels shrieked away rubber lives on the macadam.

Rick dug out like a sprinter, but his shoe struck the discarded clip, he did a comic TV split, windmilling his arms, yelling like Milton Berle milking an audience for laughs.

Smoking screaming desperately locked rubber hurled uncounted tons of metal onto him. The bumper smashed his teeth, dissolved his skull like flung egg, smeared him grublike down fifty yards of white center line in the serene lifting fog of the dawning day.

The driver made it out of his cab before he got sick.

AFTER...

TUESDAY, SEPTEMBER 2ND

AFTER . . .

Curt locked his car and started up the echoing stairs to the gym. In another week the streets of Los Feliz would be jammed with students returning to the university, but now it all seemed damned remote. Even the gym, the chromed bars and black orderly ranks of weights, seemed remote, as if his last visit had been years rather than days before.

The top half of the office Dutch door was open. Preston, at the desk, looked up and his cold blue eyes met Curt's—again, like a stranger's. But then he was on his feet, grinning his wide infectious grin, sticking out his hand. "Well, well, the prodigal returns."

After a moment's hesitation Curt shook with him. "I'm sorry about the skin-diving gear, Floyd."

"Somebody from the sheriff's office brought it back yesterday." He gestured Curt to the couch. "Going to take a workout?"

"I . . . can't. I've got a couple of ribs that . . ."

Curt stopped there; he had come intending to pick up his workout gear, break entirely with Preston. During that long night below the bluffs, he had traveled such distances, probed such depths, that a return to normal life seemed impossible. It was like what Hemingway had said somewhere about men coming of age: it was not always a matter of their twenty-first birthdays.

Into the pause, Preston said, "Your girlfriend has been calling here twice a day, leaving messages. Says you weren't answering your phone over the weekend, and that she'd been worried."

"I . . . haven't felt like talking to anyone . . ."

"Why don't you hang your head?" demanded Preston abruptly.

"I . . . what?"

The big weight-lifter sat down on the front edge of his desk. "Do you think you're the only guy who ever woke up in the morning and wanted to puke into the face looking at him from the bathroom mirror? How do you think I felt after I realized that I didn't have the guts to go down there with you?"

"That's different," said Curt coldly. "It wasn't your fight. Floyd, *I wanted to kill*. Do you know what my first thought was when I looked down at that poor dead Mexican kid the papers talked about? *That I hadn't lost my speed with a knife*. How's that, huh? All the time I was after them, I was no better than they. Just as vicious, just as sick . . ."

Preston merely grunted. "You know, Curt, when I was a kid my dad was a circuit preacher—they still had them in Missouri, places like that, in the thirties. I was in and out of a dozen rural schools by the time I was ten, which for a skinny little runt like me meant fighting. All the time, because I was the new kid in town. I got so that my first day in a new school I'd find the school bully and I'd whup him—I'd whup him because I *had* to whup him."

"But what's that got to do with—"

"Then I grew up and went into the Army and started getting regular meals and exercise, and working with the weights, and I ended up as a big guy. Big enough so I could punch a guy in the snot-locker one minute and buy him a beer the next. *But* . . . Let me feel that I've been cornered, and suddenly I'm that little guy again, fighting hard and dirty to beat the school bully."

Curt looked at him strangely. "Then you're saying that—"

"I'm saying that whatever happened down there last Friday night, you didn't have any choice. But you did have the training. And I'm saying that if a bunch of guys push another guy off a window ledge, they can't blame him for whatever he does on the way down."

"You bother me, Professor." Detective-Sergeant Monty Worden reached for a cigarette. "I underestimated you, and that can be fatal for a cop."

When Curt had come home from Floyd Preston's gym, he had found Worden's dark sedan parked in the driveway, and Worden parked on the couch in the living room. He was glad he'd talked with Preston first; it had somehow braced him for this ordeal.

"I gave your men my statement at San Conrado on Saturday morning."

Worden feathered smoke through his nostrils. "The university gave me the background, Professor. Enlisted 1942 in the British military at the age of seventeen. Volunteered for an irregular warfare group called the Special Air Services that was being set up by a guy named David Sterling. Trained in parachute and rubber-boat landings, skilled in killing with the knife, the pistol, and the hand. Awarded the George Cross in 1943 after a desert operation against some German airfields."

Curt shrugged. "Did you come to hear my war stories?"

"I came to admit that I goofed in checking you out. I should have realized it then."

"Realized what, Sergeant?"

"That you're a born killer, baby. It's in your blood, you like to see 'em die. This little exercise against these kids must have been manna from heaven to you, huh, Halstead?"

For a vivid moment Curt could see Champ's contorted face pleading up at him from the cliff; Julio's sightless eyes in the little clearing below the cliffs. A born killer? Or a man, as Preston had said, who had been pushed off a window ledge and who was not responsible for his actions on the way down? Or someone in between the two? An amalgam of college professor and wild-eyed seventeen-year-old in the desert?

"You're doing the talking, Sergeant," he said.

Worden nodded. "Sure. Tough man, played it cool right down the line. Three of 'em dead and one crippled for life with a broken back—probably worse than being dead for a simple, gentle guy like him . . ."

"Did you talk to Barbara Anderson about the gentle phone call he made to her?"

"Okay, okay," Worden said, irritably brushing it aside. "So maybe this Champ character should have been put in a rubber room years ago. But then what about that Debbie Marsden, huh? Feel good about her?"

Curt felt the sweat start out between his shoulder blades. Poor broken Debbie, used and abused and thrown away. It was so tempting to admit to Worden his stabbing guilt about Debbie; if, after all, he had quit seeking the predators . . . But Worden acted as if it was such an admission he sought, and Curt would be damned if he'd give the detective the satisfaction.

"I didn't know the Los Feliz police blamed me for that."

"Sure, okay, the punks did it, all right—after her boyfriend handed her over like a fistful of pocket change. But a blue VW was seen in the Gander driveway; and the ambulance was summoned anonymously."

"What does the girl say?"

"She doesn't." Then Worden grunted in disgust. "If the damn doctor hadn't been so quick with his needle on Friday afternoon, we wouldn't have been finding corpses on Saturday morning. As for the girl, she's okay physically—but it's my bet she'll be psyched for life. Probably the first guy tries to kiss her will get a hatpin in the chest." He leered through the smoke of another cigarette. "Not that what happened is your fault, Professor. The D.A. is buying your story, all the way down the line. Self-defense."

When he stopped, Curt said, "But you disagree."

"You bet your fanny I do." He stood up, towered over Curt, his hands fisted in his trouser pockets as if that was the only way he could be sure of not using them. "I think you lured the dummy up on the cliff, and then shoved him off. I think you conned the spic into the knife fight, and then killed him. Slashing his wrist, so he'd die the way your wife did. So damned cute it makes me want to puke."

Curt stood up also, went to the windows to look unseeingly out over the golf course. The funny thing was that if Worden had come here the day before, Curt would have agreed with him, on all of it. Even the born killer part. Now he wouldn't. Part of it was the talk with Preston, but more than that . . .

More than that, mere survival sometimes dictated bloody-mindedness, in the British sense of the word. He turned back to the detective. "And I suppose I pushed the Dean boy in front of the truck?"

"I can't fit you in there," Worden admitted grudgingly. "The driver and the time element both exclude you—you were calling our office from the all-night greasy spoon in San Conrado just about the time he got it. Funny, too—since it was his fingerprints I had lifted off that wall above the couch in the other room."

Debbie's boyfriend. It figured. The planner, the one who pushed or conned the others into it. Good family, the newspapers said, the father in insurance, $50,000-a-year class. A persuasive boy, he would have been, and a clever one. But then, if he was clever, what had brought him to the middle of that highway in the shrouding mantle of fog?

"So that just leaves Gander," said Curt. "The one who's missing."

"Missing?" Then Worden nodded again. "Yeah, you would, all right. Only I don't buy your story about walking all the way to San Conrado. I think you left the cove a lot later than your statement says, and that you hitched a ride with someone we haven't found yet."

He stopped, dug in his trouser pocket, and then dropped something on the coffee table. Curt picked it up curiously: a blackened silver skull-and-crossbones ring, very heavy and made for a large finger. He looked up, surprised an almost erotic expression on Worden's face. "This is supposed to mean something to me?"

"Some fishermen down the coast hooked into a ten-foot white

shark yesterday—one of the man-eaters. They sliced him open, just for the hell of it, and found a partially digested human arm in his belly. Wearing this ring on one of the fingers."

"You mean that Heavy Gander—"

"His old man has identified it. Funny thing, Halstead, tough old guy like that, you'd think he wouldn't give a damn. But he busted down an' cried like a baby when we showed him that ring."

"Yes," said Curt. "Well." He felt as if he had been bludgeoned, but he knew now that he would be all right. He realized that Worden had come hoping for a confession, and he knew that Worden wasn't going to get one. Even if he had been guilty, anyone but Worden. He looked at his watch. "I suppose you've got to be going. Sergeant . . ."

Worden stared at him for a long moment, then heaved a deep sigh. "Yeah, you're a tough cookie, Halstead. One of the worms. I spent the morning with the D.A., tryna convince him we had enough to prosecute. He said no; he was right, of course. On what we got, no jury would convict—not with a smart defense attorney to drag your dead wife into court by the guts whenever you needed her. So you're gonna get away with it . . ."

"Just like they would have gotten away with it, Sergeant," said Curt. He let the detective get to the front door with his hand on the knob before calling his name; trying to match his tone to Worden's, when the detective had told him almost casually that the predators would never be found or punished.

Worden turned, eyes hard and wary. "Yeah?"

"No hard feelings?" said Curt. "It's just the facts of life, Sergeant."

He stood by the open door, watching the tail of the angry detective's car disappear down the driveway between the trees. One of the worms, Worden had said. Perhaps he could operate in his world only by seeing everyone and everything in two dimensions only; perhaps police work demanded a clear-cut choice between the good and the evil. Because Curt still thought that Worden was a damned good cop.

He went upstairs to his study, sat down at his desk. The time of predators was past—at least for now—but the time had left behind a need for decisions. For endings, in fact.

Curt wrote out his resignation from Los Feliz University in longhand on his letterhead, read it through once, and sealed it in an envelope for delivery to the university. Preston had been right: The whole man was involved, you could not change your nature, you could only control it. Until Curt was more sure of what he was controlling, of just who and what he was, he knew that he no longer could teach.

Then he went downstairs to the phone, dialed a number, was aware of a tingling in his fingertips when the receiver was raised.

"Barbara? Curt Halstead here. I'm sorry I didn't call before, but . . . I had some things to work out. I . . . this evening I'm going over to the hospital to see Debbie Marsden, and I wondered if you would like to go along. And I thought that maybe afterward . . ."

His suggestion hung in the electronic limbo between them for a long time; and when Barbara answered, she seemed to have made a decision about far more than just how she might spend her evening.

"I'd like that, Curt," she said evenly. "I'd like that very much."

Curt Halstead stood for a long time beside the phone, before finally replacing it in its cradle. Yes, he thought, a time for decisions, a time for endings.

But perhaps, also, a time for beginnings.

ABOUT THE AUTHOR

Joe Gores (rhymes with "doors") was born in 1931 in Rochester, Minnesota, and now lives in northern California. He kicked around Alaska, the South Seas, and Africa as a young man and has traveled through all fifty states. He served in the U.S. Army writing biographies of generals for the Pentagon and received his education at Notre Dame and Stanford. While at Stanford he was employed as a private investigator in San Francisco where he spent twelve years on the job. He walked down many mean streets, learned some disquieting truths about human nature, and was threatened with nearly every blunt instrument known to man. Out of this experience came his acclaimed Daniel Kearny & Associates File series. He is a prolific short story writer and the author of thirteen other novels, including *Dead Man*, *Menaced Assassin*, and *Cases*, and he has also written teleplays for *Kojak*, *Magnum P.I.*, *Remington Steele*, *Mike Hammer*, *T. J. Hooker*, and *Columbo*. He is also the author of *Marine Salvage*, the standard popular work on that subject. Not only is he a productive writer, but he is a highly honored one as well, winning three Edgar Awards (best first novel, best short story, and best TV episode, for *Kojak*) and Japan's Maltese Falcon Award for his novel *Hammett*.

ABOUT THE AUTHOR

Joe Gores (rhymes with "doors") was born in 1931 in Rochester, Minnesota, and now lives in northern California. He kicked around Alaska, the South Seas, and Africa as a young man and has traveled through all fifty states. He served in the U.S. Army writing biographies of generals for the Pentagon and received his education at Notre Dame and Stanford. While at Stanford he was employed as a private investigator in San Francisco where he spent twelve years on the job. He walked down many mean streets, learned some disquieting truths about human nature, and was threatened with nearly every blunt instrument known to man. Out of this experience came his acclaimed Daniel Kearny & Associates File series. He is a prolific short story writer and the author of thirteen other novels, including *Dead Man*, *Menaced Assassin*, and *Cases*, and he has also written teleplays for *Kojak*, *Magnum P.I.*, *Remington Steele*, *Mike Hammer*, *T. J. Hooker*, and *Columbo*. He is also the author of *Marine Salvage*, the standard popular work on that subject. Not only is he a productive writer, but he is a highly honored one as well, winning three Edgar Awards (best first novel, best short story, and best TV episode, for *Kojak*) and Japan's Maltese Falcon Award for his novel *Hammett*.